THE LAST SHE

THE

LAST

SHE

H. J. NELSON

wattpad books

wattpad books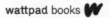

Content Warning: violence, attempted sexual assault, fighting, animal death

Published in Canada by Wattpad Books, a division of Wattpad Corp.
36 Wellington Street E., Toronto, ON M5E 1C7

www.wattpad.com

First Wattpad Books edition: December 2021
ISBN 978-1-98936-571-7 (Hardcover original)
ISBN 978-1-98936-572-4 (eBook edition)

Names, characters, places, and incidents featured in this publication are either the product of the author's imagination or are used fictitiously. Any resemblance to actual persons (living or dead), events, institutions, or locales, without satiric intent, is coincidental.

Library and Archives Canada Cataloguing in Publication information is available upon request.

Printed and bound in Canada.

1 3 5 7 9 10 8 6 4 2

Cover design and interior images by Jill Caldwell
Images © Valua Vitaly, © helivideo, © Mix and Match Studio
via Adobe Stock, © vinct, © imagedepotpro via iStock, and
© Sebastian Unrau via Unsplash
Typesetting by Sarah Salomon

To my dad,
who gave me a love of stories

ONE—ARA

I crouched below the ruined bridge and scrubbed the blood off my fingers. River rocks tinged with gray, ochre, and green wavered beneath the current. Father would have reached for one, but I didn't. Instead, I rubbed my hands against each other, watching the swirls of red disappear into the flow.

Look, Ara, three skips. Think you can get four?

All around, the trees faded to colors of blood and pus, as if no time had passed. But no traffic roared across the bridge, and the center had given way, the two ends stretched out like doomed lovers' hands. My camouflage backpack rested between the eaves of the bridge, and below it, a squirrel lay spread-eagled on a river rock. His body was laid open, his face crushed. Without a bow or bullets for my pistol, I'd had to smash him with a rock. I couldn't risk lighting a fire and had eaten only the kidneys, liver, and heart. The salty taste and chewy texture only reminded me how long it had been since I'd eaten a real meal. And that I needed a proper weapon.

1

The new tech will fail you, same way it failed the world. A gun is your new best friend.

But my pistol was empty. Which meant I was about to put into action a plan my father would never have approved. Find a group of men, steal their weapons, bullets, or both, and be gone before they knew what happened. I wiped my hands dry, fished out my backpack, and started back up the steep riverbank. The squirrel's blood had dried beneath my nails, but I let it be. My hands had been stained by worse.

I pushed through the tall weeds until I found the overgrown trail that ran beside the river and the prints I'd found fresh last night. I remembered the trail; it had once been a mecca for young families, full of expensive houses and the flashy new tech machines my father hated. Out here, on the edge of the city, the lots were large and the massive houses were built right up next to the river, with backsides made entirely of glass. Now the expensive houses crumbled, and the Midwestern city once known for its hospitality lay still.

Yesterday a group of men had stopped here for water, then left the river behind and headed deeper into the city, where the buildings grew thicker. There were prints where they'd laid down heavy packs, and if I had to bet, one of those held a weapon.

There are no such things as friendly men, Ara. Not in this world. Not for you.

I tightened the straps of my pack and followed the tracks. The city grew slowly around me, as did the silence. No low drum of cars, no hum of airships, no voices. Only the wind and lonely birdsong. The plague killed females first and fastest, to the point I knew of no other female survivors. But even if a few men had been spared, it hadn't been enough to keep the world from falling apart.

Gas stations and other businesses soon pressed in between the encroaching trees, signs faded, weeds and vines growing thick. I passed an abandoned airship lost in waves of billowing waist-high grass. The front half was crumpled, as if it had lost power and fallen straight from the sky. Growing up, almost every family I knew had the new, shiny airships that zipped through the skies, but my father had always preferred the older technologies: steel and oil. In the end, neither had brought salvation.

~

The driveway reflected the full heat of noon, and though the neighborhood should have been filled with the noise of laughing children, lawnmowers, and airships, it was quiet. Only my father's voice rang out through the dry, summer air as he loaded another jug of water into the back of the truck.

"Ara, did you put the matches in?"

"Yep, and two lighters."

"Good."

He tossed our backpacks on top of the other supplies in the truck bed. With them we could go three weeks in the Sawtooths, or even farther north into Canada. Bottled water, canned and dehydrated food, two containers of gasoline, two sharpened axes, our bows, and other supplies lined the truck bed. I'd never appreciated the supplies he kept until now. When news of the plague started just a few weeks earlier, the stores had emptied almost overnight. A week in, I'd heard Mother and Father talking late at night in the kitchen, and when I woke, she was gone. "A trip, to visit her sister," my father said, with eyes that couldn't meet mine. And then my sister Emma and I were separated. Under no circumstances were we to go into each other's rooms. My father brought us food and water. The first night I snuck out onto our rooftop and tapped on her window and her blue eyes greeted me with mischief. But three days ago, the day the electricity shut off, she answered my tap with white eyes weeping tears of blood. I nearly fell off the roof in terror.

The fear and silence when Father left with Emma that night made it hard to breathe. The world had fallen apart around me, but I hadn't cared or noticed till mine did. I sat on the roof all night, joined by the steady whine of cicadas, the distant sound of gunshots, and the steady thump-thump-thump *of earth as our neighbor dug two deep, long holes in his backyard.*

In the early dawn, they returned. Father carried her cradled in his arms. I could breathe again. He didn't tell me where they'd gone, only came to my room and told me to pack a bag. But I had a child's faith that she would be all right, that he had taken her somewhere that would make her well again. That was why we were leaving today.

Now Father's prized hunting rifle lay in the front seat, the pistol with which he'd taught me to shoot in the glove box. He'd changed into his hunting gear: a wool lined jacket, dark pants, a camouflage cap, and heavy boots. Unlike Emma, people always picked me out as his daughter. Same hazel eyes, same sharp cheekbones, same auburn hair.

He pulled the tarp over the truck bed and shut the tailgate. We were lucky he was a romantic who loved the old tech. While others had switched to airships years ago, Father kept his guns in a safe and the car under a tarp in the garage.

The leather squeaked beneath me as I climbed inside. Loki, our husky, whined from the back seat, unhappy at being alone. Usually he sat with Emma and me on either side of him.

4

"I could sit in the truck bed with Loki if Emma wants to sit here?" I said. "Then we'd still be separate?"

He started the car and began to back up, not meeting my eyes.

"It's just us, Ara."

~

The wrongness of the moment twisted my gut even now. It was a horrible thing we did, leaving her. A decision that has haunted me ever since. Maybe my punishment was that all I had now was an empty pistol and my father's final words: to go back to the beginning.

The tracks left the river path and moved west, pushing first through thick weeds and then following a dirt path that snaked through neighborhoods full of fading houses, shattered windows, and streets littered with cars and airships. Weeds, leaves, and dirt smothered all. I kept the rising sun at my back, and after an hour of walking came upon the remains of what I guessed was the men's fire from last night. The ash was still warm; if they'd started at daybreak, I couldn't be more than a few hours behind. If I could find where they camped tonight, I could steal the gun and be long gone by morning.

Rusted cars with grimy windows littered the roads and several times I passed collections of bones and dried flesh that I tried not to look at. The city grew thicker and I passed a dozen yellow buses, stationary, in front of a brick building. *FORGIVE US* had been spray-painted in white on the wall. It wasn't my school, but I stared anyway. It had been only three years since the world had ended, but I could barely remember the sixteen-year-old whose biggest problem was if she'd get back together with Sean Dennis, or if any colleges would offer her a track scholarship.

Funny, I'd once looked for others to race and now I spent my life avoiding it. My legs were thinner now, but just as fast. A fall breeze drifted between the abandoned houses, carrying scents of rot and decay. Most of the doors and windows had been boarded over, but some had been torn open, gutted clean as a fresh kill by scavengers like me. Only a few bore a red *X* painted across their front entrances. These were left untouched. The sun climbed higher, and I checked over my shoulder more and more often.

At noon, I came upon the second mistake the men made: a plume of smoke blackened the sky two miles west, dead on their current path. I scaled the largest tree I could find, a solitary oak with a tire swing attached, and surveyed the area. Trees and houses stretched as far as the eye could see. The farther I looked, the harder it was to make out the houses' missing shingles, faded paints, or fresh covering of vines. Nothing moved but the smoke drifting into the sky, all framed by the mountains rising in the distance. Why send a signal to the whole world? Stupidity? Overconfidence? Both? Part of me wanted to stay in the tree and wait till nightfall. I didn't know how many men still roamed the city. But I hadn't seen anyone else all day. Still, I was playing a dangerous game.

I left the tree behind and approached the fire slowly. The scent of burning flesh hit me well before I sidled up next to the bonfire, its warmth deceptively inviting against the chill of the day. It had been lit in the middle of a cul-de-sac, between a rusted Chevy and a blue minivan with no wheels. Buried beneath smoldering branches was the blackened body of a large animal. The scent of burning fur was almost unbearable, but even through the flames, I could see the white eyes. The animal had been infected.

The weight of the empty pistol felt suddenly heavier against my back. In the beginning, Father and I hadn't known that animals could get infected too. Then, in the mountains, we'd found an enormous bear with white eyes weeping blood; the same sign humans showed. Only this bear walked with jerky movements and charged at anything that moved. We tracked it for three days, before Father finally used two precious bullets to end it. Together we burned the body. After that we'd run into other infected animals, all grown far beyond their normal size with white, bleeding eyes, a jerky stride, and an aggressive nature beyond any I'd seen when they were wild. It made them easier to kill—they almost always charged—but the thought of meeting one now, without a weapon, terrified me. These men also must have known the dangers of the infected animals, as they'd burned the body. It made me wonder what else they knew of the plague. Not that I would ever get a chance to ask. The only thing more dangerous than an infected animal was a man.

Walking around the fire, I was unable to resist tracking the kill. A split heart, splayed wide. An elk then, and a large one at that. The tracks were spaced close where the first shot had taken him, then wide where he had run, a pool of blood where he had fallen then surged upward before the second shot downed him for good. I hadn't heard a gunshot, which meant they'd taken him with a bow. And one hell of a shot at that.

So, a group of four men, confident enough to light a bonfire in midday, armed and proficient enough to take down an infected elk. I rocked back on my heels, tracing the smoke still rising like a black flag.

They were good. But Father and I had been better.

Ara . . . I made a mistake, we all did. Go back to the beginning . . . go back . . . it's not too late.

I stood up and followed the men's tracks. Stray leaves blew

across the street, catching flame and burning dangerously close to nearby houses. I didn't bother to stop them. Let the world burn; it had never done anything for me.

The tracks became harder to follow, crossing over into cracked blacktop in silent neighborhoods where thick brush had sprung up between buildings. A sense of wrongness prickled my neck as I passed into a section of trees cut through by an overgrown dirt road. The thicker covering made my heart pound and feet fall silent, the trees full of shadows. The road wound back and forth through the trees, and I stopped next to a rusted car and tilted the mirror to me. The glass was cracked, coated in dirt, but I didn't need more than a glance to make sure my auburn hair sat tucked beneath my cap. It was too long to pass for a boy's cut; I'd need to cut it soon. The mirror showed a face thinner than I remembered, my once-pale skin tanned from months of outdoor living. My clothes were faded and baggy, for warmth and protection only. Nothing to suggest my sex. Even if anyone saw me, they would mistake me for a boy.

Something moved in the mirror. I spun. The world stopped as he stepped out from the undergrowth, not twenty feet from where I stood. The first human I'd seen in months. *A man.*

Neither of us moved.

My entire body stiffened with fear. He was tall and well built, with curly hair and strange, green eyes, like the forest itself was watching me. In a different life, I might have thought him handsome, but now I saw only an enemy stronger than myself.

How the hell had he gotten behind me?

"Beautiful day for tracking, don't you think?" He had a slow smile, almost like a dare. He took a step forward.

I pulled out my pistol in one smooth motion, even as my

hands trembled. His smile faded and seconds inched by as he took in my gun, my tattered clothes, my thin form. He lifted his hands slowly.

"Listen . . . Why don't you put the gun down? We can talk."

"I'm not much for talking." My voice was soft, but my heart was running itself ragged. Besides my father, he was the first human I had talked to in almost three years. And if I'd had a bullet, I'd have put it in him without blinking.

He took another step forward. "Look, I'm not going to hurt you. My name is Kaden, I live nearby. Let me help you."

"I said stop!" I shook the gun at him.

He stopped, but his eyes became hard. "All right, go ahead, shoot me. Can't say I don't deserve it." The gun trembled in my hands as he took yet another slow, measured step forward, his eyes locked on mine. "But see, here's the thing. I think if you were going to shoot me, you would have already. My bet? That gun is empty."

"You want to bet your life on that?"

He stopped again.

"How about this?" I took a step back, motioning with the gun. "You go your way. I go mine. No harm done."

He didn't move. His eyes flicked to the trees behind me.

It's a trick, don't look.

"How about this?" he said. "Surrender, and when we get back to the clan, I'll put in a good word for you. We could use a smart kid like you. We've got food there. You don't have to starve anymore. And my men won't hurt you."

Men?

Behind me, a twig snapped. My insides went cold.

Don't hesitate, Ara. There are no friendly men in this world. Not for you.

I pulled the trigger.

Click.

He flinched, but I'd already flung the pistol at him and vaulted into the forest. I dumped my backpack and sprinted through the trees. Better to have nothing if it meant my freedom.

Without my pack, I flew, adrenaline surging through me. They wouldn't catch me; I had the fastest 200-meter time in school as a freshman. A glance over my shoulder showed me the curly-haired man—Kaden—was still in the clearing. Another man raced parallel to my left, but he would never catch me. My feet barely seemed to touch the ground—

—until I slammed full force into a body. It was like running into a wall; a wall that wrapped its arms around me.

We went down hard and the forest became a blur of trees and grass. I caught a glimpse of red hair, long limbs. Kicking and thrashing with a vicious desperation, I gained my footing and lunged sideways when his hand caught my left foot. The forest floor rose up as I crashed forward with a flash of pain, fighting to rip my foot away.

Kaden's weight hit me, and this time the fight was different. He dug his knee deep into my back, crushing me. My fingers scraped against rocks and dirt as I struggled to throw him, but he only pushed harder, harder, until I buckled, my face grinding into the earth. I wanted to scream for Father, but I was alone, left only with the lessons he'd taught me. I got my elbows under me and tried to roll sideways, to throw him off. He pressed down harder. Black spots flickered in my vision. I couldn't breathe. A heavy hand pressed down on my lungs, making it impossible to move, to think. I thrashed, weaker now. Still, his body pressed. The harder I fought, the more the blackness filled the edges of my vision.

"Hey, hey, steady there!" He sounded concerned. "You're all right. Just calm down." His weight lifted a fraction.

He knocked the wind out of you. You're okay. Breathe!

"That's the boy who was following us?" A deep, slow voice from my left.

"Yeah, no wonder. He looks half-starved. Probably just looking for food."

This came from Kaden. God, he was heavy. But through the panic came a single thought: He didn't know I was a girl.

"Anyone with him?"

"No."

"You think he's part of a clan?"

"Nah, I mean . . . look at him."

The weight of their eyes was suddenly as heavy as the silence. I didn't like that I couldn't see them with my face ground into the dirt. Then—

"Jeb, come help me check him for weapons. He had a gun, might have a knife too."

My leg muscles tightened, screaming to run. What did checking me for weapons entail? There were a few things he'd notice if he checked too closely.

I readied myself for Kaden's weight to lift. My breaths came shaky and shallow, fingers tingling as I prepared for the race of my life. Instead, powerful hands grabbed my arms, and held me steady. For a brief moment the weight lifted as Kaden stood. I kicked wildly, making contact with someone, hearing a satisfying *umph.*

The satisfaction didn't last long. Sudden pain exploded across my lower thigh: one of the men had swung something hard against me. The pain radiated down my leg and I swallowed a whimper.

Another set of hands held my legs now, and I was shaking, blinking back my tears.

What sort of pain would I endure if they found out I was a girl? Hands worked steadily up my leg, squeezing my thigh viciously. I jerked, but the hands kept moving. Maybe he would just search my back? When he paused at my waist, I allowed myself a feeling of hope.

The metallic note of a knife leaving its sheath broke it. Slicing upward, the knife cut through my shirt and cool air swept over my back. I closed my eyes.

"What the hell is . . ." I could almost hear him making the connection in his head at the sight of my bra. I was skinny, but even then, a woman's shape was still different from that of a man.

"Turn him over."

The pressure released. My window of opportunity. Like a viper, I flipped over, kicking the man who'd been searching me full in the face.

I should have aimed for Kaden. He tackled me and was sitting astride my waist before I could get to my feet. *Damn!* His eyes blazed into mine with a sudden understanding.

He reached forward and ripped my shirt away completely, not even bothering with the knife. Then he pulled the hat from my head. Tangled, auburn hair spilled down around my shoulders. My hair was one of the few features I was proud of; thick and straight, hinting at red in the light. I cursed myself now for not cutting it. Not that it mattered. I was trapped beneath a strange man, shirtless except for my bra, my pale skin exposed to the sunlight.

Kaden spoke first. "It's a girl."

He said it with such disbelief that, had I not been terrified, I might have been insulted. I resisted the urge to spit on him. The other men came closer. My eyes burned with humiliation and fear.

"I don't know how you were raised but sitting on a girl is not a polite way to introduce yourself." Or at least, that's what I probably should have said. What actually came out was a mix of profanities that amounted to, "Get off me. NOW!"

Kaden smiled, not at all cowed. Without taking any weight off me, he looked up at the others. "It's definitely a girl."

"Can't be. There's not any left."

This from the boy with red hair, freckles, and long limbs—the one whom I guessed had been running alongside me. His eyes seemed too big for his face, and they were filled with a sort of innocent longing, like he saw in me a lost mother or sister. I didn't want to imagine what the other men were thinking.

It didn't take long to find out.

"We should check, make sure it's really a girl, all the way," said the man with the drawl and the small, rat-like eyes, the one I'd run into. He was balding and had a rash across his arms. The left side of his face was an angry red, and I realized with satisfaction that he was the man I'd kicked. His eyes traveled down my body.

"No, it's a girl." This from Kaden. Somehow, I felt like he was the leader here. His green eyes trailed over me, and my face flushed. I returned his gaze with all the hate I could muster.

Then, suddenly, the weight was gone. I sat up slowly, survey- ing the men surrounding me. Besides the boy, Kaden, and the ugly one I'd kicked, there was a tall man with a hatchet strapped to his waist who hadn't been part of the fight. His deep bronze skin was contrasted by facial hair peppered with gray, a detail worth noting as I'd not seen anyone over thirty who'd survived the plague, besides my father. I stood, favoring one leg, still burning from the hit.

"Sam, give me your jacket," Kaden said.

The younger boy, Sam, took off his jacket and handed it over. He stared at the ground, face littered with freckles and hair unwashed. Kaden tossed the coat at me. When I caught it, I considered throwing it at his feet, but settled for glaring at him instead as I pulled it on. I was outnumbered, and my leg throbbed. In a foot race, I could beat every man here, except maybe Kaden. Even standing still he looked fast, with long legs and an athletic frame.

He caught me watching him and smiled. I decided I could outrun him; but I'd put a knife in him first, to be sure. I crossed my arms. The jacket was well worn, soft, and still warm. When I breathed in the scent of leather, there was a metallic tang—blood, in my mouth. I had bitten my cheek when falling and didn't even notice.

"What's your name?" he asked. A simple question, but I hadn't been asked it for so long.

"What's *your* name?" I countered. Even though he'd already told me his name, I felt caught off guard, not sure I wanted to tell this group of men anything about me. Even my name.

"Kaden. That's Sam, Issac, and Jeb."

Sam, the youngest of them, gave me a soft, boyish smile, contrasted by Jeb's leer: he was the ugly one I'd kicked. Issac looked me square in the face and nodded, a quiet sympathy. He looked the oldest of the group, maybe even older than my father.

"Ara," I finally said. Short for Arabella.

Kaden picked up a rope from the ground, and I realized that was what Jeb had swung against my leg. He stepped forward, and I jerked back when I understood what he meant to do. "You're going to tie me up?"

He smiled, watching me through oddly long eyelashes. "Will you come with us if I don't?"

"No."

"Then it doesn't look like I've got much of a choice."

A cold breeze drifted through the trees, carrying scents of the forest, smells I'd spent the last three years in and had protected me—until now. He tied my hands in front of me with the meticulous movement of someone who knew what they were doing. I leaned as far as I could away from him, shifting the adrenaline, pain, and panic back with a plan. *They're just men. They die as easily as animals.* I could still steal a weapon. I could still make it home.

While he tied my hands, Sam ran back to the clearing and returned with my pack and my gun. He pulled out the magazine.

"It's empty," he said, sounding confused.

Kaden smiled knowingly, but I refused to acknowledge that he'd been right.

"You know," Kaden said as he gave the rope a final tug, forcing me a half step closer, "most people shoot a gun. But I like your style. Throwing one is much more sporting. Your aim is a little off, though."

"Give me the gun and a bullet and I'll show you how off it is."

He laughed. Then in a gesture that felt far too intimate, he stepped behind me and wound my hair into a bun. I tried to ignore the feeling of his hands in my hair as he pulled the cap back over my head and then picked up the rope.

"You know, princess, I don't think I will."

TWO—KADEN

Three years ago, I'd held my little sister, Kia, as she took her final breaths. I'd buried our brothers the day before, beneath a dying Montana sky, and knowing how alone she would leave me carved a fear as deep as the pain. In life, she never stood still. In death, her small body was limp, the only movement a track of blood rolling from her white eyes. *Let the horses free, Kaden.* The last words I'd heard from a female. Until now.

A cool breeze blew leaves across the street, whistling through broken windows with a high-pitched cry. The eerie sound masked the steady footfalls of our small group. My whole body felt wired, on high alert, and it was impossible not to glance at Ara as often as I looked behind us. An hour ago, I thought my biggest problem was telling Gabriel we'd failed our mission and had lost our team's gun. Now I had to tell him, and the clan, we'd found the first woman I'd seen in three years. A woman who, judging by her stiff-legged walk and angry eyes, wasn't nearly as thrilled to be with us.

"Turn here, Sam," I said softly. Sam nodded and led us off the pavement and onto a game trail that wove through the remains of a community park. Now it resembled more a forest than a clearing, with weeds and trees growing where once there had been only grass. Still, the vine-covered outline of a children's playground stood as a reminder of what this place had once been. I tried to keep my eyes on the surrounding trees and houses, tried to watch for trouble, but everywhere I looked, all I saw were those eyes, high cheekbones, and reddish-brown hair tucked beneath a cap that couldn't completely conceal what she was. It seemed unfair that the last woman on Earth would be beautiful. But I suppose God had already proved Himself a cruel bastard.

Issac caught my eye, tilting his head toward Ara in as clear a message as he'd ever sent. *Talk to her.* Yet I felt a sudden uncertainty that was as out of character as our group's silent procession.

"Sam, let's stop for water," I said when we'd reached the massive oak at the center of the park, the leaves a riot of coppery oranges and red with the fall. Sam held the trailing rope that secured Ara's hands, happy as a new kid with a puppy. The fresh scent of earth and leaves mashed the rotted scents of the city as I turned to her stiff form. "Would you like some water, Ara?"

Her eyes instantly narrowed—fair—so I drank deeply before I held the bottle out to her. She hesitated, then snatched the bottle from me and did the same. When she was done, she dumped the bottle on the ground instead of handing it back to me. I lifted a brow but didn't say anything.

"Ready?" Sam said, his eyes going back and forth between the two of us.

"After you two," I said. Sam stepped forward, Ara glaring at me until the two of them passed. Issac, the king of silent discourse, glanced down at the water bottle and smiled before he, too, continued down the trail.

"Shut up," I said, and picked up the bottle and followed after them. I thought about what I would have said to him if we had been alone. *What else could I have done, Issac? Think about what would have happened if anyone else had found her first. She had an empty gun and one backpack of supplies against a city overrun with warring clans. She was lucky to have been found by us.* And then Issac would shrug, or not say anything, which would only make me imagine a million possible answers. Like maybe I was the bad guy here. Maybe I should have helped her instead of taken her captive. Maybe this wasn't the way to treat the last woman left on the planet.

Damn Issac.

It was nearly dark by the time we came to the mall, a huge domed structure that towered over the surrounding buildings. The deepening colors of dusk masked the building's decay, making it almost impressive. An empty parking lot stretched out around it, the only visitors a few shiny airships, rusted cars, overgrown weeds, and an abandoned army tank.

"We can't get them to run anymore," I said to Ara as we passed by the tank. She stiffened, but I saw her eyes go to the open top, where the hatch lay open. "It's a good place to spend the night, though, if you're trapped out in the open. You can lock yourself in."

She didn't respond, but there was something assessing in her eyes. Something that told me that, given the smallest chance, she would be gone.

I led our small group through one of the side entrances where Jeb waited for us. He didn't always scout ahead, but today I'd thought it wise. The mall was close enough to the clan that it was relatively safe from other clans, but nothing was completely safe in this world.

The side entrance led us down a small hallway, and into a back area that was once a storeroom. It had a solitary window in the back, concrete floors, high ceilings, three steel beams that ran through the center, and most importantly, thick walls and doors. The first time we used it we dragged in a fire pit from REI and knocked a hole in the ceiling for the smoke. Now we'd added a few shopping carts and a collection of the beanbag chairs Sam loved.

"Scout out the area?" I said to Issac, who nodded and disappeared through the doors into the greater mall area. It wasn't that I didn't trust Jeb . . . but I trusted Issac more. After all, he wasn't the one who'd suggested we check that she was female "all the way." I'd had to resist the urge to smack Jeb, but that impulse often overtook me. I took the rope to Ara's hands from Sam as he set to lighting a small fire to cook the rabbit he'd shot earlier in the day. Jeb sulked in the background, watching Ara, who stared at the door where Issac had disappeared. Gabriel had assigned Jeb to our group six months ago, and even if Gabriel was the clan leader, I wished now I would have refused. Jeb was a good horseman, and had a knack for sniffing out supplies, but he would also report everything about this mission, and Ara, to Gabriel. Which brought me back to my current problem: the young woman standing straight-backed beside me. I cleared my throat and nodded to one of the steel beams. "You can sit there."

To my relief she sagged against the pole—I wasn't sure what I would have done if she had refused. I used the trailing end of the rope to tie her to the pole. *Just for while we make dinner and set up camp*, I reasoned, trying not to feel guilty. By then Sam had a small fire going, and I unpacked our few supplies to set up camp. We worked in silence, a feat that rarely occurred. Issac came back a short time later and took over spinning the rabbit roasting over the fire. With everyone here, I couldn't put off the moment I'd been dreading any longer.

I cleared my throat. "I think we should call a vote." The men's eyes turned to me, and, catching the light of the fire, so did Ara's. "The rules state we bring all captured persons to the clan. But," I paused, "this is different."

"She's a prisoner," Jeb said at once. "She was in our territory. This shouldn't even be up for a vote, *especially* because she's female. We will be heroes when we bring her to the clan. I vote we follow protocol and take her back. That's what Gabriel would want."

All the more reason to not bring her back then.

I stared into the fire. "Sam?"

Sam wrung his hands. I worried most about his reaction to all this. I'd only joined the clan for him; to give him a sense of safety and community. But Sam's concern wasn't for himself. "She'll be safest with the clan. Gabriel won't treat her like a prisoner. That's my vote."

"Issac?" I said, voice heavy.

Issac let the silence stretch out so long I didn't think he would answer. Then his voice cut through the darkness. "I vote we let her go."

There was a stunned silence, broken only by the crackle of flames. He gave no further explanation, and I knew it would be futile to ask. My eyes flicked to Ara. She stared at the flames, betraying nothing. "It's decided. We take her to the clan."

I'd hoped reaching a decision and saying the words aloud would calm the tension that made my shoulders tense and neck ache, but if anything, it made it worse.

A silence grew again. At night we usually harassed and insulted each other till the embers burned low, but with Ara watching, even I wasn't sure what to say or do. Sam pulled the bow from his back, running his fingers over the string, probably thinking he'd need to wax it soon. Today he'd stood straight-backed and sure when the infected elk charged. He wasn't the little boy I'd found hiding in a tree fort in the woods. Yet he'd held the rope to Ara's hands with a gentle care. While she glared at the rest of us, something in her eyes softened when she looked at him. The thought gave me an idea.

I reached into my bag, pulling out the last of the bread from the clan, then knelt beside Sam. "Let me take over cooking."

I passed him the bread, nodding to Ara, and winked. He smiled, understanding, and then stood up and walked over to Ara. She glanced up, eyes hard, but then, again, her face softened at the sight of him. Something about his lanky arms and lopsided smile—he could win over anyone.

"Are you hungry?" he said, just loud enough for me to hear. Her voice was soft, I missed the response. As Sam fed her the bread, piece by piece, I wished that Red was here, or any of the other horses, so I could go for a ride and rethink this whole thing. I shouldn't have tied her up. Maybe I really should have listened to Issac and let her go.

But Jeb would tell Gabriel if we came back without her, and Gabriel would tear apart the entire city to find her. She'd been following us . . . maybe if I could spend some time alone with her, she might tell me why. I stood up, stretched, then moved back into the shadows and circled around the two, just in time to hear Ara say, "Sam, will you untie my hands for a minute? Just so I can get feeling back in my fingers?"

"No." Ara and Sam started as I stepped into view. "I'll take it from here, Sam," I said. Sam ducked his head, picking up the remains of the bread, and headed back to the fire. I crouched before her. Her eyes instantly hardened; even so, it was hard not to stare. The light of the fire lit the planes of her face, the high cheekbones, the delicate lips; all the tiny differences I thought I would never see again.

"Care for a bath, princess?"

Her lips pressed together, not answering, and my chest tightened with guilt. Was she afraid of me?

"I'm going to untie you." She leaned away as I crouched behind her, working at the knot securing her to the pole. While the rope around her middle slackened, I left the one holding her arms together tight, and grabbed beneath her shoulders, pulling her to her feet. Then we made our way past the fire, and then through the doors Issac had disappeared through earlier.

I stopped just through the threshold to let my eyes adjust from firelight to the light from the night sky. We stood in an open cavern, three stories tall and impossibly long, stretching into the darkness ahead. The glass roof had caved in, starlight reflecting against thousands of shards of broken glass. Circling staircases led up to the higher levels, and hundreds of darkened storefronts branched off the main floor. In the beginning, it hadn't been hard to walk down these halls with Sam and remember the crowds and noises, point out the remains of the food court or the video game store, the last poster pasted forever in the window. Back then it felt like the world had short-circuited, and as soon as it rebooted the people would return, mop the floors, clean the windows, announce some new sale, and we'd all hop back on the capitalist hamster wheel. Instead, each time we visited, there were more weeds, more shattered windows, and more debris strewn about the once-neat stores and aisles, until I found I couldn't remember this place as it was before. Not that I had particularly fond mall memories, but I felt like I was failing Sam by filling his teenage years with memories of hunting infected animals and taking captives instead of flirting with girls at the mall or playing video games.

Ara favored her leg as we walked, forcing us to a slower pace. Though part of me wanted to ask if she was okay, and if I could look at it, the other part knew that would scare her more than leaving her alone. Jeb had hit her pretty hard with that rope, the ass, but I also wondered if maybe it was an act. She'd survived this long; she had to be clever.

Our steps echoed in the massive space as we walked between overturned benches, trash, broken bottles, and discarded clothing. We passed a lump of matted fur that I hoped was the remains of a coat and not a dead animal; hard to say here. Ara took in everything as we walked, her eyes moving up a set of still escalators that led to the second level. When we turned the corner, we found our progress blocked by a large fountain. The graceful copper statue of a woman stood in the center. She was twice the size of a real human and held a kite that fluttered away from her, the copper burnished green. Two emerald-colored children laughed as they chased her, their fingers perpetually reaching. Beside the fountain sat a water pump stained the same deep grassy tone, and behind it two escalators led to the second floor.

I led us to the lip of the empty pool then dropped the rope,

watching her as I did. *If you're going to run, here's your chance.*
The pump was rusty, so I threw my full weight into it, forcing it
down, then straining to pull it back up. Sam had found the fountain here; he remembered it from when he came here as a kid,
as a sort of tourist attraction where you could actually pump the
fountain and water would come up. It must have been connected
to some sort of well system because it still worked. A deep gur-
gling noise came from the faucet and I pumped harder. Ara took
a half step forward as red-tinged water sputtered out of the head,
then ran down a small chute to fill the bottom of the pool. A clear
flow soon followed.

"Here, let me." I moved to her, undoing the rope, and letting
it fall to the ground, and then stepped back. There was nothing
holding her now. No reason not to run. I moved to the fountain
and stuck my head under the flow of the pump, the cold shocking
me straight to the core. Then I pulled back and shook my head
wildly, spraying water everywhere.

"Come on, princess, I brought you here to work, not stare." I
gestured toward the pump, but her eyes shifted away, out into the
darkness, and she took a step back. "Unless you think you can't."
Her eyes came back to me.

I lifted off my shirt and tossed it to the ground. She arched
a brow but didn't look away when I undid my pants and tossed
them out of the fountain as well. Normally I'd bathe naked, but I
didn't want to scare her off completely. Actually, I hadn't expected
her to watch me undress. But she looked me over, head to toe,
and then, right when I thought she would bolt, stepped up to the
pump.

She grabbed the handle and forced it down, and the trickle
of water began to flow, surging each time she pushed the pump

down. I threw the water over my hands and legs, scrubbing off the dirt. Sam left a bit of soap hidden under the lip of the fountain, and I reached for it now. The dark hugged the corners and recesses of shops, and I was glad both Jeb and Issac had scouted the area. The mall was within our clan's declared territory, but it was a large territory, and besides the main central building where most of the men of our clan lived, we couldn't possibly defend it all. Gabriel liked to believe everyone respected the clan territories, but there were plenty of loners with no allegiances. And just before we'd left for our mission we'd gotten a report of a horde of men causing trouble downtown. Though the several organized clans throughout the city managed to keep an uneasy peace, it was the men who didn't stay put that were the most dangerous. They had nothing to lose. Unlike me, who suddenly had everything to lose.

"You won't make it," I said, grinning when her eyes flicked up to mine, surprise there. "I'd catch you. I ran track in high school."

"So did I."

Our eyes met, a silent battle of wills playing out. She could run, but I would catch her and bring her back. This wasn't her moment. She seemed to realize that, because she went back to pumping.

I washed the soap off, and then jumped out of the fountain and ran my hands across my body, sloughing off the water in rivulets. I'd need to change into dry clothes later. I pulled my black T-shirt onto my still-wet skin, then tugged on my pants.

"Your turn, princess."

She took a step back.

"Either you take a bath yourself," I said, "or I throw you in and scrub you myself. No offense, but you stink."

She took another step back, and I smiled and leaned back lazily. *Give it a go, princess. See what happens.* Another step backward, now ten feet away.

"Turn around while I get undressed," she said.

"Come stand by the fountain," I countered.

We sized each other up, a strange game of cat and mouse. She looked over her shoulder, and then sighed and made her way back to the fountain. She stripped off her shoes and socks, then lowered her feet over the side. She closed her eyes and pulled off her cap, letting her hair fall free and running her fingers through it. I suddenly felt like a creep watching her and threw my weight against the pump. Still, I wondered why she hadn't cut it—but was also glad she hadn't. I missed long hair, high laughter . . . well, a lot of things about females. The gurgle of water sounded again, like deep-throated laughter. The flow into the pool increased and ripples caught the moon's reflection. She stripped off Sam's jacket and my breath caught as I turned and forced myself to look out at the darkened storefronts and the mall stretching out beyond us.

"Do you have scissors?"

I almost laughed. It was such a girly thing to ask for.

"To cut my hair, I'm not going to stab you with them. A brush would work too."

I stopped pumping, trying to remember what store we'd found the soap in; it wasn't one we visited often. The sign had faded, but it was close, only one store over. "Stay here. I'll be back in a second."

I vaulted over a railing into the store. It was almost pitch-black inside. *If she's going to run, it'll be now.* Was that what I wanted? The last few years I'd broken in several wild horses for the clan. There was always a part of me that regretted it, that wondered if I should have left them free. I knew better than most the secrets and danger of the clan: once you were in, it was hard to get out.

I stumbled across a wicker basket and began to throw in bottles and things that looked soap-adjacent. There was some sort of hand towels that didn't smell too bad, and a wooden brush, so I threw those in too.

It took me less than two minutes, but when I ducked back out into the moonlight, I felt a surge of surprise—and something else I wasn't sure I wanted to name. She was still here. Long limbs, a small waist, and a tangle of long hair lit by the moonlight. I looked everywhere but at her as I walked back toward the fountain.

"Hey, princess, look—" I said.

"Look, asshole, it's *Ara*." The anger in her voice caught me by surprise. I didn't mean to, but I looked up, right at her, and then I couldn't speak even if I'd wanted to. "Not that hard, just two syllables. I could probably teach a monkey to say it, so I think you can figure it out."

I kept my eyes down as I set the wicker basket next to the fountain and went back to pumping. The water began to flow again.

"Thanks," she finally said, the sound of water splashing coming again.

"No problem," I said, keeping my voice light, even though the image of her standing there half-naked in the moonlight would forever be burned into my mind. "I thought we could go shopping tomorrow. We can't have you showing up to the clan looking like a bum." *Not that there's going to be any way to disguise what you are.*

"Where is this clan?" Her voice was careful, guarded, and I wondered how much I should tell her. Would she see the clan as a refuge or a prison? Something told me the latter.

"Nearby."

She climbed out of the fountain, and I stopped pumping

and kept my back turned. The night was cold, and I figured we would need to go find some new clothes for her; the ones she wore looked ratty. A few minutes later she cleared her throat and I turned.

"Wow, you clean up good." She'd brushed on her hair, so that it hung long and wet, and I was suddenly grateful I hadn't found scissors. "Let's get you some new clothes," I said, leading us away from the fountain and into a sort of surfer shop that still had a few clothing racks left standing. Ara followed me inside, her eyes again flicking to each exit. "Go ahead," I gestured to the clothing. "Shop till you drop."

Again, she didn't acknowledge me. Maybe I was off my game. Or maybe being the last woman left on the planet made you a bit more suspicious.

While she was in the changing room, I stepped back into the mall, glancing down the long corridors that ended in darkness. In the last few minutes the wind had picked up, blowing stray leaves and cleaning the scent of rot with the smell of rain. There was a storm coming. Maybe it would have been wise to go back to the clan tonight after all. But even if it had been the right decision, I was glad we hadn't. The moment we got back to the clan, I doubted I would have the chance to get to know her, and how she survived and came to be here. Not that I was doing a great job now. I ducked back into the shop. When she emerged I couldn't resist letting out a low whistle, to which she rolled her eyes.

She held out Sam's black leather jacket, the one he thought made him look so grown-up and cool. "Here. This is Sam's."

"Keep it. We'll get Sam a new one tomorrow."

I led us back to the others, not wanting to push my luck any further. Since Jeb lost our team's gun a few days earlier, I had only my knife, and it felt like meager protection for the most valuable person in the world. Sam had food ready for us and had arranged the five beanbag chairs in a circle, each almost as wide as a mattress and as high as my waist. After we ate, I led Ara to the largest one.

"Hold out your hands."

"I thought we had gotten over these petty trust issues?" Her voice was dry. "You really think I'm going to try to escape?"

Yes. "Nah, do you know how hard it is to climb off these things quietly?" I pushed her backward and she fell back onto the beanbag chair with a gasp. We had only one sleeping bag each, so I covered her with mine and prepared for a cold, sleepless night.

Sam, Jeb, and Issac went to sleep, while I sat by the fire, letting it burn down, and then adding more wood.

I couldn't take her to the clan.

I couldn't not.

At some point Issac woke and nodded to his sleeping bag, for me to sleep while he kept the watch. But even when I closed my eyes sleep evaded me. I wondered if I wasn't the only one who laid awake.

THREE—ARA

I woke to a man shaking my shoulder and barely managed not to scream. Kaden stood above me.

"Rise and shine, princess. We're going shopping." He held out a hand, and I didn't move, the whole of yesterday rushing back in. I hadn't meant to sleep. Why the hell had I slept? I'd meant to escape . . . but the bed, the full belly, the bath, the clean clothes . . . *damn*. He stood there waiting, hand extended, so I took it and let him haul me off the bed, stepping away from him immediately after. I realized too late I'd let the princess nickname slide, but it suddenly felt like I had much bigger problems. The room was cold, the fire from last night long dead.

"Sam, Jeb, and Issac went scouting. It's just us today," he said, answering my question.

My stomach clenched. "Any food?"

Kaden smiled. "You read my mind."

After he untied my hands, we ate a meal of some sort of dried meat and apples, and then Kaden led us from the storeroom back into the heart of the mall. The sun was already high in the sky, which meant Kaden had let me sleep in, a fact that embarrassed me, and put me on the defensive; why was he being nice to me? In the daylight, the mysterious, haunted feel of the place was replaced by a sad emptiness. I tried to remember the times when I'd gone shopping with friends, where I'd laughed and strolled down bright, clean corridors, but couldn't. That carefree girl was gone.

I watched Kaden from the corner of my eye as we walked, blushing when he caught me looking and winked. I wasn't checking him out—at least not that way. I had a theory, and a plan. Every so often he reached his right hand back to touch the lower part of his back. My father sometimes made the same subconscious movement when he wore a concealed weapon. If I was right, and he had some sort of weapon hidden there, I needed to steal it before I escaped.

Maybe I could ask him to—what, take off his shirt again? The wide shoulders and hard muscles of last night hadn't been hard to look at, but even I wasn't sure how to sell that request. I stored the problem away, deciding if I was going to spend time with the enemy, I might as well understand them.

The stupidest part of this whole thing—the part I would have never admitted out loud or to my father—was that I no longer viewed Kaden as an enemy. I believed him when he said he wouldn't hurt me. Not that I forgave him for taking me captive, or wanted to go to this clan, but of Kaden himself, intuition told me I didn't have to be afraid. Wary, yes. But not afraid.

"You come here a lot?" I said into the silence of our footsteps.

"When we're on foot we always stop here, because it's Sam's favorite and it's within our clan's territory." How like men to set up territories to fight over.

"You aren't usually on foot?" I kept my voice light.

"Our team is usually on horseback. Covers more ground."

This surprised me. "You have horses at the clan?"

"Thirty-two. I'm in charge of the stables." There was pride in his voice, but I felt cold. Thirty-two horses. How organized did you have to be to have thirty-two horses? And if they had horses, what else did they have? Dogs? Could they track me? Maybe I should just take my chances and run now.

Kaden interrupted my thoughts. "Let's start at REI, they've got some sturdy women's clothes no one's touched." *Right. Supplies first, then escape.* Even if I couldn't find a way to steal his weapon, I needed supplies to make it back home, especially with winter approaching. Might as well let him help me collect everything I needed.

Kaden led me through the aisles of REI. The glass displays were coated in dust, and the once-white floors held tracks of different rodents that I didn't bother to examine. Some of the rows looked untouched, others like a bulldozer had run through them. Together we pushed through piles of debris to find hidden treasures. I found a large backpack and a sleeping bag that, when compressed, could fit into a shoebox. I picked out hiking boots, tennis shoes, jeans, shirts, and a flannel top. I'd never enjoyed shopping, but it was fun taking things for free, almost thrilling—like I was stealing them. I even snuck a few things in when Kaden wasn't watching: a pocketknife, a journal, and a compass. Above everything else, I needed to find my way home.

"So," I said when we left REI, passing by a Wetzel's Pretzels, "how long have you been at the clan?"

"Two years now."

"Are you from here?"

"No. I'm from Montana." Was that wistfulness in his voice? I'd been to Montana before, on a family vacation. I wondered why he was here, in Boise; and then decided it didn't matter.

"What about you?"

I instantly went on guard. "What *about* me?"

"Where are you from?"

I stepped over the remains of a shriveled fern that had fallen over and spilled earth all over the grimy floor, remembering a time I'd come to the mall with Emma. She'd needed new clothes for school. Instead we got milk shakes and fries. I thought she'd eaten hers, but later I realized she was hiding bits of them in the potted plants, for the birds that lived inside the glass dome of the mall. I wished I would have taken her here more, instead of the boys I sometimes met here. It almost made me smile to think what my father would have thought of me being here with someone like Kaden. "I was from here," I finally said.

He arched a brow. "Was? So where are you from now?"

The mountains. The rivers. Wherever my father leads me. "Nowhere, I guess."

He didn't push it, and I didn't ask him more about his home. Maybe he realized that, like him, whatever family or friends I had were long dead. We kept walking, the wind and mannequins our only company. We passed a few more hours this way, Kaden leading us on a wandering tour through the mall, and then stopped for a late lunch of more apples and jerky. As the afternoon stretched on, clouds built in the horizon, the temperature dropping. My father and I would have started to look for shelter, but if Kaden was worried, he didn't act it.

"Do you need any unspeakables?" Kaden asked as we left a shoe store, where I'd replaced my shoes for a sturdy pair still light enough to sprint in. I stopped for a moment, baffled by his word choice, until I saw the pink walls and floors of the store beside us.

Oh.

"Definitely," I decided on a whim, and walked into Victoria's Secret, mostly to see if it was possible to make Kaden uncomfortable. He followed behind me, and I heard the soft double click as he turned his flashlight on. The beam moved over rows of brightly colored panties and lacy lingerie. The sultry stares of the women in the posters felt foreboding in the dim light.

"Say what you want, but this is the creepiest store in the mall." Kaden's voice cut through the silence. "Like, what is this thing?" He held up a garter strap.

Laughing, I made my way to the back of the store, past a door with an Employee's Only sign. Kaden followed behind, his tread as soft as mine. I wondered if he would make as good a hunting partner as Father. I dismissed the thought immediately; no one was as good as my father. He was patient, stealthy, and rarely missed a shot. He knew the animal's patterns better than they did. He had an instinct for the forest that I didn't realize I'd taken for granted until he was gone. It hurt to remember this, because in the end it hadn't mattered. We came into a small back room with counters running along the wall and clothing packaged in plastic bags.

"Those might be fresh," Kaden said, swinging his light to the bags. He seemed reluctant to actually touch them. I set to opening them, the light of his flashlight focused on my hands.

"What's your theory?" he said as I sorted the bag's contents.

"Theory about what?"

"Why you survived. Or why we all did."

Sure, why not discuss the end of the world while sorting through underwear? He propped the flashlight so it pointed toward me, and then crossed his arms and leaned back against the wall. "Everyone's got a theory: supervirus, vaccine gone wrong, aliens, God's wrath, the computers decided to finally overthrow us . . ."

"Computers, for sure."

"Do you think . . . you're the last . . . ?"

"The last female?" I finished.

The plague had come so suddenly, so violently, that it was impossible to know anything for certain. In the mountains I asked my father so many times why I had survived that I could almost hear his answer now. *I don't know, Ara. Maybe someday we will.* But even now I knew he hadn't told me the whole truth. I forced myself to shrug my shoulders. "I don't know . . . but I hope not." I ripped open another bag. "Doesn't really matter, though, does it? Seems like we're screwed either way."

"It matters to me," Kaden said with a grin. "I like women. Well, liked."

"I bet you did." *And I bet they liked you.*

"I like to imagine there's a city out there that's totally untouched, where the women and kids survived. And where none of the animals got infected." As he spoke, he made a pillow out of the bras and panties I'd discarded and then laid his head on it. So much for not touching them. It was such an absurd pose that I had to bury a laugh.

"Yeah, and maybe all the men died instead."

He titled his head to look at me. "Wishful thinking?"

"No. I wouldn't wish that on anyone. Though I do think it's probably bad luck to keep the last she captive and take her to some clan."

Kaden gave an overly dramatic sigh. "Can't you just give the clan a chance?"

"No."

"How about giving me a chance?"

"Also no."

He sat up and turned to me. "Isn't there anything I can do that will make you like me?"

"Yes. Give me your knife and then run in the opposite direction."

He laughed and then we fell into silence again. He hadn't corrected my mention of the knife, which was disappointing. I'd hoped it was a gun. I wasn't strong enough to take it by force, and I couldn't work out a way to trick him into giving it to me. And maybe, complicating it all, was the sudden realization that while I wanted to steal his weapon and escape, I wanted to do it without hurting him or his team. Maybe that was why he talked so freely; it was harder to hurt someone you knew something about, even if it was as small as the fact they were from Montana, liked horses, and had given you an annoying nickname. I hadn't corrected him the last time he'd called me princess; some small piece of me missed talking and joking with another human. There was something refreshing about Kaden's approach to surviving the end of the world. Not all of his choices were strictly aligned with survival. Some seemed more for fun. It was a bizarre, reckless approach that I both admired and figured would eventually get him killed. When I had found what I needed and shoved it into my pack, we headed back into the mall.

"Any other stores you want to hit up?" he said, his tone light as if we were a couple out for a stroll at a mall.

"Anything left in the food court? I could use a burger." That was always Emma's favorite.

"I could use ten burgers. But no, just rats, and only Sam's fast enough to shoot them."

"I saw some wire back in REI, I could show you some snares we could set tonight." The words were meant as a test; I wanted to know if we would be heading for the clan tonight. He hesitated before answering.

"I'd like that."

So, I had at least one more night. Good.

The daylight faded as Kaden and I finished our search, choked out early by the growing storm. A cold breeze began to blow through the open ceiling, rising and fading with an eerie howl. We had just passed the fountain again when Kaden and I turned the corner and froze.

Seven huge dogs stood before us.

The beasts snarled, revealing sharp teeth. But they weren't normal dogs. Their eyes were milky, unfocused, and weeping blood. They walked with the lurching stride of the infected. Leading them was an enormous all-black beast that looked closer to a wolf than a dog.

They foamed at the mouth, hackles raised, teeth bared.

"Gun?" I whispered.

"Knife," Kaden confirmed.

My father's words thundered through me. *Whatever you do, don't run. Running makes you prey.*

The beast in front surged forward and reason deserted me; I bolted. Kaden ran beside me, the two of us streaking over debris and rubble.

I risked a glance back. The plague made their movements jerky, slower than those of a normal wolf. Still, they gained on us.

Then I saw the green lady in the fountain. I traced the reach of her arm to the kite. It extended from her hand to the second level of the mall.

"Kaden!" I cut sideways and tore off my backpack, not bothering to check if he followed. The fountain grew before me, and without slowing, I leapt on the rim of the pool and vaulted toward the green lady. Her belly slammed into me, and I scrambled for purchase, climbing up to the arm that held the kite—it was bolted to a ledge just below the second floor.

A thud sounded from below as Kaden hit the statue and scrambled up. Snarls and howls followed. Then a high squeal. I glanced down to see Kaden clutching a bloodied knife.

"This attaches to the second level," I pointed to the kite tail. "We can climb over."

"Then do it!"

I climbed to the woman's hand and hesitated—the metal was so thin. The dogs circled below, and one of them jumped at Kaden, the snap of his jaws slicing through the air. I had to move.

I stretched out over the length of the kite, a few feet at a time, like I was crossing thin ice. *Don't look down, don't look down.* The cold metal cut into my hands, the rotting stench of the dogs rising from where they paced below.

Kaden cried out, but I couldn't risk a look. The metal grew thinner beneath me as I forced myself to continue, ignoring the snarls and dragging my body forward.

I made it to the second-floor ledge, and with a final burst of adrenaline pulled myself up and over. Behind me Kaden climbed to the top of the statue, his shirt ripped and stained red. He no longer held the knife and paused to lean on the green lady's head, his face pale and drawn, hands shaking. Then he moved slowly down the arm, toward the kite. Blood dripped from his fingertips.

I turned to look down an empty hallway, dark clouds choking out the daylight, the howl of wind overwhelmed by the sounds of the dogs. There had to be some way I could help him. Something I could do.

Instead, I saw another possibility.

This was the opportunity I'd been waiting for: I could leave right now. If I walked to the fork and turned left, I could avoid the camp and the other men. It would take only minutes to resupply. A fire starter, a water filter, a sleeping bag. I could be home in a week. I could find what my father had left behind. Kaden could stay on the statue until the dogs left. His men would save him. He was injured, so it would take them longer to pursue me, if they did at all. Maybe they would go back to the clan first.

The emptiness of the hallway beckoned, and I took a step forward, then another.

"Ara!"

The desperation in Kaden's voice made me turn. He was climbing the kite and teetering dangerously. His face was ashen, and his arm was tucked against his side as he struggled one-handed. His eyes were closed in a grimace as he inched forward on top of the thin kite string, and then stopped, as if it were too painful to continue. The kite wobbled in the middle.

He was going to fall.

"Kaden!" I ran back to the railing. "You need to move, it's not going to hold!"

I could do nothing. Kaden lay motionless on the kite, face pressed against it, his arm dangling as blood dripped to the floor. The dogs grew wilder, half-formed red prints marking the floor as they paced through Kaden's blood.

"*Kaden!*" I screamed, the same horror coursing through me as when I'd seen my sister's bleeding eyes. Everyone I'd ever relied on had left me in this awful place. They had left me, just like I had left my sister. Maybe it was better to be alone. I survived when others hadn't. But if given a second chance, I wouldn't have left her.

The metal groaned beneath Kaden, the dogs still circling below. I stretched out over the railing. "Kaden, give me your hand."

He groaned and reached forward. As soon as his hand touched mine, I threw my weight backward, crashing him over the railing. For a moment we both lay still on the ground.

"I thought you were gonna leave me."

"I was."

There wasn't time to rest. I surged up, taking in Kaden. His arm looked in bad shape, deep puncture marks where one of the dogs must have bitten him. Blood stained his shirt and flowed down his arm. His eyes were closed, his face twisted with pain.

The dogs howled below us. We didn't have a gun and I didn't know how long till they found the stairs.

"Kaden, we need to move." His eyes drifted in and out of focus. When he didn't answer, I shook him and he cried out in pain. "We need somewhere safe to hide."

"The jewelry store, it's just . . . around . . ." His words slurred but it didn't matter—I could see the store. He half walked, half stumbled as I dragged him down the hallway. Howls sounded louder below us. Over the railing, I could just see the escalators leading to the second floor as the dogs bounded up, their long bodies stretching and contracting, covering the distance at a vicious pace. They were coming for us.

I hauled Kaden forward, not caring if I hurt him. The storefront was only feet away, but I could hear the steady *slap-slap-slap* of the dogs' paws on the floor. Pulling him over the store's threshold, I dropped him unceremoniously, then jumped for the metal chain-link casing to pull the door closed. A giant wolf dog tore around the corner as I yanked the chains down. The dog's enormous paws hit the casing just as the chains crashed to the floor, throwing me backward. He bit and clawed at the metal, but it held. The rest of the pack slammed into the chains as well, maddened by Kaden's blood. I noticed a second grate, a sheet metal wall that slid out from one side. I slammed it closed, casting us into darkness, muffling the snarls.

The store had been gutted, the glass displays smashed and the floor filled with glass shards and yellowed paper. I checked to make sure there was no back door before I knelt beside an unmoving Kaden. I ripped off my sweater and began to tear it into pieces, trying to make some sort of bandage to stop the flow.

"Sam."

I jumped. He spoke to the ceiling, his voice soft.

"No, it's Ara."

He grimaced and rolled his head to the side. I tried to tie the fabric to his shoulder, the way my father had taught me, but blood seeped through the cloth, making my fingers slippery and clumsy. I had never bandaged a wound this large before.

Kaden spoke again, voice rough. "No, Sam. He's my brother."

Although they didn't look alike, there was something protective in the way Kaden treated Sam.

"I didn't know that." *And I don't know why you're telling me now.* I pulled the bandage as tightly as I could, and Kaden grimaced. "You'll see him soon."

Kaden looked at me with hard eyes. I'd never been a good liar, but I was even worse at comforting. So much for a feminine touch.

"He's my half brother. We were the only two to survive in our family. He lived on his own for three months before I got to him." He gasped suddenly, his whole body tensing. He spoke through clenched teeth. "I only joined the clan because of him. I thought it would be safer, but now I don't know . . ."

He briefly grew louder and then started mumbling incoherently. A sudden coldness covered me as I realized what I should have from the beginning: the dogs were infected. One of them had bitten him. What if Kaden was infected now? I didn't know how the plague had spread, only that it had, suddenly and viciously, until humanity was almost gone. The only infected survivors were animals, who grew larger and more aggressive, their eyes milky and bloodshot.

I scooted away from Kaden, but when I did, I was shocked to find my arms covered in blood to my elbows. Not just Kaden's blood either. My palms had several deep cuts. I had been doctoring Kaden; our blood had mingled. What if I was infected? I pushed the thoughts away. If we were both infected, from everything I had seen, there was nothing we could do. There was no cure. Once your eyes turned white, death was a mercy.

After a few minutes, the howls died to whines and mere shadows pacing the floor, then nothing. The silence was broken only by Kaden's labored breathing and the low whistling of the wind.

Kneeling beside the metal screen, I peeked through a crack. No sign of the dogs. Unless I went for help right now, Kaden would die.

The metal screen screeched as I pulled it back inch by inch. The mall stretched into the distance, the dark storefronts and hidden corners unnerving. Storm clouds gathered beyond the open ceiling, choking out what daylight remained. I pulled the second door closed behind me, sealing Kaden in.

Like a tomb.

Now only the chain curtain stood between me, the empty mall, and the dogs. I opened it enough to slide out and then pulled it down behind me. I paused to listen. Then, like a flushed bird, I took off down the hallway, my footsteps too loud in the empty space. Every dark store I passed, every corner and shadow, was another trial. Relief filled me when I heard voices ahead. Issac, Sam, and Jeb would help Kaden.

A flicker of warning, some deep instinct kept me from turning the corner and calling out. The voices rose, and this time ice slithered down my spine: it wasn't Issac and Sam.

I flattened against the wall and tried to quiet my breath enough to listen. I couldn't make out individual words, just laughter and the clashing of metal. Were they allies? Somehow, I doubted it. Why wouldn't Kaden have told me? On instinct I reached up to my cap, making sure all the hair was tucked underneath.

There were enough of them that they weren't worried about being quiet. It wasn't too late to leave. I could disappear and nobody would ever know. I owed Kaden nothing. I had to think of myself, of my family. Emma with her wide, blue eyes, my father in his camouflage cap, holding my hands steady as he showed me how to aim. He had taught me to protect myself.

But Emma had taught me the value of a single life. And the cost of abandoning one.

I pictured Kaden in a growing pool of blood. His curly hair limp, his strange, green eyes closed forever. A cold wind blew down the corridor, rustling leaves and trash as I peeked around the corner. Movement in the food court revealed five men. I pulled back, my heart thundering.

A low snarl from behind me. The black wolf dog stalked forward.

If not for its dead white eyes and bared teeth, I might not have seen it.

Behind it, the milky eyes of the other dogs lit the darkness.

A flash of lightning lit the air. I spun and surged toward the food court and the other men. The dogs howled and raced after me, the sound of pursuit pushing me faster. The first drops of rain began to fall through the destroyed ceiling. It was as if a dam had broken, unleashing chaos.

I barreled through the food court. Two men stopped and watched me in surprise. One leveled a rifle at me, but I only yelled, "They're coming!" and streaked past him. I wove a trail of destruction, pulling over chairs and tables behind me, hindering any pursuit. Shouts of surprise were replaced with shouts of horror as the dogs came upon them. Screams, snarls, shots, and howls echoed behind me.

It felt like only seconds before I burst through the doors of the room we'd slept in. Jeb, Sam, and Issac all turned and looked at me in shock.

"Dogs . . . infected . . . chased . . . Kaden . . . hurt . . . other men . . . in food court . . ." I bent over and clutched my knees. My arms were stained red to the elbows.

"Sam, stay with Ara and barricade the door," Issac commanded. "Jeb, with me." I stood stunned, as if I had spent all my energy and could only watch as they rotated like planets around me.

Issac stretched a map out on the ground. I pointed to where I had left Kaden, the men, and the wolves.

Sam took my hand and pulled me away. Before we could barricade the door, Issac turned to me again. "Are you hurt?"

The gentle way he asked was somehow disarming. Maybe because I wasn't used to anyone caring anymore. I looked down at my blood-covered hands, and then met his eyes again. "I'm fine."

Sam and I barricaded the doors as soon as they left. Then he packed equipment and bags into three shopping carts. Inside one, he placed a sleeping bag and draped a tarp over it. Then he cleaned my hands with a bottle of alcohol and wrapped them in white cloth.

After that, we sat and waited. There was something peaceful about Sam, like the eye of a hurricane. Despite the destruction around us, as long as I stayed here, beside him, I felt safe. He talked to me, soothing and quiet, as if I were a wild animal. Though I couldn't concentrate on his actual words, his voice calmed me. Finally, we heard heavy footsteps and moans outside the door.

"Open up! It's Jeb!"

Sam and I pushed aside the crate, and Jeb and Issac carried Kaden in. His shoulder was bandaged, a much better job than I had done but his blood had already soaked through. His eyes were closed, and he moaned as Sam lifted the tarp on the shopping cart, and the other two men placed him inside. Kaden had to fold up to fit, despite Sam's attempts to make it comfortable. He was too tall and masculine to look anything but comical inside.

Jeb looked to Sam, then Issac, seeming lost without a leader. He settled on Issac. "I recognized the other men from the Borah Clan. The infected dogs have them pinned in the back of the food court, but they've got at least one gun. We should make for our clan before they come looking for us."

Issac nodded once, and Sam and Jeb began gathering the remaining supplies. Issac shrugged off a backpack, holding it out to me, and I was surprised to find that it was mine. The dark exterior was wet, but I pulled out the coat I'd found this morning and shrugged into its warmth. The weight of the pack felt comforting on my shoulders.

Issac motioned for Sam to push Kaden's cart while he and Jeb took the other two, heavy with supplies. I followed behind them. We took a hallway leading out the back of the mall. The wheels of the carts squeaked in the musty corridor, and the oddness of the moment struck me.

We were the strangest shoppers to ever leave this mall.

Issac led the group and kept a careful watch, but we saw neither men nor wolves. A hatchet was now strapped to his waist. He rammed his cart into the last set of double doors, and they swung open into the rain-filled night. The dark clouds gathering earlier had grown into a gale. The downpour came in sheets, and without even stepping into it I felt the first breath of winter.

We stepped out into the unrelenting rain and walked south, away from the mountains and deeper into the city. In the sifting shadows, buildings rose and fell. It wasn't long before I was soaked, even with the new jacket. But I didn't mind. It washed away the numbness. It washed away the blood. With each step in the wrong direction, my father's voice echoed in my head: *"Ara . . . I made a mistake, we all did. Go back to the beginning . . . go back . . . it's not too late."*

I needed to go back home. Back to where we had left Emma. Her absence, and the secrets my father kept hidden, haunted me. My father had taken Emma somewhere that night, when she first showed white eyes, the night before we left. There had to be a reason for that, and a reason he told me to go back to the beginning. Father always had a plan. It had kept me alive for three years, and it would keep me alive now.

The figures of the men wavered in the downpour. Issac pushed onward, relentless. Sam's white hands clenched the cart, his head bent against the wind and rain. Kaden was invisible, hunkered under a bit of tarp. He would live. Probably. Either way, it wasn't my problem.

I had supplies on my back, and even if I'd failed to find a weapon, I knew home lay somewhere to the south of here. I took several breaths and pushed my hood down. The rain coursed down my face. I saw everything around me unhindered—the crumbling buildings overtaken by nature, an airship lying upside down beside a rusted car. The faded, yellow stripes of the road centered me. I tightened the straps of my backpack.

Lightning cracked and when the sky went dark again, I lunged forward. I heard a cry behind me, but I didn't look back. I knew they couldn't catch me.

I didn't know we were already there.

FOUR—ARA

I awoke slowly, and in pain. My head throbbed. A scratchy wool blanket covered me. The metallic symphony of rain pounded above. Whispered voices wove together. Each of these sensations came separately, and each threatened to overwhelm me.

I was in a small metal shed. No. *We* were in a small metal shed. Four cots lined each side of a rectangular room, lit by a single beam of light coming from the cot opposite my own. I blinked and Sam and Issac came into focus, talking quietly and looking down at Kaden, who lay unmoving with blankets tucked up to his chin. My cot creaked as I sat up and they both stopped talking and turned to me.

"How are you feeling?" Sam asked. I flinched as the beam of his flashlight spun to hit my face.

"Light," I croaked.

"Sorry." He dropped it back to the floor.

I retraced my thoughts of bolting, running in the rain, the taste of triumph. Then it came back to me. Turning a corner, and . . .

someone. I couldn't bring his face into focus, only a glimpse of lightning long enough to see shadowed pits for eyes, and the butt of a rifle smashing into my face. I touched my fingers to my forehead and winced. I tried to clear my throat, and Sam stood up.

"They gave us a bucket of water," Sam said. "Do you want some?"

Sam was already up and moving to the door, where a bucket had been placed next to a metal slat opening. He brought it to me, and I drank straight from it, nearly choking on the metallic taste. I cleared my throat again, this time managing words. "Is Kaden all right?" I pushed myself out of the bed and was hit by a wave of nausea. Sam caught my elbow, steadying me.

"You okay?"

"Yeah." Despite my insistence, I had to lean on Sam as I walked over to Kaden. Sam spun the light briefly to his face, and my legs suddenly felt weak. His face was pale, covered in a sheen of sweat. His eyes were tightly closed, his mouth pinched, as if he were trapped in a nightmare he couldn't escape.

"Where are we?" I turned to Sam, but it was Issac who answered.

"We're under quarantine," Issac said, voice calm. "Either he dies by the morning and they kill us, too, or his fever breaks and they let us out."

"They?" I asked.

"Welcome to the Castellano Clan, Ara." Issac's eyes were sad.

I sank back onto my bed and surveyed the heavy metal sheeting of the small shed. The only opening was a small area beside the door, where the bucket had been. Another bucket sat in the far corner. The rain pounded above, and I was thankful that at least they'd put us somewhere dry to wait. I knew little of the plague, but what I did know was the sickness came on fast and killed just as quickly. There were so many theories about how it spread: the air; the water; person-to-person touch; on surfaces. No one knew because nothing seemed to stop it. There were theories that it had been man-made, a form of biological warfare designed to lie dormant and infect the world before a single symptom showed, and that all attempts to stop it were already doomed. The why of it all hardly seemed to matter anymore. If Kaden didn't have white eyes by the morning, then we were fine. And if he did, then there would be no escape. As I looked around, I realized we were missing one of our number.

"Where's Jeb?"

Sam's eyes suddenly creased. He glanced at Issac, who stared at his hands in silence, before he answered. His voice barely rose above the pound of the rain. "You ran into one of the guards at the front entrance. Issac caught up to you before the guard could do anything more than knock you out. Jeb ran when he found out they were going to quarantine us—" He swallowed hard, suddenly looking pale. "I think one of his friends was quarantined, and they ended up burning the whole shed down the next day."

Thunder shook the shed, and Issac turned to Sam, who looked miserable. "He had friends in a clan downtown," Issac said gently, "he will be welcomed there." He put a hand on Sam's shoulder, something fatherly in the gesture.

"Do they know?" I said. "About me?"

Sam's eyes found mine again. "No. It was dark and raining. Issac wouldn't let them come near."

I was strangely touched by this. Issac had saved me? Why? I glanced over at Kaden, surprised at the way my heart twisted to see him there.

Sam followed my gaze. "You think he's infect—"

"No," I interrupted. I had always been a terrible liar, but I tried for Sam. I owed him at least that. "He will be fine. He's strong." My words hung heavy in the air. The rain drummed above us, filling the silence. The cot squeaked as I laid back and tried to find a more comfortable position. Issac took the cot nearest the door, and Sam took the cot next to mine, edging it a bit closer. I pulled the scratchy wool blanket over me, but still I could feel Sam's eyes on me. Finally, I turned to him. "You should save the batteries."

He spun the flashlight down, then clicked it off. The sudden darkness was absolute, but I could feel him looking at me.

"What is it, Sam?" I sighed.

He hesitated, and then, softly. "You don't have to run from us. The clan will keep you safe."

Unless they burn this shed down with us in it.

I pulled my legs up onto the cot and hugged them to my chest. "I don't belong in the clan."

"But you could, if you tried." His voice was pleading, almost childlike in its intensity.

"I can't, Sam."

"Why not?"

Because we live in a world where women are all but extinct. Because the men in the clan will see me as a possession and not a person. Because I already betrayed everyone I love.

The darkness suddenly felt like a refuge, a safe place to share a small piece of the truth. "I'm trying to find my family. Or what's left of them." Guilt tightened my chest, surprising me. They had taken me prisoner—why should I feel guilty? But Sam wasn't one to dwell.

"You should have just told us! Wait until you meet the clan, we can help you find them. Maybe they can come live here with us."

"Sure, Sam." I sighed and closed my eyes, too tired to tell him everyone in my family was dead, and that I searched only for answers. When I opened them again, they had adjusted to the darkness. Of course, I dreamed my father's words meant something more; that he, my mother, and Emma were all healthy and well, waiting patiently at home for me to arrive. But I tried not to dream that often. To survive in this world you had to embrace the darkness, not cling to the impossible dreams of the past. My father didn't return. My family was dead. The only way to honor them was to follow my father's final words.

A sudden crack and boom of thunder shook the shed, and both Sam and I jumped. He laughed nervously, and clicked the flashlight back on beneath the covers, so that the light was muted.

"Kaden said he came to find you," I blurted out, wanting to move the conversation into safer territory.

"He told you that?"

"He also said you're brothers."

"Half brothers. I'm surprised he told you. He never tells anyone that. Said it was better 'kept secret.'" He made air quotes and grinned.

"He told me you were brothers when he thought he was—" *dying* "—when he was hurt."

Silence stretched between us until, to my surprise, Sam laughed. It sounded strange in the cold room, amid the noise of the storm. He ran his hand through his hair so that it stuck up at odd angles. I had a moment of déjà vu before I realized I'd seen Kaden do the exact same thing.

"You know, he used to be such a jerk. He only spent the summers with us, but he was always teasing me. One time he hid my Lego castle on top of our neighbor's house. Then he showed it to me through my binoculars. He couldn't stop laughing."

"Guess we were all different before."

"No, he's still like that. Only now he stands up for me. He's one of the best unit leaders and basically the whole reason the clan has horses and cattle." His chest swelled. "It took him three months, but he came on horseback to find me. My mom somehow got him a message." His shoulders caved forward as a dark memory passed over his eyes.

"How old is he?"

"He's twenty-one. I'm thirteen."

He paused, then asked in a curious voice, "How old are you?"

It had been so long I had to think about the answer. "I'm nineteen." Strange, to think I'd become a legal adult in a world that didn't care anymore. There were no bars to try to sneak into, no one left to vote for, no colleges left to give me a scholarship, no high schools left to graduate from. I laid my bruised head against the cool metal of the shed. "You said your mom got him a message?"

"Yeah. When my dad and her first got married, Kaden left to live at his dad's ranch in Montana. That's where he learned to ride so well." Sam frowned at the memory. "I never got to visit. He said his father wasn't much of a dad." I tried to picture a wild, blond, green-eyed boy on horseback.

"Does he have any other family?"

"A half sister and two other half brothers who didn't make it. But even though we weren't raised together, he still came for me." Sam leaned against the cold wall on the cot beside me.

"Of course, he did. You're family. Families stick together."

Sam smiled, but the lie punched me in the gut. Kaden had come for his family. I had left mine.

"What about you?"

His question surprised me. I stared up at the ceiling, suddenly wary. "What *about* me?"

"You said you were looking for your family? Did you mean siblings or parents?" His question was innocent, filled with genuine concern, but I had to fight my natural tendency to say nothing. I could trust Sam . . . couldn't I?

"My mom left early on. I didn't know then, but her eyes were turning and she didn't want to infect us. She didn't come back." I stopped, the words almost too thick and painful to say. "And I had a little sister. Emma." *Go back to the beginning. It's not too late.* Not too late for what? For answers? For Emma? For me?

"Is that who you're looking for?" Sam's voice was gentle.

I didn't want to answer, and even if I did, didn't fully know how. "No. She's gone. I'm looking . . . for my father." *Or whatever he left behind.*

Sam reached over and squeezed my hand. In the dim light I couldn't make out the red in his hair or the freckles on his face; instead I saw the resemblance between him and Kaden. The same straight nose and strong jaw. Sam's face was softer and free of stubble. It surprised me—I hadn't noticed the similarity before.

"Are there others? Other female survivors?" Sam asked. Even in the dark, with the storm pounding the shed, I heard the desperation in his voice. It made me sad.

"None I've seen," I whispered.

"How did you survive?"

The sound of the rain almost overpowered his voice. But it didn't matter, because the question had echoed in my head nearly every day for three years.

"I don't know."

In the end, the world fell apart like a boil bursting open: one day there was news of a strange sickness, and the next day thousands of people had white, bleeding eyes. I remembered Father flipping through the channels, desperate, and Mother leaving and not coming back. The number of cases grew exponentially, with no idea how it spread, how to fix it, or why women were more affected. Barricades sprang up, tanks rolled by our house, reporters begged people not to leave their homes. It didn't matter. Nothing stopped the sickness. A month in, he disappeared in the night with Emma. He brought her home. We left without her. We'd driven through a city littered with corpses, the only movement great flocks of blackbirds.

Sam said, "Well, the clan is a home for the lost."

I'm not lost. I'm a prisoner. But his smile was so naïve, that I couldn't find it in myself to tell him I would never belong in the clan, or anywhere for that matter. Instead, I leaned back in the cot.

"Tell me more about the clan."

~

Hours later, it finally stopped raining, and the thick darkness of the night faded. Sam had told me story after story about the clan, broken only by the thunder. I hoped Sam's stories would reveal some sort of weakness in the clan. Instead, they featured Kaden, and the wild and sometimes ridiculous escapades he led his team into while gathering supplies and livestock around the city. It brought a fuller picture of Kaden into relief; a man who was bold, sometimes reckless, and well liked by the men of the clan. At first, I didn't understand his recklessness, and why he willingly endangered his brother. But after a while, I think I understood. The way Sam talked, it was as if the end of the world were an adventure instead of an apocalypse. Maybe Kaden wanted to make a brighter world for his brother than the one we lived in. I couldn't fault him for that.

I did glean a few useful details. The clan was led by a man named Gabriel, whom Kaden disliked. The clan was split into many sections, well defended, with enough food that no one starved. Sam had just finished telling a story about Kaden leaving a wild raccoon in Gabriel's room when I decided to push my luck.

"Why don't Gabriel and Kaden get along?"

"Some of the men think Kaden would be a better leader. But Kaden always said he doesn't want it, that even if Gabriel's a prick, he's good at organizing and making everyone work together." Light crept under the door, slowly brightening the room. "He meets everyone and decides if they can stay with the clan. Just . . . be careful." He said this in a mysterious tone.

"Why?"

"There has to be a reason Kaden doesn't like him."

"More than one I'd say."

Sam and I jumped at Kaden's voice. Across from us, Kaden groaned, turning his head to reveal tired, but clear, eyes.

"Kaden!" Sam sprang off his cot and ran to him. I stood, then stopped when my head throbbed violently, and made my way over more slowly.

I sidled up next to the cot, wondering if Kaden had heard any of the embarrassing childhood stories Sam had begged out of me last night. I couldn't meet his eye.

"Ara, put your jacket back on, and put your hair in the baseball cap."

Who died and made you king? I thought. But I did what he

said regardless, and afterward he looked me up and down before nodding approval.

"Sam, go tell the guards we're all clear-eyed and healthy. Ara, help me stand up." Sam went to the metal hatch where they'd slid the bucket through, ducking down and calling out into the morning. I grasped Kaden's forearm and bent over his bed. Kaden groaned when I pulled, and I realized from the pained look on his face that I'd need to help more.

"Something wrong?" he said, his teasing smile tinged with pain. I bent over him and slipped my other arm around his back. His skin was warm to the touch, and I was suddenly hyperaware of him: his smell, the way his hair curled, the way his skin felt under my fingers, the way he wasn't wearing a shirt.

"Thanks." His good arm rested on my shoulder for balance as I held him upright. His bandages had soaked through in spots.

"Can you help me put a shirt on?" he said, eyes and mouth pinched with pain.

"Where's your stuff?"

"Under the cot, there should be a shirt on top."

I crouched and pulled his backpack out. A moment of déjà vu hit me as I remembered crouching over my father's backpack, searching desperately through it one last time, my hands shaking. I stood up abruptly. No more memories. Not today. Something told me it was going to be a long one.

"This okay?" I held up a tattered red button-down.

"You're the girl, shouldn't *you* be giving *me* fashion advice?"

"Oh my goodness," I said in my girliest voice. "This is soooo your color, holes and stains are just *in* this year." His eyes crinkled at the sides.

I helped pull on his shirt, fully conscious of the way his eyes tracked my every move. His back and shoulders were broad, his skin warm. I hadn't realized how tall he was until I stood next to him, so close I could watch his chest rise and fall.

"Thanks."

"Yeah."

I stepped away. Silence lingered between us.

"The guard's coming," Sam called out.

The door opened, framing a thick man holding a rifle like it was part of him. Kaden stepped in front of me.

"Gabriel wants to see you all. Now."

FIVE—ARA

We stepped out into the dawn, the morning air smelling of rain and wet earth. The guard took a moment to check Kaden's eyes, decided we weren't a threat, and nodded for us to follow him. Before we could, Kaden's hand landed on my shoulder. I turned to him in confusion as he pulled a piece of rope from his pocket and gestured to my hands.

"Trust me," he whispered.

As if I had a choice. Once my hands were tied, our small group followed the guard. The shed was in an old parking lot that was mostly empty except for a few abandoned airships, their shiny silver exteriors beaded with dew. There were also a few automobiles, but unlike the airships, their doors and tops were either rusted or missing. It wasn't until we passed by one that I realized this destruction was deliberate; there were planter boxes inside brimming with what looked like wilted tomatoes and some sort of squash. Across the expansive parking lot stood an enormous building framed with wooden pillars that looked like a giant hunting lodge. Faded cursive letters were etched above the entryway: *Cabela's*. I almost laughed; I was a prisoner at my father's favorite store.

An impressive fence topped with barbed wire circled the parking lot. Even in the early morning, men with rifles patrolled the fence. It suddenly made more sense why Jeb had run. No one would be sneaking in or out.

Sam talked with our guard while Kaden and I took up the rear. Halfway to the building, Issac simply went his own way. The guard looked as if he might stop him, then glanced at his broad shoulders and the hatchet strapped to his waist, and seemed to decide otherwise. Kaden called out to the men we passed, who smiled and greeted him.

Soon the pillars of the building loomed over us. Doors that had once been glass were now covered with metal sheets. Two burly, armed men guarded the entrance.

"Heard you were detained," the guard on the left said to Kaden. *Detained.* He said it so casually.

"Thomas, Brandon!" Kaden nodded to both men. "Good to see you."

"Anything to report?"

Kaden nodded to me, lifting the rope that held my hands bound. "Just a scrawny prisoner." The guards laughed at this, and my anger flared even as I stared at the ground.

The doors screeched open and we stepped into darkness. Before they slammed behind us, I saw another set of covered doors.

Frantically, I tried to remember the layout of the store. Father liked to go on his own, but once Mother made him bring Emma and me, and we had begged for fudge. He had let us wander the store, eating chocolate, while he went to buy some sort of old-tech gun up for auction. I remembered a tall ceiling with glass skylights, taxidermied animals, and a high ledge running the perimeter of the store. But the memory was cozy and warm; this place looked repurposed for war. I stepped closer to Kaden as the second set of doors swung open, and for just a moment, thoughts of escape disappeared.

There were men everywhere—a sea of life standing before me. Young men whistling and talking, middle-aged men cooking food. Even a few souls with graying hair, not quite old but the eldest I had seen survive. I could do nothing but stare. Part of me wanted to cry; there were so many survivors here, so much *life* here. It had been so long since I'd seen people just being people. The other part of me was terrified. Every step I took deeper into this fortress was a step further away from honoring my father's words. *There are no such things as friendly men, Ara. Not in this world. Not for you.* When they found out what I was . . . my throat constricted.

Kaden tugged on the rope, and I stumbled after the group. We followed a thin cement path through the store. Most of the original merchandise I remembered had been moved to make way for stores of canned food, and other supplies and equipment I didn't have time to examine. But it was the sheer number of men that took my breath away. They cooked over open fire pits, the smoke drifting up and out through one of the broken skylights. Other men talked and relaxed in camouflage chairs. Running around the perimeter was a high ledge that once had displayed cozy outdoor scenes of tents and other stuffed wildlife. Now tents littered the ledges, as well as clothing, chairs, plastic dressers, and coolers. I even saw a majestic-looking moose with several different colors of underwear hanging from its antlers. This must have been where most of the men slept, as I could see men in various states of undress climbing out of tents and preparing for the day.

Scenes of wildlife interrupted these pockets of life, the only thing from the original store that hadn't been changed. We walked by a boulder with four taxidermied wolves, so lifelike that I watched them warily.

At the back of the store, a mound of rocks stood against the wall, crowned with taxidermied animals, each holding a lifelike pose. The mound was North American–themed, with a cougar and a mountain goat locked in mortal combat, surrounded by chipmunks, deer, an elk, a moose, rabbits, and others. All animals I had seen, fought, or killed in the last three years.

Kaden forced me to the ground at the base of the mound. "Keep your head down, wait till I say."

A bell rang out, and men began to make their way to the center, gathering around us. The rope burned into my wrist as I tried to fold my hands and slip them loose. I looked up past the wooden railing and into the jaws of a snarling wolf and the empty, reflective eyes of a white-tailed deer. More and more men surrounded us. Again, I was forced to reconsider how many were here. Three hundred? Four hundred? More?

"Good morning, brothers."

The voice was calm and measured, and only seemed loud because of how the chatter died almost instantly. But what surprised me was that it came from above, at the top of the mound.

"Tomorrow we celebrate two years of formation," the voice went on. "As such, tomorrow will be declared an official holiday, and celebrated accordingly." Cheers went up at this. "Lots will be drawn for five who will work through half the celebration before rotating with another five." The cheers lessened.

"Work will proceed as usual today. But first, each unit leader will report on the week's progress. Kaden? Would you care to report? You are almost a week late."

Something about the cold way he spoke made me nervous. Blood pounded in my ears as Kaden suddenly grabbed my arm and forced me to stand. My eyes traveled upward, past the vacant eyes of the doe and into the eyes of the man standing atop the mountain. I was surprised. He wasn't a day over twenty-five, with piercing eyes as sharp as the stuffed falcon forever perched on the ledge beside him. Unlike the grubby men surrounding me, he wore a spotless button-down and his face was clean shaven, revealing golden-brown skin and neatly trimmed dark hair.

"We spent the first week on the far north side of the city, across the river," said Kaden. "There were reports from others about a strange creature in the flooded downtown. We investigated but found nothing. We also tried to get to the testing center, but the water was too high. We will need to return with kayaks. If we don't act soon, we could lose whatever medicine still remains there."

Kaden paused, as if reveling in the absolute attention he held. Only his tight grip on my arm said differently.

"And?" The ice in the other man's voice contrasted with Kaden's smile. The two glared at each other. The man's cold eyes swept to me. At first, I tried to hold his steely gaze, but it seemed that he dismissed me. Then he looked again. This time he leaned forward, the whites of his eyes growing wide. I stared at the ground, breathing fast.

He knew.

He knew and I would never escape.

"Kaden, who is this?"

"Glad you asked, Gabriel." With a sudden flourish, Kaden dropped the rope on my wrists, pushed back my hood, and let my baseball cap fall to the ground.

"This is Ara."

The silence that covered the building was so intense that the lone birdsong floating down from the ceiling seemed intrusive. I felt the stare of every man there like a physical weight.

Damn Kaden and his theatrics.

SIX—KADEN

My shoulder throbbed, my head ached, but the moment Gabriel vaulted over the wooden fence and took Ara's chin in his hands, my whole body surged with anger. So much so that it was hard not to punch him in the face.

"Impossible," he whispered.

Ara yanked away from him, and the murmurs grew. I stayed close to her, straight-backed, meeting men's eyes and daring them to come closer. Guilt twisted my gut for putting Ara through this but considering everything I knew of Gabriel, I didn't see any other way. If I'd told Gabriel privately, he might have hidden her away forever, or tried to claim her like some kind of possession. Now that the whole clan knew, the men would come to see her as one of their own.

The voices continued to grow, the men crowded closer, and I wondered belatedly if there might have been a better way to do this. *Guess a whole night with a burning fever and a throbbing shoulder wound aren't exactly good decision primers.*

Despite their curiosity, the men kept a careful circle around us. Fear was a powerful repellant; Ara should be dead. Or at least infected. Murmurs of disbelief and shocked, almost angry, voices called out. The men inched closer, and for maybe the first time, Ara voluntarily stepped closer to me.

"Silence," Gabriel lifted a hand, barely raising his voice, and the voices died. "Kaden and I will escort the prisoner into a holding area until we decide what to do with—" he paused and glanced at Ara "—her. The festivities will continue tomorrow night as planned." His voice dropped. "Unit leaders, report to Liam. Meeting adjourned."

Mutinous silence. No one moved.

"I said, *meeting adjourned*." His voice was ice. The men dispersed, whispering and throwing looks over their shoulders. Gabriel turned to Ara, and I felt a sudden, uncomfortable foreboding at the way he watched her. I didn't often regret my decision to not become clan leader, but right now, I wondered if it had been a mistake.

"Come, we can talk in my office." He started down the path to the back of the store, and we followed.

All around the store, men turned to watch Ara, but at least Gabriel was good for something, glaring at them until they went back to work. We passed under a fake pine tree with a taxidermied cougar crouched in its limbs. Behind the tree was a shop labeled *Gun Library*. Ivory tusks framed the wooden door. Normally I avoided this part of the building, but I knew there was a back-office area that Gabriel used for a bedroom. And that there was no exit.

"Ara, if you wouldn't mind. I need to talk with Kaden alone for a moment." Gabriel opened the door and gestured her inside.

I buried a smile, waiting to see if she would listen to him. But maybe she also sensed that with Gabriel it was best to pick your battles, because she stepped into the room without a word. Or maybe she was going to figure out how to use one of the old guns inside and shoot Gabriel with it. The door had barely shut when Gabriel rounded on me, his whole demeanor suddenly changed from calm to furious.

"You've never liked my authority, but this is a new level. What the hell is your problem?" Even angry, there was something oddly controlled about him.

"I'd say my biggest one is looking at me right now."

He didn't rise to the bait. "You found a woman, and didn't think to share that piece of information with me before telling the entire clan?"

My fists clenched, and pain lanced down my shoulder at the movement. "She's not a piece of information. She's a person."

"You should have told me before. We could have met without the entire clan knowing—"

"Remind me what happened the last time we met without the entire clan knowing?"

His eyes suddenly went cold. "Everett's death was an accident. And he was my brother before he was your friend."

But neither was enough to save him, was it, Gabriel?

Gabriel cleared his throat, that calm, calculating exterior snapping back in place. This was why he made a good clan leader. The mention of a dead brother threw him for only a moment. Maybe to save humanity you had to lose your own.

"What does she know of the clan?" he said.

I suddenly regretted this entire thing. I never should have brought her here. Yes, there were good men here. There was safety, food, stability . . . but there was also Gabriel. "She knows it's a safe place," I said. "But from what I've seen, she's survived on her own so far. You should give her free rein. Let her feel like she has a choice to be here." *Or actually give her one.*

But I didn't say that, because his eyes already narrowed, suspicious of my help. Which he should be. I decided to push my luck. "She asked to be part of the horse team with Sam, she seems to really have connected with him." This would at least get her out of the main building and away from Gabriel. I'd have to remember to mention it to her.

Gabriel's frown deepened. "I see." He glanced at the door. "Does she have experience with horses?"

I never asked, but sure, why the hell not? "Of course."

I felt a sudden wave of exhaustion. All I wanted was to go to the stables, check on Red, my men, and then pass out. But I wouldn't leave Ara with this man. He seemed to realize this as he made his way back to the door. He paused with his hand on the handle.

"And what does she know of me?"

I gave him a cold half smile. "That you're the clan leader."

He stared at me with those eerie gray eyes that always reminded me of a corpse. "Tell me we can work together on this?"

On this? She's already a project to work on? But I didn't have the strength for a joke. "If she wants to belong to the clan, I won't stand in her way. I brought her here, didn't I?"

"So you did." He seemed to realize this was the best he'd get from me, because he turned back to the door. "She stays in here today, until I talk to the rest of the clan. Agreed?"

He stared at me until I nodded, and then opened the door. I followed him inside.

The walls were filled with glass cabinets containing what even I had to admit was an impressive array of guns, many of them ancient muskets and revolvers. Gabriel had insisted they be kept here, "preserving history" or some crap like that. I would have taken them down, given them to the men to try to use, but since we were short on ammunition, not guns, Gabriel got his way. He usually did. Ara sat at the long rectangular table in the center of the room, where Gabriel held his weekly clan meetings, because god forbid the end of the world also mean the end of boring work gatherings.

Ara caught my eye and I pressed my lips together, wishing I'd had more time to warn her about Gabriel. I pulled the door shut behind me, the room darkening, lit only by the light creeping through the cracks in the door.

"First, I want to welcome you to the clan, Ara," Gabriel said. I resisted the urge to roll my eyes. "My men and I will do everything in our power to make sure you are happy and well taken care of here. I'd like to spend some time with you later today, after you've rested and eaten. If there's anything you need, please let me know."

Ara said nothing, her arms crossed in front of her. Before Gabriel could speak again, there was a knock on the door, and a man holding a tray of food walked in. My mouth salivated at the sight of it. He set the tray on the table with trembling hands, staring at Ara before he turned to Gabriel and said with a squeak, "Liam said he needs you."

"I will be there shortly." Gabriel cleared his throat and turned back to Ara. "Do you have any questions for me?"

"No," she said. An awkward silence settled over the room. I lounged against the table, trying not to smile. *This is going well.*

Finally, Gabriel dipped his head. "Well, after last night, I'm sure you'd like some time to yourself. My quarters are through that door; you can rest there, and then we can talk later today." He gave her a last smile and made for the door. "Kaden?"

"I'll catch up with you," I said without looking at him. He stood there, looking between both of us, and I could almost see the tiny wheels in his head turning. But whatever he saw, he decided to leave it, and left. As soon as the door closed, I exhaled and leaned against the table. All I wanted was to sit in the chair and lay my head against the table. But I knew if I did, I might not get back up. The smells from the soup—potato and some other vegetable— wafted up to me. I swear if Gabriel wasn't so good at keeping food on the table I would have left ages ago.

"You okay?" I said, when I was sure Gabriel was gone. In the dark, it was hard to read her.

"I'm fine." Her eyes went to the door. "Gabriel's not as scary as you all made him out to be."

"That's because you don't know him yet." *And hopefully you never do.* The thought made me uneasy, and I forced myself to stand and smile through the pain. "I need to go check on the stables. They always slack off when I'm gone. You should eat." I pushed the food toward her, ignoring the way it sloshed in the bowl with some effort.

"Can I come with you?"

Her words caught me off guard and I was tempted to say yes. "No. Gabriel doesn't want you to leave this room. Just for today. Your arrival was . . . unexpected." I tried to smile. "He wants to make sure things are ready before you meet the clan again."

"And Gabriel makes the rules?"

"He does for now. Just wait. And trust me." I picked up the loaf of bread, split it, and tucked half into my pocket. Then I walked past her and opened the door to the back bedroom. "If you won't eat, you might as well sleep." I stepped into a cream-colored room with no windows. A desk and chair stood on one side, and a camp bed with a red sleeping bag and checkered blanket were tucked in the opposite corner. A perfect visual for the manically organized brain of Gabriel. There wasn't anything left for me to do or say, but I hesitated to leave. I'd just brought her to a new place, only to abandon her. Then I saw her stifle a yawn; she was tired too.

Still, I paused at the door. "Be careful with Gabriel. He's not what he seems and he'll do anything to get what he wants."

"And did you just give him exactly what he wants?"

"Maybe. But the clan isn't all bad. There are good men here. Men who would die to protect you."

She stiffened at my words, clearly not comforted. I lowered my voice, trying to make it gentle. "Listen, I told Gabriel you had experience working with horses. You can work with Sam and me in the stables. You'll be safe there. I'll teach you how to ride."

"And what happens when I want to leave?"

"Then tell Gabriel you want to join the clan. Join, and if you decide you want to leave, in a couple weeks, I'll help you."

She stepped forward, all the way up to me, so that it was suddenly a bit harder to think. "And if I want to leave now?"

"Then you'll have to take it up with Gabriel."

Even in the dark, I could see the disgust in her eyes at my response, and I felt whatever small amount of rapport we'd built crumble. I'd brought her here. This was my fault. No apology was going to fix that.

"I'll come by later with your things," I said lamely. She sat down heavily on the bed, and I wondered if there were any way to comfort her. I dismissed that thought immediately. Anything I did would probably freak her out more. So instead I opened the door, surprised when she called out to my retreating form.

"Kaden, promise you will help me leave?"

"Promise, princess."

But I wondered if it was a promise I could keep.

SEVEN—ARA

A cold wind blew over the hills, bringing with it the scents of manure and the sharp pine of the encroaching forest. Gabriel crouched beside me, gazing out over the clan and a landscape shaded with the final orange and reds of fall. I'd slept through the first day and night of my time at the clan, but he'd woken me this morning with a strange request: he wanted to show me the clan from the roof.

"The stables are just up the hill." He pointed to a rise behind the main buildings. "We put them farthest away because of the smell. We have a small barn with some other livestock and chickens just to the right." He continued to point out other aspects of the clan, and I listened intently for weaknesses. I found none. "We've mostly been hunting and gathering food from the remains, but we brought in a good harvest this year. Lots of potatoes. I've started clearing fields for—"

"Why am I here, Gabriel?" I cut through his explanations.

He turned the full force of his gray-blue eyes to me, and I

forced myself not to look away. He was a handsome man—dusky skin, those light blue-gray eyes—but there was also something shrewd about him. As if he could look at a person and size up their value in an instant, then discard them just as easily.

"This," he spread his hands wide, "is my vision for humanity. We have a chance at redemption. A chance to rebuild. I want you to be a part of it."

I looked at the men that swarmed over the ground like ants. "And if I don't want to be a part of it?"

"Then you put me in a tricky situation. I've seen the violence and horror in this city." His voice dropped, a hint of bitterness creeping into his polished persona. "At the end of everything, people didn't come together. They tore each other apart. It isn't hard to imagine what most men would do to you if they found you." I pulled my coat tighter around me.

"You might not see it this way," he went on, "but you were very lucky Kaden's group found you."

"You could just let me go."

"I could. But what would the clan, or even history, think of the man who let humanity's last hope walk out into danger? Can I sacrifice the needs of many for the desires of one?"

And just what are the needs of a group of men with one lone female? My thoughts followed a dark path, my voice not completely steady when I asked, "And what do you expect of me here?"

He looked up, his voice soft. "None of my men will touch you, Ara. I made that all very clear to them. As long as you stay within the clan, you are safe."

And there it was. As long as I remained a prisoner, as long as I followed his rules, then I would be safe. *There are no such things as friendly men, Ara. Not for you.* I couldn't trust any of them. Hadn't Kaden proved that? I'd saved his life, and he'd brought me here. I didn't for a second believe he would help me escape, even if he'd promised to. If I wanted to get back to the beginning, I would need to do it on my own. But he had given me some valuable advice: if I wanted to escape, the fastest way might be to appear that I wanted to be here.

"I guess a prisoner is the safest person of all," I said, laying my trap and waiting for him to say something equally pretentious. It didn't take long.

"Maybe we are all prisoners to the cards life has dealt us. I am a prisoner to duty, the leader of a clan. Men depend on me. We each have a part to play in the redemption of the world."

"Maybe the world doesn't deserve redemption. Maybe I am fate's final laugh."

"I'm not laughing. And neither are the men of the clan. You've brought more hope to these men in one day than I have in three years."

If he meant to flatter me, it didn't work. My only thought was they needed to find something else to put their hope in, because I wouldn't be here long. A plume of smoke rose in the distance, where some of the men were clearing a field beyond the fence. They kept the perimeter of the fence clear and there were men everywhere working. It was going to take every ounce of cunning I had to escape this place. Still, the words were hard to force out. "Then I will join you."

His smile was contained, as were his movements, but his eyes gave him away. He'd gotten exactly what he wanted. "Excellent. Come. We will make it official."

Gabriel led me back to the gun library, and then he opened a wooden cabinet beneath the guns. "Please, sit," he said, and then slid a wide, heavy book toward me. I stared down at it, and when he nodded, opened it to the first page. The page was well worn and yellowed, with a neat list of names down the front, all in different penmanship.

Gabriel answered my question. "A list of every member of the clan. They are all required to sign when they join. I find it's good to keep some semblance of order here."

You've got more than a semblance; a prison would be easier to escape. "All I have to do is sign?"

Gabriel smiled. "Not quite. Once you sign, we will have you voted in and find a place for you to work."

I examined the first page; the lines were small and the names filled the whole page. *How many men have lived and died here?* I held the first page in my hand, meaning to turn it to a blank space, when the first seven names caught my eye. They all had the last name: Castellano. The bottom of those seven read *Gabriel Castellano.* Issac had said this was the Castellano Clan, but only now did I realize it was a family name.

"Is your family here as well?"

"No." His voice was polite, but firm, brooking no further conversation, even though I wondered: if his family wasn't here, where were they?

I pushed the curiosity away. All that mattered was my own family and getting the hell out of here. "Where do I sign?"

He turned three full pages of names before he pointed to the last few spaces at the bottom of the page. "Here."

"And I know where I can work in the clan." I signed my name at the bottom: *Arabella Edana.*

"Oh?"

"I want to work with the horses."

He gave me a long look, but finally said. "Kaden mentioned you might. Are you sure that's what you want?"

"I'm sure." I'd only ever ridden a pony at a state fair. But how hard could it be? As soon as I learned to ride one of those four-legged monsters, I was out of here. Hopefully with a gun and enough supplies to survive the winter too.

He took the paper back from me, handling it as if it were precious and not just a sheet of paper full of scribbled names.

"Well, we'll get it sorted in the morning. For now, we should go to the celebration. Sam came to see you while you were sleeping, he'll want to see you now." He paused, his voice dropping. "Kaden came as well. He left your backpack."

Gabriel waited in the main room while I searched through my backpack in the small bedroom. The pocketknife I'd found at the mall lay tucked inside a rolled-up jacket. I debated taking it with me, but instead hid it deeper inside the bag. I changed quickly, uncomfortable being unclothed in a room without a lock, knowing Gabriel was just outside.

After I was dressed, Gabriel led us back out into the main area. All around us men stopped their work to stare. I held each of their eyes until they looked away but was discomforted, nonetheless.

Gabriel explained the layout of the store to me as we walked, and how every man who joined brought some sort of special skill: hunting, fishing, or farming; knowledge of edible plants; a few even had medical backgrounds. Listening to him talk, I understood why Kaden didn't like him; he had almost *too* much of a plan. We walked through the hunting and fishing sections, where I was disappointed to see all the guns were missing. Gabriel explained that leaders in each section were responsible for managing all the equipment, renting out supplies, and keeping everything in good condition. I'd seen a few men with rifles slung across their backs or pistols strapped to their side walking through the store, but there was something possessive in the way they handled the weapons. It was going to be hard to steal one. I added it to my growing list of problems.

"We also have an archery range. We're trying to train all our hunters in archery. Our ammunition supplies are low, and we need to save what's left for defense of the base. The higher tech weapons don't work at all anymore, so we're left using guns, and soon it'll be just bows. Do you hunt at all?"

I shrugged. My father was amazing with a bow, and had trained me to be the same, but I wasn't going to let him know that. Maybe I could steal a bow instead of a gun.

"The kitchen is over in what was originally a small candy shop, though many of the men cook for themselves. It's too difficult to feed this many people. It's one of our biggest structural problems." He frowned, as if the shortcoming was a personal flaw.

"Ara!" A head of red hair vaulted out of the camping section. Sam wrapped his arms around me and lifted me in a crushing hug. I gasped in surprise. I had always shied away from physical contact, but Sam's exuberance left no room for awkwardness.

"Come on, the celebration is about to start. I saved you a spot." He dragged me away from Gabriel.

"And I need to go ring the bell. See you there," Gabriel called after us.

~

The celebration was to be held in roughly the center of the store, around the biggest fire pit. Easily over a hundred men sat in camp chairs and on the ground around the fire, all talking and laughing. They quieted and stared as I approached. *You can do this, Ara. You can act like you belong here.* Still, each step forward felt like willingly walking into a group of infected animals without a weapon, every nerve on end.

"Sam! Ara! Over here!" Kaden waved us over to the very center of the circle, where two empty camouflage chairs sat beside him. I made my way through the men, hyperaware of their rank smell, their devouring eyes. My feet fell so lightly on the floor one wrong movement from anyone would send me running. As much as I didn't want to sit and present my back to the men behind me, I didn't see another option. As soon as we sat down, Kaden began introducing me to the men around us. "Ara, this is Jack, the best fisherman you'll ever meet."

Jack grinned at me, and despite the tension filling my body I had to resist the urge to smile. He looked like a human jack-o'-lantern—he had to be missing half his teeth.

He stood and shook my hand vigorously. "Real pleasure to meet you, thought you'd gone extinct, but it's a real pleasure to know you ain't."

Despite myself, I found myself relaxing a little, especially when someone brought me another bowl of soup and a hunk of bread. An air of celebration rose, and though many still stared, more began to introduce themselves. I met Tom "Hunter," who was in charge of all the hunting operations and sported an impressive beard and heavy odor. Jordan, a large, soft-spoken man who oversaw the kitchens, and a young man named Lukas, who was lanky and silly and only a bit older than Sam. I talked for a bit with Liam, the man whom Gabriel had named as his second. There was a moment of shock when I realized we had gone to the same high school. I had never graduated, but I remembered him, a grade above me. He was taller now, with bright blue eyes and an easy smile. All of the men knew Kaden, and many ruffled Sam's head as they walked by.

Names blurred together, and I let Liam, Kaden, and Sam keep up the conversations. I kept waiting for someone to try to grab me, and while many of the men stared, with Kaden, Issac, and Liam surrounding me, I felt, not exactly safe, but at least able to catch my breath.

"What did Gabriel want with you?" Kaden leaned in to be heard over the other voices.

"He wanted me to join the clan."

"What did you tell him?"

"I said I would, but only if I can work with the horses."

He laughed at this, a deep, full-throated noise with no shame. "I'll teach you. The doctor said no more expeditions until my shoulder heals, so I'll be working in the stables for at least the next two weeks."

"And after that?" I leaned in closer, the commotion around us making it hard to hear.

"Then we'll leave to collect medicine. It was what we were trying to do on this last mission, but the water was too high. The dam burst a year ago, and we've had so much rain recently we couldn't get to it. We'll need to return with kayaks."

"Sounds fun," I said dryly.

Kaden laughed. The truth was it sounded awful. The downtown area was flooded, dangerous, and the opposite direction I needed to go. Maybe this was a good thing. With Kaden gone and Gabriel believing I wanted to be here, maybe I could slip away without anyone's help. The bell rang, signaling the start of the celebration, and men from all over the store drifted to the circle. Something about what he'd said stood out to me. "So why this place? Why not one that's easier to get to? It seems like a lot of trouble."

"That's exactly why Gabriel wants us to go. Most of the hospitals were overrun in the end, the supplies used up or destroyed. But this one is so tricky to get to, so there's a chance the supplies are untouched." Kaden paused, and I saw him weighing what to tell me. He dropped his voice and leaned closer. "Gabriel told the clan he wants the antibiotics and medicine there, but that's not what Doctor Jones said. He thinks it was some sort of ground zero for the plague in this city. Maybe they were looking for a cure."

"And what do you think?"

"I don't," he winked at me. "I'm just a lowly unit leader who does what he's told."

I seriously doubt that. He turned to talk with Jack, and I almost left it alone, but curiosity pulled a final question from me. "What's it called?"

"Birmingham Medical Testing Center."

And then I couldn't breathe.

~

"Ara! They're coming!" My father's voice cut through the clear mountain air. It was almost noon, and he had been out hunting for hours. Blue puzzle pieces of sky showed through the full leaves above. It was a perfect spring day, and until now I had been enjoying the sun

on my shoulders. Now he returned, weaving through the undergrowth. Loki, our husky, bounded after him. In his last few strides, my father threw me the rifle. It was only for show—we had run out of ammunition ages ago.

Besides, weapons wouldn't help us now. In the distance, the river rumbled, high and swift from snowmelt. I made to grab my backpack, but he stopped me.

"Leave your things," he said, and it was only then I realized the true desperation of this moment. In those packs were everything we owned. I thrust my pack inside a hollow log beside his. Loki whined at my father's heels.

"Where to?"

"You know the sandstone ledge, up against the river? Meet me there in two days."

This was wrong. We never split up.

The distant noise of dogs howling sounded clear over the baritone roar of the river. Below the baying, I heard a high thrumming noise. An airship. I hadn't seen a working airship in three years, but somehow they had one.

My father surprised me then, pulling me close. He gripped my shoulders, his words whispered and frantic. "Ara . . . I made a mistake, we all did. Go back to the beginning . . . go back . . . it's not too late . . ." Loki whined louder now, pacing toward the river and then back, hackles raised.

"Everything I did, it was all to save you." He disappeared into the trees then, with only a knife strapped on his waist and a bow slung across his back.

Before they disappeared from view, I was gone. They left to give me a chance, and for them, I could not waste it. I ran swift and silent as a deer, and then spent much of the rest of the day with my shoes off, wading up and down streams to leave no scent. Though I was weary and hungry, I stepped carefully and left no path for any to follow.

For five nights I waited on the sandstone ledge overlooking the river, not allowing myself to think about what came next. The last few years my father had taught me how to survive, but always he made the decisions as to where to go next, and I followed faithfully. So, I waited. I ate huckleberries in the forest and scaled a tree when a black bear joined me to share in the harvest. I drank straight from the stream, the icy water so cold my teeth ached.

Finally, I could wait no longer.

On the sixth day, I returned to the campsite. I found the hollowed log and pulled out my backpack. It was filled with all the essentials for survival: matches, knife, tarp, water purifier, compass, tinder, a sleeping bag. I reached deeper into the log. At first there was nothing, and wild hope rose in me. Then, my fingers brushed fabric; my heart shattered as I pulled my father's pack from inside.

He had not been back to claim it.

A distant sound in the forest. I jerked upright. No one could have followed me; it was just an animal. Even so, without a weapon, I felt like a fish in a shallow stream, trapped with nowhere to hide. I crouched over my father's backpack, ripped open the zipper, and searched through it one last time. I was aimless, a ship without a rudder. Go back to the beginning, he'd said, but what was the beginning? I threw his bag on the ground in frustration, but as I did, I noticed something—a small X in the inner lining of the fabric. It betrayed a tiny pocket not part of the original design. I drew my knife and slid it along the stitches. A small piece of paper fell out. It was folded into a tiny rectangle, and well worn. I opened it, expecting something lengthy, explaining everything, but on it were only four simple words:

Birmingham Medical Testing Center

~

"Ara? You okay?" Kaden reached out to me, and I felt his hand on my shoulder. He spoke again, but the words slurred together. All I could hear, repeated again and again, was Birmingham Medical Testing Center.

I needed to go on his expedition.

~

"Tonight"—the men turned to look at Gabriel, framed by the fire's dancing light—"we celebrate two years of formation!" The clan broke into raucous applause. "But before we celebrate, we have a new member to vote in. Who will speak for her?"

A moment ago, I'd wanted to join the clan only as a ruse to help me escape; now it was essential. This whole time I'd thought the beginning my father had spoken of was home, but what if this testing center was the beginning he meant? Silence grew over the clan.

"I will speak for her." Sam stood, gangly and grinning. "This clan became my family after I lost mine. Ara lost her family too. I've gotten to know her, and I think it's time we had a girl in the clan."

Some of the men chuckled, and a few more slapped him on the back as he sat back down.

Kaden stood, and this time a different sort of silence fell over the crowd. It felt charged, tenuous. "If Ara wants to belong here, then she deserves the chance. She saved my life." I looked down, my cheeks warm.

"I agree with Kaden and Sam," Gabriel said, standing up. "Ara will make a valuable addition to our clan. All in favor, raise your hands."

I kept my eyes on the ground but heard the rush and rustle of many raised hands. Kaden gave me a sad smile. "Welcome to the clan, Ara."

The celebration consisted primarily of eating meat roasted over the fire and singing off-key, raunchy songs. Gabriel also brought out several boxes of expired, packaged sweets. Kaden and I split chewy licorice, and I saw Sam eating a Twinkie and Issac a Snickers bar.

Now or never.

"Kaden?"

He turned to me, and I took a deep breath and leaned toward him, letting my arm brush against his. "Teach me how to ride tomorrow?"

I'd never tried to deliberately flirt with someone. My few memories of flirting with boys were awkward and childish, no help with someone like Kaden, who was both handsome and older than me. But my worry disappeared instantly; Kaden was almost too easy to flirt with, even if it was just an act. He grinned and slung an arm around my shoulders. I felt my cheeks grow warm, as he whispered in my ear, "Well, the first thing you need to know . . ."

After an hour or so, most of the food had disappeared and one of the men produced a soccer ball. This led to a scramble to go outside into the parking lot and set up teams. Several men invited me to play, but I turned them all down.

"Did you play soccer at all growing up?" Kaden asked as we stood against the side of the building. Even with the game going, guards patrolled the long fence.

"No, it was the same season as track." I shrugged. It seemed absurd that I'd once run for the fun of it, not because my life depended on it. "Feels like a different lifetime to be honest."

"I'm sure Sam would teach you if you asked."

Go back to the beginning. It's not too late. I turned to Kaden, and took a deep, steadying breath. "Not if you teach me how to ride. And take me on your expedition."

"We'll be taking the kayaks through downtown. It'll be dangerous."

"All the more reason to bring me. You might need someone to save your life again."

Kaden smiled, looking out at the game as I held my breath, waiting for his answer.

"Why do you want to go?" he finally said, and I heard suspicion beneath the curiosity.

There was one moment, when I looked into his green eyes, that I thought about telling him the truth. For so long my only goal had been to avoid others, to find food, to follow my father's words, that I'd forgotten what it was like to work with someone.

But Kaden had brought me here. So, I told him what I hoped was the right answer. "I don't want to stay here with Gabriel; not if you aren't here."

He nodded, looking back to the men, seeming to accept this as we fell into silence and watched the game. He hadn't given me an answer, but he also hadn't said no.

When it got too dark for the men to see the ball, everyone went back inside. I saw the guards who were walking the perimeter trade off with other men, who lit torches dipped in some sort of oil before they began to walk the same path. Inside, men climbed rope ladders up to the second-floor ledge, a few scaling only a knotted rope that had been dropped over the edge.

"Do you sleep up there?" I asked as we crossed the dark store.

"Nah, too smoky," Kaden said. "I sleep in the stables. But I'll come get you early tomorrow." I wanted to ask to sleep in the stables, too, but I'd already pushed my luck today, so instead I stayed silent. A few muffled conversations carried on at campfires scattered throughout the darkness, and this time I realized the fires were placed strategically below broken skylight windows, so most of the smoke drifted outside. We passed beneath the fake tree before the gun library, and I could just make out the cougar crouched in its limbs.

"Do you still have that knife in your bag?" Kaden asked suddenly. I looked up, surprised. I hadn't realized he knew, but he had been the one to bring my bag back to me.

"Yes."

"Good. Sleep with it next to you."

We stopped before the wooden doors.

"Careful, Kaden, we're getting dangerously close to becoming friends."

I meant it as a joke, but his face was serious when he said, "Too late, princess."

I realized how alone we were. His green eyes cut through the dark, and I suddenly felt awkward beside his tall form.

"Well, good night." I turned and stepped inside, pulling the door firmly shut between us. I heard Kaden laugh softly on the other side before his footsteps receded.

He's a means to an end, nothing more.

Nothing more.

EIGHT — KADEN

Red chewed at one of the wooden posts, his tail like a red flag as he whinnied and paced back and forth. For the first time since joining the clan, I hadn't taken him out on his morning ride across the hills. It was also the first day thirty men who weren't assigned to me had turned up to help at the stables.

Help might have been too strong a word.

The men leaned up against the wooden posts, watching what was happening in the center of the corral.

"Like this?" Ara called, and flashed me a grin as she pushed the gentle mare I'd chosen faster. Red whinnied again, but I ignored him.

"Good," I called out, "Now turn her the other way."

She pulled the reins and Dawn, the gentle mare, turned and followed the new path. It was a clear day, and leaves blew across the arena, the trees almost bare. I would have preferred to be alone with Ara, but I couldn't send the men away, the same way I couldn't look away as she pushed the horse faster.

From the corner of my eye I saw Gabriel striding out of the main building and up the hill to the stables. I smiled and ducked under the fence.

"Good, now stop."

"Whooaa." She pulled back the reins and shot me another grin. Her red hair caught the sunlight, and though the day was cold, I suddenly felt warm.

"When do I earn a saddle?"

"When I say so. Lean forward." I swung up onto the horse behind her, showing off just a little bit. She tensed for a moment but didn't pull away, her body pressed fully against mine.

"All right, Liam, open the gate, we're going for a little ride."

Liam's eyes lit up, that hectic blue always game for trouble. He was a favorite among my men, and a diplomatic choice as Gabriel's second. Gabriel might be a controlling ass, but he wasn't stupid. He knew there were men in the clan who'd rather I lead. With a slight squeeze I urged the mare forward, and her ears pricked forward at the open gate and the open hill beyond. I didn't have to turn to know Gabriel was probably running up the hill after us—in fact, I could hear his voice now. But then I dug my heels in and the mare took off. I wrapped one hand around Ara, but instead of screaming she let out an excited whoop.

Catch us if you can, Gabriel.

~

We stood atop the hill, looking down on the clan, both of us breathless after the ride. I'd dropped my hand from her waist when we'd stopped, but she hadn't pulled away from me. I noticed Liam and a few others had saddled up and followed us, but they kept their distance. I guessed Gabriel had sent them, but even if I had wanted to piss him off, I knew not to take Ara farther out of eyesight from the clan. Gabriel wasn't the most dangerous thing in this city.

I pointed out over the hills, to where you could make out the tall buildings of downtown. "The clan owns everything from the edge of downtown up to these foothills."

"Really?" Ara's voice was skeptical. I laughed.

"Well, Gabriel thinks he does. Our clan is the biggest in the city, and we patrol the territory, but it doesn't stop other smaller clans or loners from coming through." The wind caught her hair so that it tickled my face and neck, but I resisted the urge to catch a piece in my fingers.

"You ever think of leaving it all behind?"

For the first time today, her voice held a touch of bitterness, and maybe longing. Despite the easy banter between us, I had still captured her.

"All the time." Maybe I shouldn't have been so honest, but I felt like she deserved the truth.

She was quiet for some time, looking over the city. The clouds made a pattern of light and dark over the valley and the wind carried the fresh, sharp scent of sage.

"It used to be such a beautiful city," she finally said.

"It still is." But I wasn't thinking about the city. Ara turned back to look at me, the closest I'd been to her full, bright eyes.

"What would Gabriel do if we just rode away?" Her eyes held a mischievous, daring look.

"Lucky for you, pissing off Gabriel is pretty much my favorite hobby. He'd probably mount a full aerial assault, somehow get the airships working again."

Ara turned from the city to look back to the foothills that climbed toward the mountains, longing written over her face. I wanted to ask how she had survived the last three years, where she had gone, who had been with her. But I held back. Like with a wild horse, slowly, carefully.

"Would he catch us?" she asked finally.

This time I caught her eye. "If we were riding this horse, maybe. But if we were riding Red? Never. Red could race the wind and win. We'd disappear into the sunset and never be seen again."

Or more accurately, Issac, Sam, and I would take half the herd, my herd, and drive them through the mountains and down the coast. Sometimes when Gabriel was unbearable, I found myself filling in the details, and now, just as easily, I added another: a red-haired girl riding beside me.

"When do I get to ride Red?"

With her red hair and that wild look, she and Red would make a deadly pair.

"Not for a while. Red's a lot to handle."

"I can handle more than you think."

Something warm and hungry rose in me. Then she surprised me, kicking Dawn forward, and we rode back to the clan.

~

Gabriel was angrier than I'd ever seen him, and insisted he stay and help in the stables. I only had full use of one arm, and though I hadn't planned on making Ara do the dirty work, it was worth it to shovel horse crap the rest of the morning just to see his sour face. Every time Ara met my eyes, we both had to look away to keep from laughing.

Several times that day, Ara brushed up against me, her hand touching my shoulder, or brushing a piece of hay off my shirt. I couldn't tell if she noticed the response it brought out in me. I hoped not. She was sharp and quick-witted, and teased Sam and I mercilessly. I was surprised at how well she fit in here. When the sun was full above, Gabriel left for what he called "clan business." While the clan belonged to him, the stables belonged to me, and the cool looks of the men, thrilled that Ara had chosen to work with us, didn't go unnoticed by Gabriel. Before he left, he stepped into my path.

"Kaden, report after dinner. Ara is required to be inside an hour before dark every night." He turned and left, wiping the smile off my face.

The stables might be mine, but I understood the message in his cold eyes: Ara wasn't.

NINE—ARA

Kaden shook my shoulder, waking me. I sat up, pulling the blankets to my chest.

"Get up. We need to go before sunrise. Everything is ready."

"'Kay," I mumbled. I was used to waking to the cold sunrise, dew heavy on my tent, with the fresh scent of pine. But for the last two weeks I'd woken in a dark room, warm and dry. I worked every day in the stables with Kaden and his men, though Gabriel had kept a much sharper eye on us, and we hadn't left the inner perimeter since our ride into the hills.

Time blurred when I was with Kaden. I found it harder and harder to remember that I was flirting with him for a specific purpose. He'd also lost his family and told me stories about his journey on horseback through two states to find Sam, making it sound like an adventure and not the horror it must have been. I surprised myself, sharing a few details of my life in the mountains with my father—how he would hide feathers for me to find, how he would sing around the campfire—moments I hadn't realized I treasured till I spoke them aloud.

But maybe the thing that bonded us most was planning this expedition, and the secrecy it required, like it was some exciting covert operation. It was a tricky problem, but Kaden settled on speed; we would act at the last possible moment and tell as few people as possible. In the hours before dawn Kaden's men had loaded the kayaks and supplies in the wagon. Boden, a quiet, tall man from the stables, would take us to the edge of the water, and then drive the wagon back to the clan alone. Kaden knew a place where we could leave the kayaks after we were done; apparently, he had several of these secret hiding places scattered across the city. I also got the impression they might have been more for his use than the clan's.

My hands shook with nervous excitement as I pulled on clothes, hefted my backpack, and made my way into the next room.

Kaden's eyes flicked over to me. "Ready?"

"Hell yeah."

We paced through the quiet clan. Today he led me out a small door in the back of the kitchen, the only exit besides the heavily guarded front doors. For the first time, escape wasn't first on my mind. Finally, I was close to finding the beginning my father spoke of.

Outside the day was cold and windy, the dawn still an hour off. Clouds covered the sky, and I shivered and settled deeper into my jacket. Leaves blew across the parking lot, and the horses that were to pull our wagon, loaded with kayaks, stood heads bowed against the wind.

I didn't know what we would find, but if I was right thinking this was the beginning my father had spoken of, then I hoped he'd left something for me, and this was the last I would see of the clan. The thought buoyed me, but also made me want to appreciate what might be my last moments with men who had somehow become friends.

Issac was already huddled in the back of the wagon, and Sam sat at the front beside Boden, ready to drive the horse team.

"All right, let's get going and see if that stupid ass—" Kaden stopped suddenly as Sam ran his hand across his throat in a slashing motion. Gabriel stepped out from the front of the wagon and smiled at us both.

"I thought it might be wise if I joined you."

Kaden and I both exchanged glances—his full of incredulity, mine fear.

"Gabriel . . . what—what are you doing here?" It was maybe the first time I had seen Kaden almost lost for words.

There was a moment of quiet tension. We all watched Gabriel, waiting to see what he would do. But he just pulled his hood up against the wind. "Yesterday I received a troubling report about one of the clans downtown. I thought you could use some extra manpower, just in case."

Kaden looked over at me, the shock on his face comical. But the fear on mine was gone. For whatever twisted reason, Gabriel wasn't going to stop us. So what if he came? I was on my way back to the beginning. And maybe he would be worthless at kayaking and sink like a rock.

I winked at Kaden and then jumped onto the back of the wagon and patted the space next to me. Kaden laughed, unapologetic, and joined me, both our legs hanging over the edge. I didn't miss how Gabriel watched us, but I also didn't care. Sam slapped the reins and the horses began trudging toward the flooded downtown.

Though I didn't lean into him, Kaden's leg rested against mine, warm against the morning chill.

It wasn't often I had the chance to watch the city pass me by. I'd been looking forward to this time with Kaden, but now, with Gabriel sitting in the wagon, I wasn't sure what to say. Kaden decided for me.

"So, what was the *oh-so-troubling-report* that's got you worried enough to come with us?" he asked.

Gabriel's eyes flicked to me, and I felt a surge of anger. Did he think I couldn't handle it, or did he not trust me with some secret clan business?

"Yes, Gabriel, do tell." My tone was as mocking as Kaden's, but Gabriel didn't react, instead staring at the skeletal remains of a business we rolled past.

"The Timberline Clan is gone," he finally said, his voice soft in a way I'd never heard from him. Kaden and Issac exchanged a quick look I didn't understand.

"Gone, like moved?" Sam said, swiveling back from the front of the wagon to look at Gabriel. Even Boden glanced back.

"Gone like one of our teams stopped by to trade, and the livestock were slaughtered, the buildings burned, and every man dead, left where he'd fallen. The only thing alive was a dog scavenging the remains." Whatever I'd expected him to say, it wasn't that. Beside me, Kaden had gone perfectly still.

"I knew men there, and their leader," Gabriel went on. "He was levelheaded and prepared for winter. It doesn't make sense. Why kill the livestock? Why burn the buildings? They could have taken the clan, stayed there through the winter or longer."

I surprised myself by speaking first. "Not everyone wants to rebuild the world, Gabriel." *Some men just want it to burn.* He stared at me, and for the first time, he didn't look like a clan leader. He looked like a man lost.

"What kind of a man wants the world to burn?" he stared out the wagon at nothing. No one answered, but the answer still came to me: *a very dangerous one.*

After a moment, Kaden cleared his throat, and the men turned to him. "We'll be extracareful. Boden can leave the wagon at the edge of downtown and ride bareback to the clan. Once we get on the water, we'll be out of reach of anyone on land."

The men accepted this new plan, and information, in silence. It wasn't the cheery expedition I'd imagined, but it fortified my resolve. Whatever it was my father had left for me, these men had their own problems. And after today, I wouldn't be one of them.

~

It was noon by the time the downtown section rose around us, and we unloaded the kayaks and then slipped into the water. At first it was shallow, lapping at the tires of rusted cars, but quickly it deepened, replaced by an entirely foreign aquatic landscape of sunken buildings and streets. As we paddled out I stared down into the wavering, submerged world until the water deepened, the human world below masked by dark water. Even the scents of the road—grass, damp earth, and wood—faded, overwhelmed by scents of cold water and decay.

Kaden's kayak bumped into my own, and I flinched, the soft thud drowned out by the treacherous sounds of swirling water beneath us. Towering skyscrapers rose from the dark water and blocked out the sky, creaking in the dim light.

"You all right?" his voice was soft.

"Something moved under the water." I searched the swirling current for the strange way the water had shifted a moment before. Almost as if something huge . . . No. I didn't want to think it. Already I doubted myself. Maybe something large, like a city bus, had been caught in the deep current. The water did that sometimes, made you see things that weren't really there. "It was nothing," I finally said.

Kaden nodded. "Stay close, we're nearly there."

Mist swirled off the rippling surface and cold water leaked onto my fingers as I dipped my paddle in and out of the current. I tried to remember this place with people, lights, traffic . . . but couldn't. The water had drowned out and silenced anything below in its grasp. We turned a corner and I saw it, an imposing steel gray building with black lettering.

Birmingham Medical Testing Center.

My heart clenched, terrified and longing.

As we drew near, the building loomed tall and I wondered how we could even get inside. Then, Kaden propelled his kayak through the water and aimed it directly at one of the large glass windows. Just before he smashed into it, I saw what he must have already seen; the window was already cracked, a large hole a few inches above the waterline allowing water to flow freely in and out. He rammed his kayak into the window, a crack spiderwebbing across the full pane. Then he lifted his paddle, breaking chunks of the glass free, the steady thunk followed by the softer splash of glass hitting water. When the opening was big enough, he glided through. Sam followed, the bright orange of his life vest disappearing into the hole.

"Go ahead, Ara." Gabriel gestured me forward.

I moved to follow, but I fumbled and went farther to the left than intended. The glass tore into my shoulder, ripping straight through the jacket. I swore as I drifted inside, lifting a hand to my arm and coming away with a smear of blood. *Shit*. I wiped the blood on my pants, tugging my jacket down to cover the cut.

The interior was full of shadows. I switched on the flashlight attached to my helmet, the beam joining the others already slicing through the gloom. The ceiling was only a few feet above me, the room cavernous. Trash and debris littered the water. I could just make out a tiled floor beneath us.

"Come on through, Issac." Kaden called out. Issac glided into the room without a problem.

"All right, Gabriel . . ."

No one came. Outside the window there was only murky water. I tried to orient myself to look out of the gap we'd left in the window, but it was difficult with the floating debris and the current. Then Gabriel coasted through the window, a troubled look on his face.

"What's wrong, Gabriel? Wishing you hadn't come?" Kaden taunted.

"No. I thought I saw something." Gabriel looked over his shoulder.

"Saw what?" Kaden's voice was filled with annoyance, and I swallowed the urge to say I'd seen something as well.

"I'm not sure, something beneath the current."

"There's a whole city beneath the current," Kaden said, dismissing him, and turning his headlight to the door. "We need to get to the higher levels."

Silence fell between us as our lights cut through the gloom of the half-submerged room. Water dripped from the ceiling and lines of green scum marked the walls.

"Who'll get out and open the door?" Sam said. The building groaned as the water lapped at the walls, and I sent up a silent prayer that it wouldn't collapse around us.

After a moment of silence, Kaden sighed. "Me, I guess." He jumped out of his kayak and swore at the sudden cold. Sam and I both laughed.

"The floor is solid at least." He grimaced and waded through the water, opening the door and pulling his kayak after him. "I'll find a way to the next floor and then come back for you guys." Kaden pushed his way out into the hallway, and though none of us said it, the room suddenly felt ominous without him. We all waited in tense silence, the minutes stretching long.

He came back some time later and pulled Issac after him, then Sam. When it was only Gabriel and I left, I glanced out at the current swirling beyond the window. The question was out before I could stop it.

"Gabriel, what did you see in the water?" The hair on my neck prickled, the sound of lapping water growing sinister.

"I'm not sure. Something . . . big."

Finally, Kaden pushed through the door, grabbed my kayak by the nose, and pulled me through without even acknowledging Gabriel. The water lapped at his waist as he maneuvered my kayak into the stairwell. It was a tight fit, but the stairwell doubled back, the turn just above the waterline, and he heaved it up there.

He steadied me as I climbed out of the kayak, his hands taking my waist for a moment, a touch that I felt all the way to my toes. The water lapped at the walls, the only sound in the gloom.

"Everything okay?" I said when he didn't speak.

He glanced over his shoulder. "Ara, listen . . . this place . . . There's something I don't like about it. Promise me you'll stay close to one of us at all times?"

He sounded so different than the teasing Kaden I knew. "Of course." The words slipped out of me before I could consider what they might cost. I wasn't here for the same reason he was.

He nodded. "All right, guess I better go get the deadweight." He sighed and then waded back to get Gabriel. "Sam and Issac are just through those doors," he called over his shoulder.

I adjusted my headlamp and pushed through the door—and then stopped. Kaden's warning suddenly made sense. The half-submerged floor below felt otherworldly, but this floor was ominous all on its own. Some sort of luminous mold grew in cracks in the walls, lighting the room in a soft green glow. Long white cabinets and counters coated in dust held a few forgotten glass vials and metal instruments I had no name for. On the far wall, Sam and Issac stood before something long and metal hanging from the walls. Chains.

"What is this place?" I followed the trail of the chains, not wanting to ask what they were for.

Issac lifted a chain, and then let it fall, the cackling sound breaking the oppressive silence. "They were testing for a cure."

"Issac, Ara, look." Sam pulled open a door to a side room not lit by the green glow. I approached with growing apprehension. Sam's flashlight slowly cut through the darkness and moved over cages set in the walls. Empty, except for—I jerked back at the sight of a hand and shriveled body, and thudded straight into Kaden. He held me for a moment, just long enough to restart my heart.

"They were monkeys," Kaden said, voice sad. "I saw them

when I came up. I should have warned you. Guessing that's what they were testing on. Must have gotten left behind . . ."

Kaden pulled the door closed. I was glad. I didn't want to think about what it must have been like to die in a cage, forgotten. Kaden cleared his throat, all our headlights suddenly turned to him. I was thankful for the sudden distraction.

"Gabriel, Sam, and Issac, you three start by searching this floor. When you're done, move up to the next floor. Ara and I will go to the top of the building and work our way down. We'll meet in the middle with whatever we've collected. I don't think we'll make it out tonight, so search for a place to sleep too."

He pulled out a red whistle from one of the empty backpacks we all wore for collecting supplies. "Stay with your group. One whistle if you've found something we should see, two if you need help, and three for trouble. It's unlikely there's anything left alive but be careful anyway."

The building creaked and our flashlights cut the darkness, casting monstrous shadows. Apprehension and fear alike built inside me. Had my father been here?

"Let's get moving," Kaden said, and our circle splintered. I nodded to Sam, who smiled back, and then followed Kaden to the stairwell. I didn't look at Gabriel, but I could feel his eyes follow me and Kaden.

We climbed the concrete steps to the top of the building in silence, the rushing sound of water fading the higher we walked. The stairwell was empty except for dust and the light of our flashlights cutting back and forth. Only when Kaden stopped did I realize we'd reached the top floor.

The climb had me breathing hard, but I took a sharp, sudden inhale as I looked at the door on the final floor. It was different than the others we'd seen, a silver metal that reminded me of the airships that had fallen from the sky back when this all began. It wouldn't open.

"Why is this door the only one that's locked?" Kaden said with a frustrated sigh.

The blood pounded in my ears as I stared at the door. "Same reason for all locked doors . . . there's something valuable behind it."

"Maybe I could get Issac to try to open it with his hatchet?"

"No, that won't work." My voice was distant, unfocused. Because I'd seen a door like this before. I know I had, I just couldn't remember where. It tugged at me now, like an itch I couldn't scratch.

"Princess?" The light of Kaden's headlamp hit my face and I flinched, looking away.

"It looks pretty solid," I said, backtracking. "I think maybe we should try it last. Otherwise the others will find everything while we spend an hour trying to break it down."

He stared at the door another moment before he turned. "Good point. Who knows, maybe we'll find a key." He gave a half-hearted laugh that said he didn't think it likely.

The floors below the strange door were disappointing, full of desks, faded paper, and computers covered in dust. The closest thing to helpful we found was an old vending machine we raided for snacks. When we came to a new floor with floor-to-ceiling windows and an open reception area, Kaden switched off his headlamp and jumped up onto what was once some sort of check-in counter.

"Well, princess, that's more than half the floors. I think we deserve a break. The others should be up here soon."

I let out a deep breath, secretly glad to be done searching the windowless, musty rooms that seemed to grow smaller and smaller. Whatever my father had left behind, I didn't feel like it would be there. Here, with the fading daylight streaming in, I could breathe again. Even if I hadn't found what I was looking for, I felt optimistic, and when I glanced at Kaden, a warm feeling rose in my chest. I'd once hated being called princess, but now, I had to pretend to dislike the nickname. When had that happened? Kaden pulled a small white box from his jacket.

"What's that?" I leaned forward, but he didn't answer. He pushed his fingers into the small white box and—"Kaden, are those cigars?"

"Nicked them from Gabriel," he said with a grin. "He keeps all these crazy private stores, trying to ration things off to last forever. Uptight prick." He stuck one of the cigars in the corner of his mouth and smiled. "But they're going bad soon. And who knows how long we'll last."

"Those things will kill you."

"That's the dream, isn't it? To live long enough to die by your own foolishness." He put his leg up, the other swinging back and forth, the picture of youth in a crumbling ruin.

He took the cigar out of his mouth and gave me a rakish grin. "Every man needs a vice. And since mine can't be women . . ."

"I hear women are in short supply. Even rarer than a nice Cuban cigar."

I jumped onto the counter and bumped into Kaden, trying to knock him off. He pushed back, and after a short struggle I settled next to him. He draped his arm over my shoulder. I held perfectly still as he whispered in my ear: "Princess, you don't even know what a Cuban cigar is. Now, cheers."

He handed me a cigar and I held it between my pointer and middle finger, like I'd seen in the movies. It had a faint, earthy scent.

"To the end of the world," I held up my cigar, a pathetic gesture that even so made me smile. Kaden held up his from the bottom, all his fingers supporting it as if it were truly precious.

"To the end of one world—and the beginning of another. From the ashes may we rise reborn," Kaden said with quiet reverence.

"Hear, hear."

We tapped our cigars together like you might glasses in a toast, and we held them in salute, at once heroic, comic, and tragic.

"Correct me if I'm wrong, but don't people generally light cigars?"

"Ara, this is why I'm so glad the female species is still around. You are unequivocally bright. No man would have spotted such a thing." I elbowed him in the stomach, and he continued with a grin. "Sadly, I have no lighter. I actually intended to use the cigars in some way to piss Gabriel off . . ."

There was a sound from the stairwell, and Kaden muttered, "Speaking of," when the doorway opened and Gabriel marched inside, looking cross.

Issac and Sam came after him, and I could tell from Sam's grin, and Gabriel's stiff walk, that something had happened.

"You guys find anything?" Kaden asked, not moving his arm from my shoulder. Gabriel stopped, looking from him to me, his eyes growing darker. I liked the casual way Kaden's arm sat around me, but I slid off the counter regardless.

"Just a ghost or two," Sam said with a grin that reminded me of Kaden. "They weren't happy to see Gabriel."

"This is a mission and should be treated as such," Gabriel responded stiffly.

Kaden grinned but seemed to resist the urge to ask more, and instead said, "Did you find anything?"

Issac shook his head, and Kaden rocked back on the counter and swore.

"I'm taking it you didn't find anything either?" Gabriel said.

Kaden placed the unlit cigar in his mouth and talked out of one side. "No. But there's a door up top we couldn't open."

"I'll take a look at it," Gabriel said, turning his headlight back on and returning to the stairwell.

Kaden barely waited until the door had shut before he turned to Sam. "What's up his ass?"

"I hid in a cage and then reached out and grabbed his leg when he walked by. Can't believe you didn't hear him scream."

Kaden laughed so hard he nearly fell off the counter.

~

We set up for the night in the same room with the reception desk, as it had the most natural light. Camp wasn't much more than a collection of sleeping bags and a tiny backpacking stove with a burner and pot to boil water, but even so, I'd made do with far less. One by one the others went to sleep while Kaden and I sat beneath the large windows and ate the rest of the vending machine snacks.

"God bless Americans and their preservatives," Kaden said with mock reverence, tearing open another pack of Doritos. "All right, your turn now." He turned his green eyes full force to me, and I had to look away to come up with an answer.

"Hot baths . . . and school."

"One of the two things you miss most about the world is *school*?

As in high school? As in the place they lock up young people and torture them with learning?"

I laughed at his incredulous tone. "Fine, what would you pick?

He ate another Dorito, then, "Fast food. And movies."

I reached for another bag of the rock-hard candy we'd collected when a sudden sharp pain in my shoulder made me wince.

"You okay?" Kaden said, suddenly concerned.

"I forgot that I cut my shoulder earlier. It's nothing."

"Let me see it," Kaden sat up, moving over to me.

"No really, it's fine."

"Ara," he said, raising both his eyebrows. "Take off your jacket and let me see. When we get back, I'll take you to the hot springs Sam and I found up by the river. You can have your hot bath and I'll teach you some biology."

He winked, and I rolled my eyes but pulled off my jacket regardless. A shiver ran down my back at the sudden cold. His fingers brushed against my arm, lifting it into the light cast from the moon.

"It's not deep," he said. "But we should clean and bandage it, just in case. We brought a first-aid kit with us."

Without my jacket the cold bit deep, but Kaden's fingers worked fast, sure, and warm. He wiped the wound, and I felt the sting of alcohol and saw a glimpse of bright red on white.

And just as suddenly, I remembered where I'd seen the door. I knew how to open it.

"Did I hurt you?" Kaden asked, aware of my sudden change.

"Oh, no, well just a little, it's fine. I'm fine. Thanks. I think I'm just going to go to bed."

"You sure you're okay?" he said, looking at me oddly.

"What? Yeah. Just really tired all of a sudden. Good night."

I stood up and made my way over to my sleeping bag, my entire body surging with adrenaline. I tried my best to mime a yawn and crawled into bed—which wasn't easy with electricity pulsing through me.

How had I not remembered before?

A few minutes later, Kaden returned to his sleeping bag and fell silent. The moon stretched deeper through the windows as I forced myself to wait for deep, even breathing from the others.

Finally, I got up and silently moved to the stairwell, easing the door open and making my way all the way up to the top floor. I'd forgotten my jacket and held only the flashlight from my headlight to guide the way.

When I reached the door, the light reflected off it and my chest tightened. Suddenly I wished I had more than a flashlight for a weapon. It wasn't too late to go back and tell Kaden . . . tell him what? That I'd tricked him into bringing me here? That there might be some secret behind this door that would explain my father's final words?

No. I was alone.

I ripped the bandage off my arm and then squeezed the wound, wincing at the sudden flash of pain. My fingers seemed to move in slow motion as I wiped a smear of red across the door.

Nothing happened.

I stared at it, wanting to reach out and pound my fists against it, kick it, anything but stand here in silent disappointment. I'd seen a door like this before, as a child, just once. We were visiting an old friend of my father's who lived so far back in the mountains I always fell asleep on the drive there. Late at night I'd woken up and crept downstairs only to find the door to the basement open. When I peered down the stairs, I saw my father at the bottom, standing before a strange, silver door. He had raised his hand, cut a line in his palm, and then brushed the blood against the door. And it had opened.

This was the same type of door, I was sure of it.

What had I done wrong? I leaned forward, pressing my head up against the cool metal. The door moved. I froze, and then pushed hard, the door swinging open before me.

Heart pounding, I stepped over the threshold.

TEN—ARA

The room inside was so different from the rest of the building that it felt like I'd stepped into an entirely new world. The walls were the same silver metal as the door. The green moss I'd seen on the lower levels grew in branching patterns all over the ceiling and walls, lighting everything in a ghostly green glow. There were no windows. I stepped deeper inside, my eyes drawn to a group of glass tubes that spanned from ceiling to floor and were large enough a person could have fit inside. Green tinted water bubbled and swirled inside, giving off a low humming noise. I wiped a single finger across the glass. No dust.

"Edana?"

I spun, terror closing around my throat.

A man stood in the shadows, between myself and the door. I didn't know if he'd been there the whole time or had only just appeared. My heart thundered, and I realized I wasn't wearing the whistle Kaden had given me, and had only a flashlight for a weapon.

Stupid, stupid, stupid.

But I didn't try to run, because somehow, impossibly, he had just spoken my last name. I took a slow, steadying breath. "How do you know my name?"

He stepped out from the shadows, the green glow illuminating a long nose and dark eyes. He had the appearance of a man who had become old too quickly, his body not matching his wrinkled face and wild hair.

"You aren't Charles," his voice was angry, disbelieving, expanding and filling the room. "The blood reading said it was him. Only he could have opened that door."

I moved backward, almost tripping over a metal crate set on the ground, and then quickly put it between the two of us. His eyes narrowed, and as he came closer, I noticed his hands trembled beneath a white lab coat. "You look a bit like Charles, though." Understanding filled his eyes. "You're Ara." It wasn't a question.

"You knew my father?"

I glanced down at the crate, cold all over again when I saw it was a cage large enough for a human. I could still make out the dark stairwell.

"We were friends. Your father and me." His voice was rough, as if he wasn't used to using it, but it captivated me completely. "And colleagues. The things we worked on together . . ." he paused, shaking his head. "We thought we were going to change the world." Then he turned away from me, striding across the room. His sudden change made me feel off balance. Again, I glanced to the stairwell, a gaping black hole in the green lit room. He bent down next to a cabinet, and I could see he struggled with a glass, his hands still trembling. Was he making himself a drink? "I suppose we did," he continued softly, "but not the way we thought."

"Have you seen my father?"

He paused, and my heart sank when he shook his head. "No, not since this all began. We had a disagreement. Concerning Emma."

"M-my sister?" He laughed at this, as though he found it funny, though I couldn't begin to guess why.

He turned his back on me, then said softly, "The last time I saw him was when he brought Emma here, when things were ending." So this was where he'd brought her the night before we left.

"Why?" All I could think of was that night, his words—so that I barely noticed the man turn, each silent step bringing him closer. "Why did he bring her here?" *What was here that my father had risked so much for?*

"Because I told him I could use her."

His words pounded through my head. My body trembled. My voice wasn't wholly steady when I whispered, "Use her for what?"

"To make a cure, you stupid girl." His eyes narrowed, became snakelike. "But your father was crafty, more so than I gave him credit for. It was only after her that I figured out who we really needed."

He stepped closer. A deep animal instinct screamed at me to run. "Who?"

"The person he protected above anyone else. You." And then he surged forward. His arm caught mine and he wrenched me backward. I spun, ready to punch him, but only managed to catch his other hand as he brought a needle to my neck. Terror pulsed in my veins.

"Kaden!" I screamed. "Help!"

Would he hear me? I stopped resisting, using his own force to spin the needle down and toward his thigh. He cursed, dropping the needle, and I managed to rip free. I jumped away when my foot caught on something, and his full weight fell on top of me, my breath rushing out. I couldn't scream—he had me pinned. Struggling beneath him, I tried to draw breath. I could see him scrambling for the needle.

Then, a sudden, sickening crunch. His weight went slack.

I scrambled out from beneath him. Only when I was free did I put the pieces together. Kaden, standing to the side of us, a crowbar in his hands and a murderous look upon his face. And the man, lying prone on the ground, a deep dent in his head and eyes that had been calculating a moment ago now empty.

No. He couldn't be dead. I needed him—the answers were so close. Or at least, they had been.

"Why did you do that?" I spat at Kaden, who jumped back as if I'd hit him.

"Do what—I—he was attacking you." Kaden stared down at the man, and then me, confusion in every line of his body.

"You didn't have to kill him!"

"I wasn't trying to kill him!" His voice rose to match mine. "I was trying to save you."

I turned back to the body, frustration filling me. That's all men were good for, killing. I must have said it out loud, though, because Kaden responded.

"I'm good for more than just killing. What did you expect me to do?"

"I needed him," I said, unable to look at him.

"Needed him for what?" I could hear that he was trying to be patient, trying to understand, but I couldn't bring myself to look away from the growing pool of blood.

"Answers. He knew my father." I pulled the piece of paper from my pocket and tossed it at Kaden.

He was quiet for some time. "Is this why you wanted to come here?"

Something in his voice made me look up. "Kaden—" I swallowed, then quieter, "Yes."

The paper trembled in his hand, and he stared down at it in disbelief. "Gabriel said that you had some other reason for coming. I didn't want to believe him." He took a step back, the warmth in his eyes gone. "Might be the first time he was right."

Guilt tightened my chest. I wanted to explain why I'd lied, why I'd used him, but even now, I held my father's secrets close. "I'm sorry," I whispered.

He dropped the crowbar, the noise immense in the sudden silence between us. His shoulders hunched, his stride not his usual confident swagger as he walked away. I thought he would leave, but he stopped at the door, took a slow deep breath, and turned back. "We should start looking. Once Gabriel finds . . ." he glanced down at the man on the floor and swallowed. Then he cleared his throat and looked at the room, not meeting my eye. "What are we looking for?"

"I'm not sure," I whispered, my voice so dry it barely made a noise. My hand shook, so I fisted them at my sides, and forced myself to take in the surrounding room, burying the sudden panic that rose like vomit. If this wasn't the beginning my father spoke of, then what was? Our house? The thought of not having a path forward was more terrifying than the dead man at my feet.

Kaden's eyes softened. "Let's just start looking for medicine, okay? If Gabriel comes up here we'll tell him we came up here to . . ." he paused, seeming to realize exactly what Gabriel would assume if he found the two of us up here alone together, in the middle of the night. "We'll tell him we came to look for the medicine."

"What about—" I glanced down at the man on the floor.

"We tell the truth; he surprised us and I accidentally—" he stopped, then forced the words out "—killed him."

The pain in his voice made me want to go over to him and do something, anything, to comfort him. Instead, I turned to the first set of drawers, hiding my shaking hands by opening drawer after drawer.

Tears hid just behind my eyes, and I both wished for a moment without Kaden to break down, but also didn't think I could handle being here without him. The more I tried not to look at the body on the floor, and the growing pool of blood, the more it drew my eye. The two of us moved in silence as we searched the room. What we found painted a confusing picture. Undeniably, some sort of new tech was powering the water tubes—and the rest of the floor—that was set up like some sort of laboratory. It was the only new tech I'd seen working since the end of things. The floor was also well lived in; there was a room for sleeping, with a shelf of books above it, and a bathroom with a pipe that had been rigged to empty into the water far below.

"He found a way to use the new tech again," Kaden said as he tapped the glass tube of glowing green water for which neither of us could find any purpose. His eyes darkened. "I haven't seen anyone do that for years. Gabriel will be furious he can't recruit him." He paused, turning to look at me. "What do you think he was trying to do here?"

"He was looking for a cure." And he was willing to do whatever it took to find one. Which meant this couldn't be the beginning my father meant. He wouldn't have sent me to a man who would try to hurt me. Even if this was where he had taken Emma that night, ultimately, he'd brought her home. Back to the beginning. That's where I needed to go. Home, not here. I stood and turned to him. "No. My father came here, so I thought there might be answers here for me. But I was wrong."

We walked down the stairs in silence. Before opening the final door, he stopped and turned to me. "Ara, you don't have to do everything on your own. I can help you. If you just tell me what you need, I'll help you find it."

My eyes flicked to his, and I wished they hadn't—the hope there felt like a knife to my gut. He stepped forward and I could feel the tension in the space between us.

Go back to the beginning. "No one can help me, Kaden."

"Then whatever it is, let it go." He stepped closer, voice pleading now. "We'll leave the clan with you. Issac and I have talked about it before. Taking some of the herd and driving them out to Montana. Or down the coast to Mexico. Wherever the hell we want. You could find a new family. With us."

I wished it weren't so easy to imagine it. Wished I didn't instantly wonder what a new beginning with Kaden would mean. Because I already knew my answer. "I don't want a new family, Kaden. I want my old one back." *I won't give up on them. Not again.*

We stared at each other, disappointment in his eyes, resolve in mine. "Okay," he finally said. Then he stepped through the door, leaving me in the darkness.

My body ached when I finally crawled into my sleeping bag, but sleep evaded me. I stared into the darkness, replaying the nameless man's words. Why had my father trusted him with Emma? Why had the man thought I would help make a cure?

And though I didn't want to think of it, I couldn't help but replay that brief, impossible moment, when Kaden offered me a glimpse of a life I couldn't have without betraying my past. Because the man's death had also shown me something else my father had taught me: I couldn't trust or rely on anyone. All these men, even if they meant me well, only stood in my way.

I was well rested. I had supplies. There was only one way to honor my father's words: go back to the beginning. The beginning that had to be home.

It was time I left the clan.

ELEVEN—ARA

A mist came off the water, the cold autumn wind whistling between buildings as we kayaked below. The sun wasn't even over the horizon, a soft pink light our only guide. No one spoke.

I slept only a few hours. Part of me wanted to take a kayak and leave right then and there to begin the journey back to my house. But the water was treacherous enough in the day; I didn't want to face it alone in the dark.

When we woke, Kaden led us up a final time to the top door. Gabriel couldn't find a way to open it, for which I was glad. I didn't want to face the questions the room would have brought, when so many of mine had gone unanswered. So many thoughts swirled in my head that I barely noticed when Sam rammed his kayak into mine.

"You okay?" Sam glanced at Kaden, and then back to me. Kaden had been polite this morning, if a bit cool, and Sam was like a lost puppy trying to figure out what was wrong between us.

"Yeah, I'm fine."

"Well, keep your eyes up, Kaden said the water gets tricky ahead."

I nodded. I turned my head to look at the remnants of a tattered flag when my kayak suddenly jolted sideways. I nearly dropped my paddle as I threw my weight to one side, overcorrecting and almost tipping into the water. My heart raced as I steadied myself and searched the water for what had jolted me.

Nothing.

The dark water rippled.

"This way," Kaden's voice drifted over the water. Something was wrong. The current was moving differently than it had been a moment ago. Then a long form broke the surface, a spine that shed the water easily three times the length of the kayak. Just as quickly as it had come, it disappeared back into the gloom.

"Kaden," I whispered. "There's something in the water."

Kaden stopped paddling, and we stilled as one. A fall wind whistled between the buildings, the only noise besides the slap of the water as we drifted silently forward. Water dripped off my paddle, the darkness and depth suddenly terrifying.

Kaden cleared his throat. "Let's just keep mov—"

There was a rush of water, and a flash of black scales. Sam yelled as he pitched sideways.

"Sam!" Kaden and I both yelled at the same time. The water began churning a foamy white. I lost sight of Sam.

A wave rose and smashed into me. Gabriel's kayak tilted sideways in front of me, and I saw a flash of red brick a moment before I collided with the side of a building. The water roiled, and the world tilted as the waves slammed me into the wall again and again. I curled forward, trying to protect myself. My ears rang and I tasted blood. Everything was cold water and pain.

Someone was screaming my name. Gabriel was gone, the bright pieces of his kayak bobbing in the water.

I couldn't see Sam anywhere. *Lifejacket. He's wearing a life-jacket. He'll be fine.* But all I could think of was the infected bear my father and I had burned, twice the size it should have been.

"Ara!" Kaden smashed his kayak into mine. "Go! Get to the ledge!"

I turned to where he pointed, my body seeming to move slower than my mind. Past the building, where the street took a sudden turn, a ledge jutted out above the water, the remnants of some collapsed building. It was high enough I could jump from the kayak and climb to higher ground. Fear made my hands rubbery as I pulled for the ledge. I imagined the strange way the water had moved, imagined that creature following me, and pad-dled faster. My breath came in tight, frantic hitches, as if my lungs had shrunk. Terrified, I looked back over my shoulder.

Except for the angry *slap, slap, slap* of the remnants of the wave, the water was still. Nothing moved except Kaden. He was now in the middle of the dark water, where the monster had first appeared. Sam's kayak floated upside down as Kaden frantically searched the water. I shook with fear, praying the monster was done and would not suddenly emerge and swallow him whole.

Across the water, Gabriel had crawled onto the back of Issac's kayak. Together they made it to an alley between two buildings across the way.

I reached the ledge and abandoned my kayak, jumping onto the wall, scraping my hands bloody as I scrambled up the short distance and then turned and surveyed the water from the higher vantage point.

Nothing but swirling debris. And then—"Kaden, there!" I

shouted. I could just make out a flash of red hair under the water, floating ten feet from Kaden. He followed my gaze, and dove.

He was underwater for what seemed an eternity.

A flash of movement. Then, Kaden's head burst from the surface, Sam limp in his arms. The life vests held them up, but something had wrapped around Sam's body, and Kaden struggled to free him.

Oh God, please, not Sam.

Kaden struggled to pull Sam onto his kayak. Had he always been so small? A steady *thud-thud-thud* echoed across the water as Gabriel and Issac tried to smash through a window to safety. Kaden cradled Sam's limp form. He crouched over his brother, trying to pump life back into him.

The water was still.

At some point Sam coughed and turned over, retching out water. Numb with relief, I watched as Kaden paddled to the building Gabriel and Issac had entered, and then he too disappeared. It was several minutes more before I realized someone was calling my name. I looked up to see Kaden yelling from the second story of the building across the water, the one Issac and Gabriel had forced their way into.

"Ara, wait there!"

He stopped as my eyes met his, cold as the winter that had come over my heart. For a moment we stood like this, two statues separated by an abyss.

"Ara, no . . . please . . ." his voice was soft but carried well across the water. Even now, he saw through me, knowing what I was about to do a moment before I did.

"I'm sorry," I whispered.

Then I turned and ran, leaving behind monsters both real and imagined.

TWELVE—KADEN

Ara ran. Her retreating form hurt more than the cold water and my aching limbs combined. God, I was so stupid. Sam coughed and moaned on the floor and I turned away from the window to crouch beside him. Issac wrapped a cloth around a deep gash on his forehead. The plague had made animals bigger, stronger, but that thing in the water . . . I didn't want to think about it. All that mattered was that it had let go of Sam. He was breathing now, but shallowly. He'd coughed up so much water when I'd pulled him up.

"We need to follow her," Gabriel said, leaning out one of the windows, and making it too easy to imagine giving him a shove.

"Go find someone who gives a shit, Gabriel. I'm not one of your minions."

He was perfectly controlled when he turned and faced me. God, I hated him.

"We need to follow her. Now. She already has a head start."

As much as tormenting Gabriel gave me pleasure, there really wasn't much more I could say without showing him the truth. Ara didn't need or want me. Part of me wanted to sink my fist into the drywall just to feel something crumble. Instead I ground my teeth. I wouldn't show this maggot my pain. Maybe it was better this way.

Let her have her freedom.

"Ara has decided to leave the clan." I tried to say it with a smile, but it came out bitter. I pushed away some of the wet hair plastered to Sam's forehead, refocusing on what was important. He was deathly pale. "We need to get Sam back to base camp. He needs a doctor."

"No." Gabriel stood looking out the window now, his back completely turned on Sam.

"He could die—"

"It doesn't matter."

There was a cold silence. I stood slowly, my body beginning to shake.

"Nothing matters but saving her," Gabriel said. "We should never have let her come. It was a mistake on my part, but I thought she might be one of us after this. What if something happens? She could be our last chance at rebuilding humanity. We need her."

"I don't care!" I did care, but Sam was my brother. I couldn't do anything for Ara until he was safe. "Sam needs to go back to the clan."

"Kaden, you know her more than anyone else. We have to go get her back."

"She made her choice!" I looked down at Sam and Issac. "And now I'm making mine."

"This isn't your choice. You signed an agreement to follow my orders when you entered the clan. You think that you can—"

I swung without thinking, smashing my fist into his face, his words suddenly cut off. He stumbled backward and fell, perhaps the first look of surprise I had ever seen on his playdough face. Blood trickled from his nose.

"To hell with your agreement. To hell with you." I towered over him and he stood back up slowly. His eyes were eerie and calm, too bright on his dark face. My fist stung, but I didn't care so long as his face hurt more.

"Careful, Kaden," he whispered. "Is this what you really want? You won't be accepted back into the clan if you do this. You won't be able to use our doctor."

I smiled for the first time. How like Gabriel, always thinking he was one step ahead.

"Not if we beat you back."

"And what makes you think you will? She's *one* girl. How hard could it be to catch her?"

I threw my head back and laughed. "Just one girl? That girl is gonna put you through hell and high water. If I'm lucky, you might not even come back when she's done with you."

Gabriel stood, and I could almost see the tiny wheels turning in his brain. Always so logical. Always so controlled. He hadn't even tried to hit me back.

Ara was going to eat him alive.

After a few deep breaths, and neatly wiping his bleeding nose, he turned to Issac. "Every second, Ara gets farther away. Let's go, Issac."

But Issac didn't even look up at him. I was filled with a sudden warmth as I realized I was not as alone as I'd thought.

Gabriel froze, as if surprised, and then spoke quietly. "Then I go alone." He turned to leave, his footsteps echoing in the quiet, broken only by the faint rush of water below.

THIRTEEN—ARA

I ran until my muscles burned, my throat ached, my lungs couldn't fill. I pushed my body to the limit. Ignoring any thoughts—not about Kaden's green eyes, the way he had watched me, knowing. Sam, how I had left him without even knowing if he'd lived or died. Not about my sister, my mother, my father, the man in the glowing green room.

I could only run. Through the wreckage of the first building then into a connected parking garage, then up the slope onto an elevated bit of highway. Then following the highway until I met water and could go no farther. Finally, I collapsed, head tumbling between my knees, gasping and choking, trying to breathe. My hands shook, and I forced myself to stand and pace with my hands over my head, like my track coach used to make me do after a race. My throat burned tight and dry, each breath stinging as it went down. My forehead was bleeding and bruised.

I need a plan. That's what Father would have done.

The flooding had spread through most of downtown's low-lying parts, leaving the high ground free, so that a sort of maze had evolved. Without knowing where to go, I could be lost for days, forced to double back again and again each time I hit water. Theoretically I could move faster with a boat, but I wouldn't get in it even if I had one. Swimming in the treacherous dark current was out of the question. And then it came to me: I needed a bird's-eye view.

It took only a few minutes to find the tallest building in the area, a concrete behemoth on a small rise overlooking a square. After smashing in a base-floor window, I crawled through, landing like a cat on all fours. The inside of the first floor was lit by several floor-length windows, and afternoon light streamed in, igniting bits of swirling dust. It had an elegant, ghostly feel, like a decadent ship sunk beneath the ocean. There were six large elevators off to the side of the lobby, and I pressed the button just to humor myself.

I found the stairwell and shivered in the dim interior as I stopped to think. The days were growing shorter and colder. I needed dry clothes, food, water, and a place to stay for the night. The few supplies I'd planned on stealing—including the headlamp and camp stove—were either still in the kayak or lost in the water forever. I couldn't go back or risk them finding me. But even if the others did come looking for me, they wouldn't find me here.

So instead of continuing to climb, I started exploring. On the fifth floor, I found a small kitchen with a dirty counter that held an old coffeemaker and a microwave without a door. A table tilted sideways in the center. But in the corner, like God's own gift to mankind, were four vending machines. Two were soda machines, but the other two were filled with Twizzlers, Skittles, Pop-Tarts, Reese's, fruit snacks, beef jerky . . . I felt a pang of guilt remembering the snacks Kaden and I had shared the night before. I broke a wooden leg off the table and went into one of the side rooms where I found a huge teal-colored tote and emptied it of its contents. A wallet fell out. I opened it and read the driver's license. *Sarah Saveroh.* A middle-aged woman smiled at me, with soft graying curls and a round, kind face.

"Thanks for the purse, Sarah Saveroh." I threw her license on the ground and then finished emptying the mammoth bag. I saved her lip balm and brush, a few strands of brown still mixed in.

"Batter up." I stood in front of the vending machine, holding the table leg like a bat, my elbows up and feet shoulder length apart—how my father had taught me. I swung hard, laughing at the shock and shatter. Then I swung a few times at the pop machines. I wasn't sure what I was trying to accomplish here; they dented, bending inward like a man kicked in the gut, but I couldn't break into them. It didn't matter. One of the other machines held water and Gatorade, and I loaded all six of these as well as snacks and candy into the tote. There were two small bags of jerky, and I opened one of them and began to chew. The meat was hard and dry, even for jerky, but I swigged a bit of water and eventually managed to swallow some of the meat.

The sixth floor had an odd smell to it, but I searched the first two rooms regardless and found nothing. When I opened the third door, a strange, sour smell assaulted me. My body realized what it was a moment before my eyes found the bodies in the corner. I turned and ran, slamming the door behind me, sprinting through the hallway and up two floors before I stopped. *They're dead, they can't hurt you.* But still the smell haunted me. I sank to my knees in the stairwell. I wished Sam was here with me, or Kaden, or my father.

But I was alone.

I forced myself to return to searching the building.

On the seventh floor the offices became more ornate, the windows larger, and the rooms smelled only of dust and disuse. Still, I opened doors and jumped back quickly. In one of the larger rooms, some sort of executive's office, the oak desk held a beautiful silver lighter alongside a box of cigars. For a moment I almost put the cigars into my bag, thinking Kaden would like them, before I realized I would never see him again. The thought made me sad. I took the lighter instead.

Another office held a coat hanger with a single peacoat. It smelled a bit musty but was otherwise clean. I took off each of my wet layers, wringing them out and hanging them on the rack until I stood completely naked in the office. Then I pulled the coat on and wrapped it around me. The shoulders were a bit large, but it was dry and with the tie around the waist it fit me well. Leaving my clothes to dry, I continued on.

Accessing the rooftop was difficult, and I ended up battering down a rusty lock to reach the outside. The stairs opened up to a roof without any guardrail. The wind was cold and grabbed at me, and I crouched, not wanting anyone to see me from below. I pulled the coat tight against me, grateful for its warmth.

I crawled to the edge of the building, surveying the land. Off to my left was a highway that rose above the flooded area, a mass of water and mazelike streets before it.

A flicker of movement caught my eye. I dropped even lower, gravel digging into my knees. There on the street, someone was coming toward me. Adrenaline made my breath quick, and I laid still, a perfect contrast to the disbelief blooming inside. How had they found me so quickly? Kaden would be angry beyond belief.

But as I watched, I realized I was wrong. Six men walked around a corner. Three of them carried the long, thin form of a gun. Kaden and Gabriel hadn't found me. Someone else had. Gravel dug into my side as I lay flat across the roof. The six men came closer. What would I do if they entered the building? Hide? Run?

But they didn't. Instead they began dragging trash and pieces of furniture into the square in front of the building. I didn't understand what they were doing until one crouched beside the stack and a trickle of smoke began to curl upward.

They were making a fire.

Soon two of the men left the fire while the others continued to add to the growing blaze. I watched uneasily. Twenty minutes later, the two men returned, but this time with an additional three. Another two left. A sort of schedule emerged, and each time two men left, more returned. The day passed this way, men leaving and returning with more as I watched from above. After a few hours, I crept back inside to nibble on the food I had collected and tried to warm up. But always the fear of the men drew me back to the rooftop.

Soon the shadows began to lengthen. Still the bonfire grew larger until I feared it could be seen from anywhere downtown. Maybe that was the point. At least a hundred men were gathered below.

And I was stuck above them.

Finally, curiosity, cold, and hunger got the best of me. I returned to the room I'd left my clothes in. They hadn't dried completely, but I pulled them on anyway. The dampness clung to my skin and goosebumps crawled down my arms. I pushed the lighter into my pocket and then downed as much water and food as I could.

In the door frame I paused, feeling like I'd forgotten something. My throat tightened when I realized I was waiting for someone to stop me, to tell me this was a terrible plan, to stay here and wait them out.

There was no one here but me. And I had only myself to blame.

I made my way down to the second floor. Several of the second-story windows were broken, like a mouth full of missing teeth. One of the openings beckoned me forward, a breeze drifting through and bringing the scent of smoke and the voices of the men. I chanced a look through the shattered window, the silhouettes below framed against towering flames.

They can't see you, not when they're looking at the flames. Still, I kept my back pressed against the wall, my heart thundering to know they were so close.

The voices shifted suddenly, growing quiet and then excited. I pushed myself up again and peered out into the night.

It took a moment to process the scene, but when I did, my throat burned, all the food I'd eaten earlier threatening to reappear. They had a prisoner. Someone tall, with wide shoulders.

Please, not Kaden.

A group of four men flanked the prisoner, forcing him toward the fire. A few spat at him, and others reached out and pushed him. He stumbled to one knee, and one of the men aimed a kick at him. He fell once but quickly stood, straightened himself, and continued forward.

His hair was dark. I breathed again—it wasn't Kaden. Then I peered closer, at the way the man held himself, the short hair, straight, angular features—

No.

I didn't want to be here. I didn't want to watch. But I couldn't tear my eyes away. The men forced Gabriel to his knees, and one of them pointed a gun at his head. Their voices were lost in the wind.

The firelight cast them all as silhouettes, like a painting of hell with brushstrokes of red and black. The man with the gun screamed at Gabriel, but the jeers of the others washed out his words. Whatever they wanted, he wasn't giving it to them. The man rammed the gun into Gabriel's chest, but he only shook his head. Finally, the man held up his hand, and the crowd quieted, as if waiting for an answer.

Gabriel spat at his feet.

A shot ripped through the night, and I jerked forward, knocking a bit of glass from the window. The glass hit the ground below and shattered.

My body moved on its own, forcing me to the ground. I lay flat, hands clenched over my mouth, heart pounding. Silence. The crackle of the flames. The creak of the buildings.

Then: "The hell was that?"

FOURTEEN—KADEN

Sam coughed and turned in his sleep, tucked into the kayak we carried him in. I reached back and felt his forehead. It was damp and hot. Issac and I had trudged through miles of waist-deep water until both our lips had turned blue. Now on land, it was hardly any easier. My wet pants had rubbed my legs raw and the kayak seemed to grow heavier with every mile.

"You okay?" I called to Issac. He grunted in return, and I smiled. The day Issac complained was the day humanity was truly damned.

"If it gets any colder, my balls are going to freeze off," I muttered.

Issac laughed, a deep, pleasant sound that few had heard. Usually Issac's calm presence steadied me, but tonight the silence made my thoughts run wild. *Where was Ara? Was she safe? What if she ran into trouble?*

"You have family, Issac?" I said. "Before all this?" The steady crunch and drag of our steps filled the night. The silence dragged on, grating at me. I didn't think he would answer, but then—

"A wife. And a little girl . . . Gracie."

"You think about them a lot?"

"Every day."

The silence stretched between us. Again, Ara's face tormented me.

"What'd you do back then—for a living?"

Issac paused again before answering, as if remembering a past much further than three years back. "I was a high school teacher."

I laughed, for a moment forgetting the deep ache and pain. "What'd you teach?"

"English."

"You're joking."

"'*Death . . . that hath suck'd the honey of thy breath, / Hath had no power yet upon thy beauty: / Thou art not conquer'd; beauty's ensign yet / Is crimson in thy lips and in thy cheeks, / And death's pale flag is not advanced there.*'" Issac's voice trailed off, and I looked back at him in wonder. His smile was tired. "*Romeo and Juliet.*"

"I know, some pretentious high school teacher forced me to read it."

Issac chuckled.

I looked down at Sam, a deep twisting fear in my gut as I thought of the two foolish lovers. Issac's hand felt heavy on my shoulder.

"He will make it."

"And if not?"

"Then we go on. We will meet him again someday."

I scoffed at his words, and started trudging forward again. "I used to believe in God like that too." *Before he took everyone and everything I ever loved.*

"And now you don't?"

I hadn't expected the question, but Issac didn't rush my answer, our steps filling the silence until I said, "He's a cruel bastard. Why would He let all of this happen? He's supposed to give a shit about what's happening, but I haven't seen Him around lately."

Issac didn't answer for several steps, and then, "I believe in the sun even when it's not shining. I believe in love even when I cannot feel it. I believe in God even when He is silent."

Despite everything, I laughed, and shook my head. "Issac, you really are a teacher."

But I thought about what he had said. Maybe the truth was, I envied Issac's peace. This world turned men into monsters, but not Issac.

"Who said that?" I finally asked.

"Someone who also lived in darkness and managed to find the light."

Another cryptic answer, but it made me smile nonetheless. Sam was the only light in my life. But then I thought of sunlight on auburn hair and deep, serious eyes.

After a few more hours, the tall buildings of the downtown sector receded, and we trudged down a raised highway that was mercifully straight and free of obstruction. We took turns dragging the kayak, but I worried about our pace. How long could Sam hold on?

As I looked back, I noticed a bright light in the tall buildings. The light held my eye, and not watching, my feet tangled and I fell hard. Pain lanced up my leg, and had my throat not been parched and burning I would have cried out.

"Issac, look!" The light grew into a towering beacon of fire. We stood for a moment, watching in awe. It lit up the night. At first, I thought it must be an enormous bonfire, but it continued to grow, upward and brighter.

"It must be an entire building on fire!" I said in awe. Issac nodded slowly, a deep frown etched on his face. "Who do you think did it?" I wondered aloud.

Issac shrugged, already turning and beginning to pull the kayak forward. I stood frozen, oddly drawn to the light.

I looked back often through the night. The fire burned steadily for a few hours and then slowly diminished. Soon after, light leaked over the mountains, and a foggy, cold dawn greeted us. Birds began to sing, and the monotonous sound of our feet and the kayak lulled me to sleep, so that my head jerked down and back up as I walked. Though he said nothing, Issac began to walk heavily on one leg, and coughed deeply. Both of us wore damp clothes, and I knew to stop moving now would mean death for us all.

"Kaden, look." My head jerked up with a sudden surge of adrenaline. There, on the horizon, I could just make out six figures on horses. An immediate burst of hope filled me, followed by dread. The men could be from our own clan, in which case they would help us. Or they could be from another.

In which case they would kill us.

I came and stood next to Issac, a silent agreement between us. If the riders were from our own clan, we could wait here for them to help us. And if not, it was already too late to escape them. We stood, stoic and quiet in the cold dawn, and waited.

The men drew nearer, and I reached over to Issac, clapping him on the shoulder and smiling.

I knew these men.

"Kaden? Issac? That you?" Tom called out as the clopping sound of horses' hooves grew louder.

"'Bout time you showed up," I called back, barely recognizing my own voice. Then I saw Red, bringing up the rear.

The six men pulled their mounts to a halt before me, and I held up my hand.

"Sam needs warm clothes, and I need Red, and as much food and water you can spare. Issac will explain the rest." A surge of pride filled me when not one of them asked me to explain.

Pulling Liam aside, I said, "Liam, don't take this the wrong way, but I need your clothes. I'm freezing my ass off."

He laughed, and began to strip, some of the other men throwing insults at us as we both shivered in the morning air. After pulling on warm clothes, I ran my hands over Red. He snorted and pawed the ground, ready to run, while the others worked to get Sam warm and discussed the fastest way to get him home. He was in good hands. Even so, I felt the crush of guilt that I wouldn't be returning to the clan with him. I dropped my voice so the other men couldn't hear and turned to Liam.

"If Ara comes back, protect her. Keep her away from Gabriel."

"Where are you going?"

"I'm going to get her back." Or, at least, help her find her family. Maybe she had used me to go on the expedition, but the long night of thinking, I realized I would have done the same for Sam.

"Kaden," Liam paused. "We need you back at the clan. Without Gabriel there, maybe this is your time?" His words surprised me. My distaste for Gabriel wasn't a secret, but I had always planned on leaving the clan, not leading it. There wasn't time to think about that.

"Gabriel will be back soon."

"And if he's not?"

"Then I will be back soon."

I walked over to Sam and kissed his head. Issac's hand fell on my shoulder again. "Take care of him," I said, my voice thick.

Issac pulled me into a hug, the first he had ever given me. "I will."

I nodded, unable to say anything else. It seemed a cruel joke that it had taken the end of the world for me to find true friends. I turned to Red, ready to ride hard. The saddlebag was full, with enough food and water to last a week. Red threw his head, snorting as I touched his strong neck and ran my hand through his tangled mane. This was where I was born to be.

"Wait." Liam reached up, handing me the holster and gun he always kept slung about his waist. "It only has two bullets left."

I nodded, throat tight as I strapped it to my waist. "Thank you, Liam."

Then I swung a leg up and over Red. Already I felt stronger, the saddle warm against my thighs. Red felt my fervor and pawed the ground, prancing and tossing his head, eager to run.

I turned Red into the light of the rising sun. I bent over his neck and dug my heels into him, barely needing to urge him forward. We left the others behind as his body stretched out, eating the ground beneath him, and even though I hadn't spoken to God in three years, I prayed to Him now.

Let Ara be safe. Give me strength and speed. Let me reach her in time.

FIFTEEN—ARA

The voices of the men blended together, rising like a storm. I was paralyzed on the floor as Gabriel's words came back to me, words I should have thought of earlier: *What kind of a man wants the world to burn?* What if below me stood the horde of men who'd killed an entire clan of men for no reason, and whom Gabriel had just insulted? It made a sick sort of sense, why Gabriel had spat at their feet, and then I hadn't seen Gabriel fall, but I'd heard the gunshot, and couldn't imagine they'd missed, not at point-blank. Either way, I needed to move. The men called out below me, the voices drawing nearer, and with it flames. They were coming to look in the building, and carrying torches. As much as I wanted to look out the window, to see Gabriel, I couldn't risk it.

And another part of me didn't want another man dead because of me.

Glass tinkled as I crawled across the floor, but I didn't dare stand until I was free of the windows. Then, my footsteps carried me swift and silent down the hallway.

A steady pounding of feet from the stairwell. I threw myself through an open door, some sort of supply closet, shrinking back just as the stairwell doors creaked open and the flickering light of a torch lit the hallway. Male voices drifted closer. Their footsteps were heavy and unguarded. Careless.

"—he didn't see jack. Knew we shouldn't have burned down that last building . . ."

"Why'd they choose this building anyway? Remember the hotel . . ." The voices faded.

My heart beat unsteady. If they'd burned down another building, did that mean they were going to burn down this one? Or were they going to spend the night here? Either way, I needed to get the hell out of here.

Fear brought everything into sharp focus: my hand reaching for the doorway, the low creak as it opened, the moonlit corridor stretching into darkness. My track coach had often remarked how I ran almost without a sound; now my feet barely seemed to touch the floor. The men had come through the stairwell; I couldn't afford to get trapped there. So instead I ran toward the elevators. I chose the one with the more battered-looking doors and wedged a piece of metal inside, straining in silence. Finally, the doors yielded just enough to force half my body through and look down. Besides a slight, protruding ledge, a shaft of darkness with no bottom greeted me. A rush of blood made me dizzy as my body begged to move away from the ledge.

Noises from the stairwell—I was out of time.

Stepping onto the ledge, I shuffled sideways, reaching for the cables. The crack in the door gave the barest light to the darkness. For one terrifying moment, my fingers reached into nothingness. Then, finally, they brushed the cold metal of the cables. I clung to the wall, forcing myself to take long, steadying breaths. On touch alone I descended into the dark.

The thin cables bit into my palms as I lowered myself, but I found I could reach down with my legs and find something to brace against, then lower my body. My arms shook, but I forced myself to keep descending. I reached down with my foot when suddenly my hands slipped.

I fell into darkness.

A moment later, I hit the ground hard, crumpling into a heap at the bottom of the elevator shaft. A hysterical whimper escaped my lips—I had fallen fewer than six feet. It took a moment to restart my heart, my hands searching my body for damage I couldn't see in the dark. I whimpered when I touched my left ankle. Still, it held my weight as I stood and limped for the door. My hands trembled as I imagined myself trapped in this dark hole. Finally, I managed to cram my fingers between the metal doors and they slid open enough for me to squeeze through.

The basement spread out before me, twenty feet across with large cylinder tanks in the center. It smelled of rotten eggs and was lit only by a single small window set high in the wall. Piping led away from the room in four different directions, down narrow tunnels of concrete just wide and tall enough that a short person could stand.

I reached into my pocket for the lighter I had found earlier. My fingers pressed against the flint wheel, ready to push, when something stopped me. The smell. It was familiar.

My eyes adjusted to the darkness, and for the first time the labels on the cylinders came into focus: *G-Tec Natural Gas*.

There was a leak in the building.

My knees suddenly felt weak, and I stuffed the lighter back

into my pocket, not even wanting to touch it. Behind the cylinders a metal cabinet stood open. I'd almost dismissed it, wanting to get as far away from this place as I could, when something red broke the darkness. *No way* . . . I stepped closer, eyes growing wide. Four gasoline containers. The last time I'd seen gasoline containers was when we'd loaded two into the back of my father's truck. It was old tech, and hard to get. But liquid sloshed inside as I took the first one out and unscrewed the cap. The hard, noxious smell of gasoline greeted me.

I paused, staring into the darkness. If the men above me were the horde that Gabriel had spoken of, then they'd already killed an entire clan. Who knew what else they would do if left unchecked? This was still my city. If all they wanted was fire and destruction, then I would give it to them.

The container was heavy, but I took the time to pour carefully. Soon a long trail of gasoline followed me down a tunnel, chosen because it looked to lead farthest away from the building. The sharp smell overpowered any other, the glug and splash of liquid covering the sound of my footsteps. Finally, light shone from the edge of the tunnel.

The light grew into a thin window set into a door. A steep set of concrete stairs led up to the surface, blocking my view. If anyone was waiting up there, I couldn't see them.

The trail of gasoline disappeared into the darkness, like an unanswered question, taunting me. It wasn't too late to do nothing. I hadn't known the men in the other clan, I didn't even fully know if this horde was responsible for their end. But I had known Gabriel. He might not have been my favorite person, or even a friend, but he didn't deserve to die on his knees.

With that resolution, my actions became easier. I propped the empty gasoline canister in the door at the end of the hallway for an easy escape. Then I returned to the end of the gasoline trail. My fingers trembled as I flicked the lighter once, twice. On the third time it caught.

"For you, Gabriel," I whispered.

The trail exploded to life, surging up and away from me. In the same moment, I ran for the stairwell, bursting out the door and taking the stairs two at a time.

A breeze swept over me, fresh against the heavy smell of the gasoline. I had come up south of the building, almost two full buildings away, into a space blessedly empty of people. A feeling of lightness grew in my chest as I ran.

The feeling died when three men emerged from the shadows, looking just as surprised to see me as I was to see them.

"Who the hell—"

There wasn't time to go back: I rammed full force into the first man's chest, taking him by surprise and nearly making it free. But then the man behind him grabbed my jacket, and before I could rip away, a fist to my stomach bent me double.

The night exploded, and suddenly the men weren't my biggest problem. A wall of pain and sound threw me flat. My lungs were fire, my ears ringing as the ground rocked and tilted. Another explosion shook the night, burning comets flying high above.

Not comets: pieces of the building.

My head tilted as the world rippled. *Run, Ara, run.* My legs moved slowly, as I forced myself to crawl away. A wall lent its support, my fingers gripping the solid cement to move farther and farther away.

The cement had carved deep gashes into my hands and knees, my ears ringing so loudly I felt dizzy. But I didn't stop, afraid of what the men would do if they caught me like this. I turned a corner, cutting into the darkness, when a body stepped from the shadows. Thick arms wrapped around me. A hand covered my mouth, choking me with terror.

"Ara! It's me!"

He spun me around. It was like placing my hand on an electric fence; the current pulsed through me, but I couldn't let go, couldn't look away. Half his face was covered in a sheet of blood, twisted in pain. His right ear was gone, a bloody stump with blood still pulsing out of the wound, running down his side.

"Gabriel?"

His hands relaxed, but he didn't release me.

"They shot you."

"They tried, but apparently someone in a nearby building dropped something, made him turn at the last second." Blood trickled down from his ear, it took some effort to look away from the stump. "Was that you?"

"Not on purpose." Now that I knew he wasn't dead, all my warm feelings toward him had disappeared. His sudden appearance didn't erase the fact I had just blown a horde of men sky-high. Already voices rose in the distance.

"We have to go." Gabriel grabbed my hand, pulling me back down a narrow alleyway between buildings. "Most of the men were outside the building."

There wasn't time to argue. Together, we ran.

Time moved oddly after that, ebbing and flowing. The ankle I'd fallen on in the elevator began to throb, until every step burned fire up my leg. My head pounded, but Gabriel didn't stop, pulling me forward when I lagged. I hadn't even realized how much time had passed until soft light trailed over the mountains. Heavy gray clouds hung over the horizon, and as the dawn grew, flakes of snow began to fall.

"Gabriel, I need to stop . . ." My body weighed a thousand pounds. It was hard to think, even harder to keep putting one foot in front of the other.

"We're nearly there."

There? He pulled me inside a huge metal warehouse as the snow began to fall thicker and faster. My body trembled. Even so, an alarm went off in my head. *You need to get home.* But it was snowing outside, and winter had come early. I wouldn't survive out there without weapons or supplies—even Father would understand that. Just a night or two. To rest.

Inside, the warehouse was empty with high rafters, almost like a barn. My body trembled, weak and heavy, as Gabriel crouched and ran his fingers over the floor. Then he dug them into a crack and heaved upward, a square section of floor swinging up. A deep hole with a ladder led straight down into the darkness. For the first time in hours, my head cleared.

No way in hell.

Gabriel must have understood the expression on my face, because he positioned himself between me and the exit. "We both killed men last night. They will be out looking for us. Trust me."

"See, that's the thing, Gabriel. I don't."

We stood glaring at each other. Every part of my body ached, and I was so unbelievably tired. I needed food and rest, but I *did not* want to go down into that hole.

"It's your choice, Ara. I can't make you. But we've got food, and a warm, dry place to sleep."

Damn him. Over my shoulder, the door beckoned. And then a shiver wracked my body. So I stepped forward and began to descend the ladder. *If I never have to climb down into a dark hole again, it'll be too soon.* Before I could reach the floor, the trapdoor swung shut above us. Total darkness. I froze.

"Gabriel?"

"Just keep climbing, the ground isn't much farther." I went slower, reaching out with my feet until I brushed the ground. Gabriel climbed down beside me. The darkness was so complete I could have had my eyes closed and not known. Then the room flared to life. Two men stood before us, both pointing guns at my head. I jumped back, but Gabriel's arms wrapped around me, holding me in place.

"It's okay! It's just me!" Gabriel held me pressed against him.

"Damn it, Gabriel, you scared us." The shorter man lowered his gun.

"Ara, meet my brother, Dax," Gabriel said as I stared at Dax in complete shock. I had assumed all his family was dead. But he had never said that, had he? Dax was a smaller, less handsome version of his brother. He stared at me with a sort of venom Gabriel never had.

"And this is Ralph," Gabriel said almost reluctantly, nodding to the second man. Ralph was handsome in every sense of the word, almost too much so, with a huge, white smile and hair that belonged in a commercial.

"What is this place, Gabriel?" I tried to fight the slow, building panic as I took in the table, lanterns, blankets, and a corridor that led away from the room. I'd thought Gabriel had led us to a small bunker to hide and sleep for the night. But now I wondered: Did these men live here?

"A safe place. For members of the clan," Gabriel said.

"Why? What are you afraid people are going to find?"

"Us," Dax said. His eyes had not left me since I entered.

"You are afraid people are going to find two grown men hiding in an underground bunker? And what"—I gestured to the lone piece of furnishing—"steal your lantern?"

Dax's mouth formed a hard white line, and his eyes tightened. For the first time since descending the ladder, I felt the ground stabilize beneath me. "You are just a child," he whispered coolly.

"Oh, really?" *A child who just blew up a building with men inside it?*

"Dax, stop. We need to get along if this is going to work," said Gabriel.

Going to work? As in stay *here?* His words were ice around my heart. I couldn't stay here. I needed to get home. But it was snowing up above. Could I survive winter alone? With supplies and a rifle, yes. With nothing . . .

"There is someone else I want you to meet," Gabriel said, gesturing to the hallway opposite us. I jumped as I realized there, in the shadows, a small figure watched us. They were so slight they could only be a child, face shadowed in a deep hood.

"This is Addison," Gabriel said, and the figure moved toward us, throwing off the hood as gray-blue eyes met mine. "My sister."

SIXTEEN—KADEN

The buildings of downtown towered over me, blocking out what little sun the bleak day offered. The sun had never really risen, and what had started out as snow had quickly become an icy drizzle that soaked through my clothes. Winter was well and truly here. And I was well and truly screwed.

It had been a week of drudgery, walking Red through the cold and muck of the downtown sector. There was barely any sign of human life, let alone clues that might lead me to Ara. I had ridden hard to the building I'd seen burning that night, thinking it some sort of beacon, but when I reached it the place was deserted and the building a ruin.

Today my back ached, and even Red seemed ready to go back to the warmth and food of the stables. The buildings before me showed the reflection of a long-legged red horse, and a man in dark clothing.

A flash of movement. Behind us. There then gone.

Red shifted uneasily beneath me, his ears flicking forward and then back, raising his head to smell the winds.

No clan is dumb enough to live in the downtown sector. Must be a couple loners. Nothing Red and I can't handle.

My hand fell on the cold metal of the pistol. Red's hooves echoed on the street, a lonely sound. Two bullets and a good horse versus whoever followed us.

"What do you think, Red? Two shots sound like enough to you?"

He lifted his head and turned to look back at me. I remembered when I'd first bought him as a long-legged colt. My dad had been furious, and I'd slept in the barn for the next two weeks just to make sure he didn't try to return him. I'd woken every morning to curious, brown eyes. Those same eyes watched mine now. Besides Sam, Red was the only link I had to my old life. I'd burned that home to the ground, buried my siblings, killed my father when his eyes turned white, but through it all, Red had been there.

He whinnied. I cocked the gun and patted his neck. "I was thinking the same thing."

Red's head rose as I turned him around, ready to run. Reins in one hand, pistol in the other, like a cowboy of old.

We surged forward, a grin rising as I imagined the surprised faces of whatever group trailed us scattering before his hooves. We rounded the corner.

And then all I could think was, *well, shit.*

There were so many men before me, it might as well have been an entire clan.

But I'd told Red to run, and he wasn't about to stop now. He flew forward, rearing up when one of the men jumped in his path, hands raised. I kicked him forward and he crashed into the crowd. More men poured out of the alleyways from each side.

Shit!

A break formed between them, our only hope for freedom. Red surged forward, making for the gap. We were going to make it. And then a net fell from the sky, tightening around my chest, and we crashed to the ground.

My shoulder exploded in pain and my gun spun away, across the cement. Each movement made me more entangled. A gunshot ripped through the air. But my body was whole, even as the noise echoed. The bullet hadn't hit me, they must have missed.

Red screamed, a noise I'd never heard him make before.

"Don't kill the horse!" someone yelled. "Dammit, be careful!"

I twisted, trying to make out Red. My face was ground into the dirt, the gravel cutting into me. A heavy foot forced me into the ground, but I managed to lift my head enough to see Red. He reared backward, men pushing closer to him, hands outraised. The whites of his eyes showed as he reared back, hooves flailing.

"Stop it!" I yelled. "You're making him—"

Then, a sudden, lancing pain to the back of my head. My vision blurred, and rough hands bound me, my head stuffed in a sack that smelled of rotten food. Hands lifted me, dragging me forward, and I could do nothing, see nothing. When I was finally slammed down into the concrete, my head throbbed, and a thick liquid ran down my back. Blood.

"I'm bleeding, please . . ." A swift kick caught me in the gut, knocking the wind out of me. With nothing else to do, I curled into a ball, waiting, hoping Red would be all right.

Well Gabriel, you were right. There is a horde of men. And I don't think they want to be friends.

Hours later, someone ripped the hood from my head. Dark figures blurred across a roaring fire. Chilled concrete pressed against my back, and slowly my senses sharpened—and with them the pain. I was just outside the warmth of the flames, propped against a wall. My mouth was gritty and dry, and I tasted blood. I tried to reach up and wipe away the dried blood at the side of my mouth only to realize my hands were bound tightly behind me, chafing and raw.

There were at least a hundred men, maybe more I couldn't see, every one of them armed with a strange assortment of weaponry: pipes, sharpened bits of metal, javelins, a few guns—though I wondered if they still had ammunition as they had only shot once. It came back to me then in a rush. Red. Where was he?

We were situated between several buildings, in a wide court-yard, the fire at the center. It was natural to hide when traveling the city, but these men were broadcasting their presence, which made no sense. A large group, moving through the city center, just as winter set in? Were they suicidal or just insane? The part of me that had led clan expeditions for the past few years wanted to smack the loudest ones upside the head.

A man stumbled toward me, laughing and singing.

"Where's my horse?" I didn't have time to flinch away from the sudden kick. I doubled over, struggling to breathe as he laughed. The sharp scent of urine filled the night as the man relieved himself on the wall.

Then a huge man with a long, braided beard and ragged hair stepped up onto a rusted car and the men grew quiet. He wore an ugly vest of what looked like real fur.

"Tonight, we celebrate!" The crowd roared at his declaration, raising canteens and mugs into the flickering light. He held up one hand, and instant silence fell.

"We celebrate finding yet another hoard of supplies." He held up the can in his hand, and I suddenly realized: these men were drunk. And they hadn't even offered me a sip, the bastards.

I redoubled my efforts to pull a hand free from the rope on my hands. If they were drunk, now was the time to escape. The large man continued: "And we celebrate finding the man who blew up a building with some of our men in it. Let him burn!"

A hundred eyes turned to me. I stopped working my hands, frozen beneath the weight of the fevered, blood-hungry crowd. *Shit.*

"Wait, stop, you've got the wrong man! You want Gabriel!" My shouts were useless. The men surrounding me only laughed, grabbed at my legs, hooked their hands under my arms, and hoisted me into the air. The fire loomed closer, and the man chanted over and over, "Burn him! Burn him!"

Fear muffled all sense of reason. I struggled and thrashed. Then, somehow I met the eye of the man with the braided beard, his arms folded across his chest.

"You want a man named Gabriel!" I yelled at him. "I can show you where he keeps his supplies, take you to his stores, he—"

My nose exploded in pain, I didn't even see the fist. The ground rose up too fast; blood ran down my nose and into my mouth. The world swam. When the world refocused, the huge man stood over me, his face contemplative.

"How do you know Gabriel?" The man ignored the angry hisses of the others. He had saved me from the fire. My next few words were the difference between life and death.

"I was in his clan, but I've left it now." I spat out blood, raising my voice. "I can take you to his supplies and weapons. I can take you to him."

"How can I know you aren't still with him? What happens when we find him?"

I grinned through the blood running down my face. "If we find him, I'll kill him myself."

The bearded man smiled at this, and then stood up. "Untie him." Men jumped forward to do his bidding instantly. When they were done, I stood in the middle of the group. It was my first chance to see them unhindered, and what I found was unsettling. In addition to the weapons, many wore fur coats or coverings like the man before me, and they were haggard and dirty.

"This presents us with an interesting opportunity," the bearded man said. "Burning men has grown boring; I think we could all use a little sport." The group of men yelled in agreement, shaking spears and other weapons. He lifted a hand and they fell silent instantly, "Who accused this man?"

The crowd shuffled, no one making eye contact, until an enormous man with thick scars down his cheeks stepped forward.

"I did, Colborn. I saw him the night the building exploded."

The man was ugly, with thick arms and an even thicker neck. He carried a spear with a wickedly sharp bit of rusted metal strapped to the end.

Colborn smiled, then pulled a knife from the thick belt at his waist and tossed it at my feet. My body froze, my heart picking up speed as I understood the look in his eyes.

"Time for a sudden death tryout. The man left standing will join us, and the other," he paused, and the firelight made his grin demonic, "well, the other will be dead!"

The crowd roared with laughter, bloodlust in their eyes. The circle contracted to the single man before me. He licked his lips, then rolled and flexed his arms and shoulders, grinning as he hefted the spear. The men began to chant, "Brutus! Brutus! Brutus!"

I picked up the knife. I didn't have a choice.

Across the circle, Brutus rolled his shoulders and played to the crowd. Only Colborn stood apart, arms folded, watching me with a sort of cold curiosity that said he couldn't give a damn who won and who died. I lifted my knife and saluted him, earning a dark smile. *Thanks for the knife, bastard.*

Then I stepped forward, letting the circle contract.

Brutus roared as he leapt forward, swinging out his spear. I sidestepped toward the fire. He was fast, but unlike my dagger, his spear was heavy and ungainly. The jagged piece of metal at the end had been inexpertly fastened in place. *Doesn't matter how sharp it is if it never touches you.*

We circled each other. I found myself smiling, taunting him.

"Don't tell me your mother actually named you Brutus." There was laughter in the crowd, and his face reddened, rage filling his eyes. "You must have been one ugly baby."

He bellowed and surged forward. I lunged for the flames, the fire roaring up hot before me as I seized one of the burning logs and flung it at his face. He caught the log, a heartbeat later his high scream mixing with the scent of burning flesh. I retreated, but didn't expect the fury or the speed with which his spear came ripping sideways. The jagged end tore into my side and sent a shockwave of pain radiating all the way up my body. The men roared, sensing the battle nearing an end.

The spear is too long—one more swing and I'm dead.

He was a full head taller than me, but I didn't have a choice: I surged forward and tackled him. We grappled on the ground, and he dropped the spear, his hands suddenly wrapped around my throat, crushing me till black spots flickered in my vision.

I buried the knife in his neck. Once. Twice.

His eyes widened in surprise. Blood flowed out, a hot, thick river, baptizing me. I threw him off me and staggered to my feet. The world tilted around me.

I didn't want to watch the growing pool of blood. Instead, I looked up, and somehow it was Colborn's eyes that found mine. There was no sadness there, only satisfaction. He nodded once. I tightened my grip on my knife. I was one of them now. A monster. The fight hadn't even taken five minutes.

Colborn stepped over Brutus's body without looking down. A long sword was strapped to his back. Unlike Brutus, if he wanted to kill me, I didn't doubt that he could. He strode up to me but looked at my side. I followed his gaze, feeling almost removed from my body. I was covered in blood, but not all of it belonged to Brutus. The cut on my side seeped steadily. My life pulsed out of me. I smiled as I saw it, a strange warmness coming over me.

I hadn't won. We had both lost. I didn't bother to cover the wound—this was the fate I deserved.

But Colborn only laughed, breaking the awful silence that surrounded me.

"Hold him." He spoke softly, but his words were instantly obeyed. Men surrounded me in an instant, grabbing me by the arms and legs, holding me firm. I struggled, suddenly confused.

Colborn strode to the fire, and I watched with growing fear as he pulled a metal beam from the flame. The end glowed white-hot.

"Take his shirt off." The men ripped the fabric from my body, and he approached slowly. He eyed the gaping wound on my side. I thrashed, trying to rip free, but couldn't. My breath came in hitches, and the warmth that had come over me disappeared, replaced with a cold, paralyzing fear. I hardened my heart, trying to prepare myself, trying to think of Ara, of Sam, of anything to distract me.

He was going to cauterize the wound. I held his eyes as he smiled, the glowing metal in his hand inching closer.

"Welcome to hell."

And then there was only screaming pain.

SEVENTEEN—ARA

What followed was the worst winter of my entire life. Which was saying something, considering the previous winter, Father and I had survived in a rickety cabin with only a scrawny deer carcass and some canned goods.

But I couldn't survive the winter outside alone, without supplies, food, or a weapon. I needed to bide my time till the snow melted. Even Father would understand that. Without the sun, the days melded together, until I woke up one morning and realized I'd lost count of how long I'd been here. Five weeks? Six?

In the early morning silence, I turned to look at Addison, her mouth open and her dark hair spread around her like a halo. Sleeping, she was beautiful, like a doll with lustrous raven curls and tawny skin, bright even in this sunless place. She had the same striking gray eyes as Gabriel—from their mother, I learned. She was only eleven, but precocious in a way I never remembered Emma, or myself, being. In a few minutes she would awaken and begin our exhausting daily ritual. She chose my outfits and fixed my hair, always remarking on its color and lack of curl. She smiled and talked and laughed, while I held my silence. Then the two of us prepared meals, canned food, or completed other projects Gabriel assigned us. Two of the three men—Dax, Ralph, or Gabriel—left via the trapdoor and returned with food, supplies, and girly bows or dresses that Addison constantly requested.

Always the door was locked behind them.

I'd thought of convincing Addison we could overpower the one man left behind, steal supplies, and make our escape together, but it was more a desperate fantasy than an actual plan. The biggest mistake I ever made was leaving my younger sister. I wouldn't take someone else's away. And, besides our gender, I had nothing in common with this wide-eyed child, who seemed to have little grasp that the world—and her sex—had all but ended. I'd finally met another female survivor, and yet I felt more alienated than ever.

Today I didn't have the energy for her enthusiasm. I slipped out of the bed, grabbed the first jacket my hands touched, and made my way down the narrow corridors to the kitchen. It was one of my favorite rooms in this windowless, underground prison. It was always warm, and the iron fireplace lit up the room—it was the closest thing I had to daylight anymore. Next to the fireplace, a thick stack of logs took up an entire wall.

This place had brought a different vision of Gabriel and his family into view; though their parents hadn't survived, they must have been extraordinarily wealthy to have designed this place and kept it secret. Besides the kitchen, there were bedrooms, a living area covered in patchwork rugs, and deep below, an eerie room that connected to an underground river where we pulled up water for bathing and drinking. As much as I hated to admit it, Father would have loved this place. He always talked about having a safe place to hide away. He would have seen this place as a dream, not a prison.

"I made you breakfast."

Gabriel's voice cut through the room and I jumped; I'd missed him sitting in the chair by the fire. *You're losing it down here, Ara.* He wasn't wearing his outdoor gear, which meant he'd be staying in today. We'd had an argument yesterday, the same one we always had. I wanted to go outside; he insisted it wasn't safe.

I took a deep breath and decided it was time to try a different tactic.

"Thank you, Gabriel, it looks delicious." Greasy lumps floated in the soup as I ladled it out and handed him a bowl. "So, what are we doing today?" I tilted my head toward him and smiled. *See, Gabe, I'm just a meek little creature that you should let outside . . . preferably with a gun.*

"I got some supplies to make arrows," Gabriel said in that steady way he had. "I thought you could show me how?"

This took me by surprise. Making arrows was something I had done with my father. The thought of actually enjoying my time with Gabriel felt like some sort of trap.

"Should we wait for Addison?" Typical, the one time I wanted her here, she was gone.

"No, she's working on something else today. Come."

Yeah, prolly her hair. I hesitated, then followed him to a part of the bunker I rarely visited. It wasn't like I had anything better to do.

"This is my room," he said and held open the door to one of the only rooms I hadn't searched.

I stepped inside, feeling somehow unsure about being alone

with him. The room had a military efficiency, with a single bed in the corner and a stack of books on the side. I picked up the top book, smiling as I turned over the cover. "*The Princess Bride*. This was one of my father's favorites."

"One of mine too," he smiled and gestured for me to sit on the bed. "Please, borrow it, I've read it too many times to count."

I weighed the book in my hand, both wanting to keep it and not wanting to accept yet another thing from him.

"It's just a book, Ara."

"Maybe to you."

"Ara, why don't you like me?"

His directness caught me off guard. "I don't . . . *not* like you."

"But you don't like me?"

"You locked me up here."

"For your own protection."

I threw the book back on the pile, suddenly cold. "That's not your call to make. You can't just use people, Gabriel. This is my life."

"And if it isn't?" His voice was as cool as his eyes.

"I . . . what?"

"If your life belongs to the world, and not just to yourself, is it still your decision what to do with it?"

I turned to him, putting every ounce of venom I could into my voice. "Yes."

He looked down at his hands. He slowly nodded then looked up at me. "All right then, when spring comes, I will give you whatever supplies you require, and you can go. It will be your choice."

His words caught me by surprise, a hundred other angry arguments I'd been practicing suddenly void. *There's always a catch.* So even though I didn't fully trust this new promise, I decided to play along. "How can I be sure you're telling the truth?"

"You can't. So you may as well come help me make some arrows."

~

To my surprise, it was the best day I'd had in a long time. Gabriel was all right when he stopped taking himself so seriously. Even more surprising, he loved to read. Together we talked about our favorite books, our least-favorite ones, and even argued if anyone would ever write stories about this time. I said no, but Gabriel proved me wrong, telling me he had kept a journal from the beginning. I rolled my eyes—it was such a Gabriel thing to do. I showed him how to make arrows, and even surprised myself by telling him about the first time I'd ever gone bow hunting with my father.

I was shocked when Addison poked her head in later and told us it was almost time for dinner.

Gabriel jumped up. "Actually, I've got something special planned for tonight." He held out a hand to me and pulled me up, smiling. "Why don't you two get ready and meet me in the carpet room?"

Getting ready consisted of two forced outfit changes and Addison begging to do my hair. I finally relented, for fear I'd starve. An hour later she brought me to what we called "the carpet room." Different rugs had been piled over one another, and the outer ring of the room held an eclectic assortment of shabby yet comfy chairs.

Ralph smiled at us as we came in, a shiny guitar in his lap. The chair next to Gabriel held several boxes wrapped in shiny red paper with snowflakes.

"What's the occasion?" The present caught me off guard.

"I thought we would celebrate Christmas." Gabriel smiled broadly, and Addison shrieked out loud and wrapped him in a hug.

"Is it even December?" I asked a bit suspiciously.

"We aren't exactly sure what date it is," Ralph said. "But it did snow again yesterday."

I shrugged and took the closest chair to the door. It took some willpower not to take the comfy-looking chair, but then I would be forced to sit between Gabriel and Dax.

"I'll get my present first." Dax stood up and walked out of the room. We had developed a relationship like that of two cats forced to live together—we pretended the other did not exist unless forced to interact, and then it was with the utmost distaste. He alone seemed to resent my presence in the bunker, and I didn't care to convince him otherwise. Gabriel and Addison laughed and joked together across the room as we waited, making me feel oddly left out after our day together.

Ralph smiled from across the room, his grin growing wider as I sauntered over to him, sliding onto the seat beside him.

"Can you actually play that thing?"

He grinned and winked at me. "'Course I can, anything you want."

Emma always loved music, and Christmas. But I didn't want to share that. "How about one of your favorites?"

"My favorite is a duet, I need a female to sing with me."

"Then I'm sure Gabriel can help you," Dax's dry voice interrupted us. "I shot a wild turkey for dinner tomorrow." Dax stood in the doorway, a bag in his hands. Jealousy surged through me; had he brought the turkey down here just to show off? But then he stepped forward and emptied the bag, tumbling free two pairs of winter boots. "And I found these for the girls. I noticed your shoes are getting a bit worn, Ara." His voice was cold, even if the gesture was friendly.

"Thanks, Dax. Sorry I didn't get you anything." *Like a dead rat.*

He slouched into one of the chairs, spinning it away from the rest of us.

"Mine next!" Addison grinned as she handed me one of the larger packages.

Now I felt guilty. "You should have told me, I didn't get anything for you guys."

She grinned in that devious catlike way she had, cutting a sideways glance at Gabriel. "You have. I've never seen my brother happier." I hid my embarrassment by opening her present. It was a mint-green dress. I laughed. At least she was persistent.

"Thanks, Addison. It's beautiful." I wondered how long until she would force me to wear it. Probably tonight.

"Here, open mine next," Gabriel said quietly. I wanted to force someone else to go and take the attention off myself, but he watched me with serious eyes.

I opened the small package slowly. It was a stunning necklace, with an emerald pendant lined in what looked like diamonds. It was beautiful, and totally useless. But I was spared saying so when Addison opened her own present and shrieked at the diamond necklace inside.

Ralph strummed his guitar in the corner and then stood. "And the entertainment tonight shall be provided by RRRRALPH!" he announced. I tried not to snicker that his present to us all was himself.

His voice was deep and strong, some old country hit that my mother had liked. Addison grabbed me and pulled me off the chair, swinging me around with her, spinning in a crazy circle, her head thrown back and singing lyrics that I couldn't remember. We spun faster and faster, until she let me go and I flew away from her. But instead of crashing into the concrete, I smashed into a solid chest and a thick set of arms. I froze, but Gabriel only laughed, grabbing me by the hands and pulling me back into the center.

Addison forced Dax to dance with her, and I let Gabriel spin me in a circle. His hands were sure, and he spun me away from him and then back close. Addison shrieked as Dax hoisted her into the air. I laughed with her, caught in the moment.

Our voices rose, and nearly overpowered the sound of the guitar, but Ralph only sang and played louder, determined not to be outdone. We danced until we were breathless and sweaty, and when I sat back on the couch, it was maybe the first time I wasn't thinking of escape.

~

"May I walk you to your room?" Gabriel asked sometime later. Against the warmth of the couch my head had begun to droop. He offered me his hand and I let him pull me up.

He kept a careful space between us as we walked back to the room, and I wondered what his actual motive for walking me back was; it was a big bunker, but it wasn't *that* big. Maybe he was going to go back on his earlier promise? But when we reached Addison's room, he surprised me by turning to me, his eyes clear.

"You accused me of using you, but that has never been true. I only want to protect you. The truth is, I am afraid to open up and share, I'm afraid of losing the ones I love, I'm afraid of not being good enough." He stopped for a moment, searching for his words. I heard the frustration in his voice. "I'm afraid of failing, of not protecting my family, my people." He stepped closer, took my chin in his hands, reminding me of that first time I had met him. He forced me to look him in the eyes.

"But I'm not the only one who is afraid, Ara. I see you too." He leaned forward, my face in his hands, and his lips brushed mine. The kiss swept through me. Passion might have held him there, but it was something else entirely that held me in place.

"Good night," he whispered finally. Then he turned and left, leaving me paralyzed. Finally, I sank to the floor, the solid door against my back my only anchor to reality. For the first time, I felt as if I hadn't just lost my way.

I had lost myself.

EIGHTEEN—ARA

The next day, I stood beside Addison in the kitchen, kneading my bread and staring into the flames of the kitchen fire. I'd lain awake all night thinking about Gabriel's kiss, and his promise. I knew exactly what Gabriel wanted from me, and there was no way I was going to give it to him. But I also wondered if it were a coincidence that the same day he promised me my freedom he also kissed me. Was this the catch I was looking for? Because the longer I stayed here, and the more I gave to Gabriel, the less I felt like myself. First it was a kiss, but what came after that? How far was I willing to go to buy my freedom? Maybe I was a fool to trust him and instead of waiting for spring I should make my escape now.

And maybe, strangest of all, was the thought that when Gabriel kissed me, I'd wished that it had been a different man kissing me, one with green eyes and an easy smile. If I left this place, I wouldn't for a moment look back, but I thought often of Kaden, Sam, and Issac. I hoped they were well, and together, laughing and joking in some place better than this hellhole.

"Something wrong?" Addison's voice surprised me; I'd almost forgotten she was there.

"No, of course not. Why would you say that?"

"Because it looks like you're trying to murder that bread."

My hands paused, abandoning the bread for a moment. "Addison, your brother told me that he would let me leave when spring comes, what do you think of that?"

She shook her head slowly, a confused look in her gray eyes—striking even in this sunless place. "But why would you want to leave at all?" she finally said. "We're safe down here."

"Because there's more to life than being safe," I nearly shouted. Like the wind running through your hair or the smell of pine on a cold mountain breeze. Like the gaze of a man who made you tremble.

"What about you and Gabriel?"

I froze, and now I was the one who couldn't make eye contact. "What *about* us?"

"Aren't you guys . . ." She gave a suggestive tilt of the head.

I shook my head fervently, not believing I could blush this much in front of a child.

"So you've never . . ."

I regretted bringing this up at all. "Well, he kissed me, but—" I was almost knocked sideways by Addison crashing into me. She wrapped her arms around my middle, crushing me.

"I knew it! It's so obvious from the way he looks at you! I always wanted a sister!" Heat flooded my face, and I tried to push her away.

"Addison, stop, please, it's not like that."

A sudden determined look came over her face. She grinned. "Oh really? Come with me."

She pulled me out of the kitchen, and I laughed, a bit flabbergasted. We practically ran down the hallway, and this time she took me into a small closet. The back of the closet was paneled wood, but she dug her fingers into the paneling and pulled. A child-sized door creaked open.

She pulled me inside after her and whispered, "This is a hiding place Gabriel made for me, in case anyone ever got into the bunker. But he didn't realize the vent system connects to their planning room. They meet there almost every morning and night."

The tiny space held a short stool and a metal vent set high in the wall. She motioned to the stool. I climbed atop and looked through the vent, just able to make out a barren room with a table and four chairs.

"It's empty," I whispered.

"Stay here, and when they come in, listen to how Gabriel speaks about you."

"What if they come back?"

"I'll cover for you back in the kitchen." She grinned and turned to leave, but then turned back. "He loves you, Ara. I know it."

Then she left, abandoning me to my swirling thoughts.

I didn't love Gabriel; I was sure of that at least. All I wanted was for him to let me go, so I could honor my father's words and go back to the beginning. But down here, even those words had begun to bring despair. I wanted to believe he'd left me something, or, in my wildest hopes, that he would be waiting there for me. But what if I was wrong again, and the beginning wasn't home? Or, worst of all, what if I made it home and found nothing?

In the darkness, it was nearly impossible to measure time. I was about ready to march back to the kitchen, sure I would find

Addison and the men all having a good laugh at my expense, when I heard low voices. I stepped onto the stool as quietly as possible and risked a look into the room. Ralph and Dax entered and sat down. Gabriel paced before them.

"Maybe you need to man up and make a move," Dax said, starting up on some conversation I hadn't heard the beginning of.

"I have, and I'm finally making progress with her," Gabriel responded. I bristled. *Progress?* "But I think it's too soon; I might lose her again if we go back now."

My heart rose. Were they talking about returning to the clan?

"We can't wait. It's already been too long," Dax said. "The longer we wait, the more dangerous it becomes. Our escort will be here soon."

"And if I lose her again? What if she stays loyal to Kaden?"

"Then make sure that doesn't happen." Dax sounded almost bored.

"What are you suggesting?"

"No one has even seen Kaden since he left. We both know there are only two reasons he would return to the clan. One, for Ara. Make her yours completely and he won't come back for her."

If he had been standing before me, I would have slapped him. *Make her yours.* Was this some sick game to them?

"And the second?" Gabriel's voice was so light I almost missed it.

"The boy. Sam."

"But he's been healing well. He should make a full recovery." Ralph's voice again, this time with a hint of worry. I pictured him picking at his nails or fixing his hair.

"And if he doesn't?" Dax's voice was low.

"What are you suggesting?" Gabriel again.

I didn't want to hear what came next.

"If Sam dies, Kaden will leave the clan forever. We all know the boy is the only reason he stays. And with Kaden gone, Ara will be yours. Kaden is dangerous, Gabriel, you've always known that. The men like him, and it sounds like Ara does too. Make it simple: don't give her the option of making the wrong choice."

Dax's voice changed then, lower and smoother. "You are a good man, Gabriel. The best of us. But you know more than anyone, sometimes the ends justify the means. Are you going to let one boy stand in the way of humanity? It could be done quickly, humanely, no one would ever know. It's too late for Addison, but not for Ara." His words made no sense. Addison was only a child, how could it be too late for her? "Once she's carrying your children, you would be the man who saved the world."

I suddenly felt sick. No. Not Sam. Even Gabriel wouldn't do that.

But the next words were Gabriel's and with them my entire world changed, as if the floor had become the ceiling.

"See that it's done."

~

Lunch was a quiet affair, and even with the fresh turkey, Ralph had lost his usual pompous and bouncing air, unable to carry the conversation by talking solely about how wonderful he was.

"Something wrong, Arabella?" Ralph's voice startled me; no one but my father called me by my full name, and only when I was in trouble.

"I'm fine, just tired," I said through gritted teeth.

"Tired because you've been working so hard, *Arabella*?" Dax dragged my name out like it was a dirty word. "Maybe you could hunt for our food for a change."

"Give me a bow and I will," I snapped.

"Enough, Dax." Gabriel's voice was sharp. He turned to me and smiled gently. "Actually, I have something I would like to announce." He cleared his throat. I could feel his gaze upon me, even as I stared at my plate. "We will be moving to the clan soon."

I glanced up. "What about the snow?"

"Most of the snow is melted from the last storm. We want to move before the next big storm hits. And the clan has everything we need to make it through the rest of the winter. We think you'll both be happier there. It will be a good change, for all of us."

And what about your promise, you worthless, sniveling excuse for a human being? What about the innocent boy you would hurt to get what you want? What about the fact that I will never, ever be yours? I stayed quiet.

"The men should be here by tonight, or tomorrow morning at the latest. We need to be ready by then. Ara, I thought you could work with me—"

"Actually, Addison and I wanted to wash our hair first, so it'll be dry before tonight."

Gabriel paused, and then Addison began to plead and he conceded. Addison took my hand and we descended down the corridors into darkness to the river room. The walls were made of stone covered with green scum. The room ended abruptly, sheared off, the water roaring below, visible only as a black rippling path. I shivered at the sudden chill. Addison turned the lantern on, its glow lighting a corner of the room. The river threw undulating patterns onto the ceiling.

"I'll get you a fresh bucket of water and we can wash our faces, all right?"

"Addison?"

She turned, and it struck me that down here, in the shadows, she looked older.

"Why haven't you gone to the clan before? Why now?"

For just a moment the smiling shell cracked. "Gabriel didn't tell you about me from before?"

"No." I'd always assumed it was because she was so young. What older brother would want to bring his younger sister to a clan full of men?

Her deep eyes gazed off into the distance, her body still for once. "I was sick."

She stopped and wrapped her arms around her, as if remembering made her cold.

"Ovarian cancer, which was really, really rare in someone my age. I was sick for a long time. It was awful, all these horrible treatments." She paused and then finally looked at me. "And the treatments stopped. The whole world stopped. Gabriel brought me here. He said, when I was ready, he would take me to the clan." She reached out and took my hands, her eyes shining, her voice so warm and sincere I wanted to curl up in a ball and disappear. "And now that you're here, too, I want to go."

I stared down at my toes. How had I spent weeks in this underground prison and never known Addison had cancer? Did it change what I was about to do, what needed to happen?

"Now, let's get some water," she said and leaned over the edge to grab the rope that lifted the bucket. For a moment she teetered on the edge of the dark river, one tiny step the only thing between falling and being swept away. I stepped forward and grabbed the rope. Together we hauled up water until there was enough for us both.

I cupped the water in my hand, but the wavering reflection seeped away.

"I knew the first time I saw you," she said, her voice lilting and happy again, as if our previous conversation had never happened. "I knew from the way he looked at you that you two would be together."

I flinched.

"We will finally be safe when we get to the clan. We will be a family."

I stood slowly. "Addison, do you want to play a game with me? Gabriel said we should practice it."

Her eyes lit up as she turned to me, my insides churning with guilt. It was either this or jump into a deep, icy river in the middle of winter.

"Do you remember, a long time ago, when you were in school, and they would do fire drills?" She nodded, her eyes wide. "Well, we are going to practice what would happen if someone broke into the bunker and tried to steal you. Only the men are going to be the men who already live here."

"Like Gabriel, Dax, and Ralph?"

"Yes, exactly!" Her smile widened, dancing on one foot to the other.

"Now listen close, because this is the most important part. Your brothers and Ralph are going to call out your name, and sound really upset, and say whatever they can to get you to come out. But no matter what they say or do, you *have* to stay hidden. Understand?"

Her head bobbed up and down in excitement.

"Good." I pulled her to me, in a final hug, then held her out. "Do you know a place to hide where they won't find you? The most secretive place you can think of?"

She nodded, and I bopped her on the nose. "Good. Then I want you to go there right now, and I'll go tell the boys the game has started. Remember not to leave no matter what they say, don't leave. And if they can't find you for at least an hour, you'll get a superspecial surprise. Now go!"

She spun and ran away from me, and I was surprised that a bit of emotion twisted my chest. Maybe I would miss Addison after all. I felt inside my coat pockets for the few supplies I needed: a pocketknife and some matches. Father had taught me to survive with so little.

Tears filled my eyes. I didn't stop them.

Let the games begin.

Then I ran, faster and faster up the stairs, screaming as I burst through the door to the main room. The three men looked up at me in surprise.

"Ara, what's wrong?" Gabriel jumped up and crossed the room.

My breath came in hitches. "Addison slipped, she fell in the river."

Gabriel finger's dug into my shoulder, so painful I gasped.

"Can you still see her from the tunnel?"

Tears ran down my face, and I shook my head no.

"The current was so fast. She was just . . . swept away."

Gabriel turned to the men, only a slight hitch in his voice betraying his panic. "Ralph, come with me. Dax, go down and check if you can still see her."

All three rushed from the room.

Their footsteps faded as I watched the trapdoor. The cracks in the door glowed, sunlight leaking through. I wiped the tears from my eyes and moved toward the door that had been locked for weeks.

Everything depended on them having forgotten to lock it, just this once. I climbed up the ladder, touched the handle, and then twisted. Blinding sunlight hit my face, tears of elation and pain overflowing from the sudden brightness after so long in the dark. But I didn't let it stop me. Pain was a small cost to pay for freedom.

"I'm coming, Sam."

NINETEEN—KADEN

Winter deepened, the weeks stretching out as my side slowly healed and I came to realize the true cost of joining the horde. The plague had created a cruel world, where men sometimes had to kill to survive, but Colborn didn't kill for survival; he killed for fun. And his grip over the horde was absolute. They were like a swarm of locusts, devouring everyone and everything they encountered. You either died horribly or became part of the monster. Anyone who spoke out was silenced.

Today was no different. A cold winter sun watched me in silent judgment as I led the horde down a steep set of stairs that had once led to an underground bar. Colborn moved ahead of me, and as I stepped into the dark interior, I felt like I'd missed a step. There were new supplies here, things I hadn't added. Colborn lifted the lid off the top of a barrel, and his sudden predatory smile made my throat constrict.

"Very nice, Kaden." Colborn hefted a gun in his hands, turning it over, admiring the way the wood of the handle caught the light. He opened another wooden barrel, revealing a collection of rifles.

"Won't do your men a lick of good. I've seen the way they aim." My uneasiness deepened as Colborn nodded to the men who greedily awaited his command. They fell upon the weapons, each fighting to grab one.

So far, I had led the horde to five other storage units filled with canned goods and other nonperishables, all devoured within days. But I had no idea that Gabriel had the gall to add weapons to one of them. I couldn't decide who I was angrier with, Gabriel for stockpiling an arsenal of dangerous weapons, or myself, for giving them to a horde of violent men. At least they didn't have bullets.

Yet.

I turned to go back up the stairs, clutching my side as I did. Even though the wound had healed, it still ached in the cold. The night Colborn had cauterized the wound was a hazy blur, the following days marked with agony. Any gratitude for the care I received vanished as the weeks passed and I led Colborn's men through the downtown sector, showing them the storage sites I had added to over the years with my expedition team. As much as I hated handing over supplies to the horde, I worried that if I didn't, they would take the supplies from another clan, and kill them all in the process.

We had run into only two other men, haggard and starving. Colborn had made them fight to the death, each with only a brick as a weapon. It was a gruesome fight, but I watched it all, aware of Colborn's eyes on me. The winner had joined us. The loser we left broken on the pavement, the buildings above a desolate graveyard. It was then I realized Ara was right: some men just wanted the world to burn. Most men dreamed of the world we'd once had; Colborn seemed to glorify in pushing this one closer to chaos.

Which made planning my own escape difficult. I had only two reasons to stay. One: Ara. Our horde fanned across the city, and if she was still here, we would have found her. But there was no sign of her. She had disappeared, and I hoped she'd finally found whatever it was she was looking for. The thought of this horde finding her made me shudder.

I bent to pass through the narrow wooden door and came out into the winter sunshine, pale on the dirty snow. The second reason I stayed pawed the ground in front of me. Red. I smiled as I watched him. He pushed his velvet nose through the snow, searching for grass.

"You've done well. Everything you promised." Colborn bent to exit through the door frame, and then stretched in the weak sunlight before settling against the wall beside me. He smiled up at the sky. His good mood made mine darker.

"What about what you promised? I'm going to die an old man at this rate." *If I don't die at your hands much sooner.* He draped an arm over my shoulder, and though the gesture seemed friendly, I wondered if he had murdered men just moments after embracing them as brothers.

"So eager to leave. Just a bit longer. I have one more thing left I want you to help us with. Then you can go."

"With Red?"

He waved a lazy hand. "Of course. That's what I promised, isn't it?"

He drew away. I was foolish to trust his promises. But what choice did I have? The men watched me carefully, now that I'd proved valuable. I would never escape on foot—I needed Red. But it was also more than that. Red had been with me through everything. He'd literally carried me through the darkest days of my life. I wouldn't leave him behind.

"Come, let's get some dinner." Colborn motioned for me to follow him.

I took one last look at Red, and the four men who guarded him. Too many. He raised his head and looked at me, nicker-ing softly. Though it pained me to do so, I forced myself to turn and follow Colborn to the campfire, the sun sinking beneath the horizon behind us. The men had made camp tonight in a narrow apartment building. Typically, they preferred to sleep outside, but the winter night was bitterly cold, and snow was piled up around the door. I stepped into the building. It stank of sweat and piss. They had cut a hole in the ceiling above the fire, but the place was still hazy with smoke. It felt like a den of hell.

Colborn sat on a bench by the edge of the fire. Immediately the other men on the bench moved and I joined him in the now-empty space. Men sprawled on the ground and huddled up against walls. A few stood guard against the night, but more to watch for infected animals than other men. *We* were the men oth-ers worried about.

Colborn and I both ate a dinner of canned beans and assorted fruit in thick syrup, courtesy of the latest storage site I had shown them. Colborn had a weakness for the fruit and set stores of it apart for himself. At the center of the room, a few men were try-ing to roast a Canada goose. When it was cooked, they would offer a choice portion to Colborn. But for now, Colborn looked curiously at the pile of discarded food cans in the corner.

"So, will you return to this clan you once belonged to? Or will they be angry at you for giving out all of their supplies?" Colborn watched me, the light of the fire dancing in his eyes, and I wondered if this wasn't another one of his games, set to entrap me.

"The clan leader never much liked me anyway."

"Why's that?"

Oh, you know, the endless pranks, the disrespectful attitude, the barely concealed contempt, or the fact that I ruined his one chance to rebuild the world. Take your pick.

"It's a long story."

"You have something better to do?"

A strange, freeing feeling came over me as I realized I sat beside a man I could say anything to, and he wouldn't blink. I would never tell him of Ara, but there was an earlier reason for the hatred between Gabriel and I.

"Most people don't know this, but Gabriel wasn't the eldest brother, or the first ruler of the clan . . . Everett was." I stopped, surprised at the sudden thickness in my throat. "We were friends, and it wasn't long before I was overseeing the stables. Then one day, Everett calls in me and Gabriel. He tells Gabriel that he's going to name me as his second. Gabriel erupted, shouting about family and betrayal, ranting almost, and stormed out. But then the next day, Gabriel calls us both to his room, cool as ever, and tells us that we need to make a plan for how to tell everyone about Everett's choice. I agreed, but before we could talk again, the two of them left on a scouting expedition, alone. The next thing I know, Gabriel's back at the clan, screaming about an infected animal, and that he and Everett had got separated. Every man in the clan searched, but by the time someone found Everett, it was too late. His eyes had turned. They killed him before I even got there, and then we burned him where he lay." It was a day I didn't like to think back on. So I shrugged the thoughts and feelings away, finishing the story. "It didn't seem the right time to tell everyone Everett had named me his second, and by the next day it was too late: Gabriel had named himself successor."

"When you say 'they' killed him before you got there, who do you mean?" Colborn's voice was cool, almost conversational, like he barely cared to listen. I buried the sudden surge of anger. *He's trying to make you angry. This is a game to him, don't let him win.*

"A couple of Gabriel's men found him first. His eyes had already turned, so they gave him the only mercy they could, and killed him." I stared into the fire, trying not to show him how much I hated this, wishing I hadn't told him in the first place.

"So let me get this straight: the day after Everett betrays his brother, and names you his second, Gabriel leads Everett out of the clan alone. Gabriel comes back without him. And then Gabriel's men happen to find him first. Sounds to me like Gabriel had a plan for Everett. Same way Cain had a plan for Abel. But it wasn't mercy."

The roasting goose suddenly fell into the fire, sparks flying as I suddenly understood what he was saying. "No . . . not even Gabriel . . ."

Colborn smiled. "How often did Gabriel and Everett leave for scouting expeditions, just the two of them?"

I paused, then ground my teeth together. "That was the first time."

"And that expedition, was it planned?"

"No, but I assumed it was because Gabriel wanted to talk to Everett alone about his decision, to try to persuade him otherwise."

Colborn laughed, the sound so jarring I jumped. "Oh, he wanted him alone, all right."

I wanted to wipe the twisted smile off Colborn's face. "You don't know that. Not even Gabriel would murder his own brother." But suddenly, I wondered. Gabriel was a man who would do anything, *anything*, if he thought it was for the good of the clan.

Colborn leaned closer, "I do know. Because it's exactly what I would have done." He paused and let the horrible suggestion swirl and thicken like the layers of smoke in the room. *This is what he does. He gets to people. Not even Gabriel would kill his own brother.* But I couldn't help replaying the look on Gabriel's face, the burning rage I'd never seen before or since. What if his anger hadn't disappeared, but had warped into a dark and insidious plan to assure control of the clan? I didn't want to believe any man could murder his own brother, but now that Colborn had introduced the idea, I couldn't forget it.

Colborn suddenly laughed and slapped my back so hard I jumped. "But I'm sure your own brother is safe there. Or, if not, maybe he could join us." The thought of Sam, here, with the horde, was enough for me to place my plate on the ground, the rest of the food untouched. All this time I'd thought the safest place for Sam to be was part of the Castellano clan. Now I wondered if that was true.

Colborn gave a deep sigh. "You think you're so different than us, Kaden. But I saw the bloodlust in your eyes when you killed that man. You belong here."

"I will never belong here," I spoke without thinking, regardless of the consequences.

He smiled again, that dangerous, glinting look. "But you belong back at your precious clan? If Gabriel murdered his own brother, he'd murder your brother just as easily. Maybe you should go ask him, just to be sure."

It's another one of his games. But I couldn't help but ask, "What do you mean?" Was he letting me go?

"A group of fifty men just left Gabriel's clan. The biggest number I've ever seen. I want to set an ambush for them."

An ambush. Against the clan. My insides tightened, the wound shooting slivers of pain down my side. Gabriel prided himself on being well prepared, but the horde was a monster they'd never seen before. It would be a bloodbath.

"What else do you know?" I finally asked. Maybe I could find a way to warn them, or stop it.

"They've been traveling for three days, but Gabriel isn't with them."

"Why not attack them now?"

Colborn grinned, and the way the shadows played on his face made his smile appear twisted and demented. "Patience, Kaden. He must be guarding something extremely valuable to send such a substantial number. That's why we wait until the group has whatever it is and is headed back to the clan. Then we take it." He swiped his hand through the air.

"What do you think he's carrying?" A terrible suspicion played on my mind. What if Gabriel had never made it back to the clan? What if the valuable cargo he had wasn't something but some*one*?

He shrugged. "Weapons, explosives, gasoline, maybe all of them." His nonchalance showed me the truth. Colborn didn't just want what Gabriel had—he wanted the satisfaction of taking it away from him. This was another game to him.

"Why should I help you?"

"Help me and you can have your precious pony and leave. But

not before you ask Gabriel the truth. Find out how Everett really died. And then step into darkness. Maybe you'll find you're one of us after all."

I sat up all night, watching the flames grow lower and lower until only embers remained. I tried to think of Sam, of Ara, of what was still left. Of what remained.

Instead, I was haunted by a vision of the last time I had seen Everett.

His eyes were dull, his body swollen. I couldn't see past death to the laughing, confident man whom I had believed could lead the clan through the darkness. All I saw was a cloud of flies over a bloated body. We weren't allowed to bring him back to the clan, or even touch him, for fear of the plague, so we'd burned him right there.

I'd lit the fire, and when his ashes burned up into the infinite blue, my hope for the clan burned with him.

TWENTY—ARA

I surged out the front door and then stopped.

An entire team of horses and more men than I could count stood outside in the snow, looking just as surprised to see me as I was to see them. The winter sun beat down on us, the cold already reaching through my thin jacket, showing me just how unprepared I was. My breath clouded before me.

Sam needs you. Bluff.

"Hello . . . everyone." I tried to sound casual. It didn't quite work. "Gabriel sent me up to say hello and grab some supplies. I'll be back in a few minutes."

I jerked forward, forcing myself to walk straight through them. Every crunch of the snow made me wince. My insides screamed at me to run, to fight, but I continued walking.

"Hold up," said one of the men on horseback. I kept walking until another man stepped in front of me, hand on his rifle. "Gabriel sent you out here, all by yourself, to go get supplies?" The man had an impressive scar across his cheek and face, and a part of his nose was missing. He slid off his horse, and I felt the men around me contract.

No! Sam!

I gave him a look of disdain, arching a brow. "It's not like there's anyone else out here. And if you don't believe me, take it up with Gabriel."

He paused, weighing this.

Then the door sprang open again, and Gabriel appeared. His eyes were thunderous and found me instantly.

Too late. Always too late.

He glanced at the men, his anger shuttering as he pasted a smile on his face and walked over to me. "I wondered where you'd gone. It's freezing out here. Why don't we go back inside to talk?"

I just stared at him. I saw it in his eyes—the ugly truth. That I didn't trust him, didn't want him.

"Come back inside, Ara." All the warmth in his voice was gone.

"No," I whispered. "I will never believe anything you say, ever again. I know what you were planning. To kill Sam, so you could own me."

He sighed, shaking his head. Not contrite. Not apologetic. Finally, the rage that had been building inside me exploded and I turned to the men. "Your perfect leader was going to kill a child to get to me!"

There was silence, only wind blowing over the snow. None of the men moved, they just stared at me with dark, empty eyes. I'd never felt more alone.

Gabriel took my arm, pulling me after him. "We need to get her inside," he said to the man with the scar.

I fought against him. "I TRUSTED YOU, YOU SICK—"

I didn't see the slap coming, but I felt it so hard my head

whipped to the side. The sting was nothing compared to the shock. Then Gabriel grabbed my shoulders, shaking me and forcing me to look up at him.

"Grow up, Ara. You think my men care if I kill one? I've killed hundreds to keep the peace. And I'll kill thousands more if that's what it takes to rebuild the world. My men are loyal to me. Never forget that." Then he turned to one of them, presenting his back to me and striding away. "Put her in one of the boxes on the wagon."

I fought, but against so many it was more to make a point than to accomplish anything. I was thrown into a sort of crate in the back of the wagon, a blanket thrown in with me, and then locked in. Only then did the full weight of what had just happened hit me.

I'd failed.

But Gabriel also knew I'd found out about Sam. Did that mean Sam would be safe? Either way, I had to find a way to warn him and Kaden. I shivered and pulled the blanket over me, unable to get comfortable. Before long the wagon began to move, and sleep became impossible. The bottom of the crate was dirty and smelled earthy.

I'd traded one prison for another.

~

It was hours later when the crate was opened. I uncurled from a ball and blinked at the bright, piercing light. For a moment I thought it was the sun, but then it switched off and a cool breeze swept into my crate. It was night, and a cold one at that.

Two men I had never met hauled me out of the box. My legs were numb and tingly, and spasms of pain shot across my body as my limbs stretched for the first time in hours. The men let me move and stretch for a minute before taking my hands and tying them in front of me.

We were inside, all of us, even the horses. Huge glass windows stood behind us, the ceiling rising high in what once was a magnificent room but now seemed eerie and forgotten. In front of us was a huge board listing films that had played many years ago.

An abandoned movie theater.

Ralph came over and smiled at me, taking the rope that now trailed from my hands in his own. The two men flanked us as he led me to a small bathroom just off the main room. I had never liked Ralph more than in that moment.

"There's no other exit, so please don't make me break down the door to get you." He winked and then handed me a bucket of cold water. I nodded numbly and went inside, closing the door behind me.

Water seeped through my fingers as I scrubbed my face raw. It was tender and swollen where Gabriel had hit me, and the mere reminder of that made me furious, and terrified at the physical reminder of what Gabriel was capable of. What if Sam was already . . . No. I couldn't think like that.

"Ara, you okay in there?" Ralph knocked. With a deep breath, I opened the door. He must have sensed I didn't want to talk, because he turned and began to lead me deeper into the theater.

"Come on, we've got a cot made up for you."

We walked through the huge entryway. I understood now why they had chosen the theater. A biting winter wind roared outside, a storm not far off, and the horse and wagon could both fit inside the huge lobby area, like a giant bubble with its soaring glass walls, that, while filthy after years of neglect, still provided shelter from the wind. Arcade games littered the area now filled with men and horses.

Ralph led me farther inside. The next hallway was large and spacious as well, enough to accommodate all the men. The carpet had once been a royal red but had since faded from its former glory. Now it seemed the color of dried blood. I shivered at the thought, and looked up and met the eyes of the men as I passed by. A few I recognized from the clan. I forced a smile as I passed.

Ralph led me to the very center of the room, to a concession stand with a chest-high counter in a large circle. Along one side was a tiny gate. I almost smiled at the absurdity of it. The world lay in ruins, but that tiny, little gate still worked. There were only two cots set up within the small circle, and Addison already sat on one, brushing out her hair. When she saw me, she stopped, turning away and crossing her arms with a dramatic sigh. *Perfect*.

"You can sit there," Ralph gestured to the cot.

"Great, but first, could we just go stretch our legs for a bit? I just need a bit of air."

"Ten minutes."

I froze at Gabriel's voice behind me. "But take two other guards with you and stay within sight of us at all times."

Ralph grinned and nodded, oblivious to my silent glare, and we walked back toward the entrance. Ralph let me pause beside the huge, chestnut draft horse. The horse's head was lowered, but he raised it as I began to pet his neck. His fur was soft and so thick I could bury my fingers into it. He pushed his warm, soft nose into my hand, searching for food, and I smiled.

The other men watched us curiously, wary at first, but before long two of them joined us.

"Hi, Ara, good to see you again." Liam smiled at me, his sky-blue eyes shy for a moment.

"Liam, it's good to see you too." And it was. I gave him a smile that might have rivaled Ralph's. He lit up in response.

"This is Dusty." He patted the neck of the enormous horse. "Would you like to feed him?"

"Yes, please."

Liam poured a bit of ground oats into my hand. He didn't comment on my hands being tied, but instead took them in his own and showed me how to hold them flat. His hands were warm and callused, and I liked the way he casually, and unnecessarily, touched mine, not afraid of me as others were. Maybe if I would have tried harder to make friends in the clan, and not spent all my time with Kaden, someone would have helped me escape. I laughed at the warm, hot breath and the way the horse's lips flapped as he ate the oats.

Together the four of us walked along the glass windows, looking out into the night. The cold seeped through, frost growing up the windowpanes. Outside, snow had begun to fall, and I wondered, if it kept falling, if we would be able to continue in the morning.

As we walked, one of the exterior doors suddenly blew open, wind blasting inside. Ralph jogged over and looked out into the night, flakes of snow swirling inside. The sudden impulse to run into the night made me rock forward on my toes, and then back on my heels. I was fast, they wouldn't suspect it . . . But then what? I had no flint, no weapons, no supplies. Liam watched me closely—but even I could tell it wasn't because he thought I was about to escape. It was a sort of power—one I didn't know how to use.

"Hey, Liam," Ralph said, "Where'd the sentries go?"

A crack rang out before Liam could answer. Liam wrapped an arm around me in a protective gesture. We looked all around, confused at where the sound had come from.

Then Ralph turned around.

The whole world stopped. His eyes met mine, and for the first time, he didn't smile. His face was lined with shock. He lurched forward and then looked down at the blossoming red wound on his chest, where a bullet had ripped through him.

Liam grabbed me, dragging me backward. Bullets ripped through the night. Screams filled the air as chaos erupted. The glass windows shattered and fell, like a waterfall of ice thundering to the floor. Dark forms rushed toward us through the night.

Liam half dragged, half carried me backward. Men yelled, trying to organize against the enemy charging through the night. Some of our men hid behind ancient vending machines, already firing back at the attackers. Others crouched behind the wagon. Four men tipped an old ice hockey table on its side with a tremendous crash, and then sheltered behind it. Others crouched behind the ticket counter. I wanted to look behind me, to see the faces of the men who had shot Ralph. Only Liam kept me moving forward. I watched as two men tried to calm Dusty, but the enormous horse reared up, his feet striking out as he threw his head back in terror. Liam pulled me through the door to the hallway before I could see what happened next.

In the hallway, Liam set me on my feet but kept pulling me forward. Men surged past us. I was reminded of movies of old battles, one side caught unawares and then slaughtered. But seeing it myself was different. I could smell the sweat and blood, my ears ringing with the sounds of gunshots and shattered glass.

Then Gabriel came through the crowd. He gathered the men around him, leading them forward. Beside him, Addison had never looked smaller or more terrified. Then, standing before me, he slipped a knife between my ropes. I looked down in numb surprise, forgetting they had even been tied. He put the knife in my hands and turned to Liam, giving Addison a push forward till she folded her body against mine.

"Liam, take her and Addison, go to the back of the theater, hide in one of the rooms. Don't come out until the fighting is over." Then, eyes on me. A great distance stood between us, and even though I knew this could be the last time we ever spoke, that he went to protect me, maybe even die for me, I still hated him.

"Be safe, Ara."

I looked away, following Liam.

I never was the forgiving sort.

~

Liam led the way down the empty hallways away from the fight, a pistol clutched in both hands, his headlamp slicing through the darkness. I tugged Addison along after me. Long-ago movie posters clung to the walls, two-dimensional faces watching us with faded, tired eyes. I suddenly wished I would have asked one of the men for a cap to hide my hair. I'd once loved having my hair fall free and long, but now it made me feel vulnerable.

Away from the glass windows the hallways grew ever darker, the dim interior eerie with the distant sound of raised voices and gunshots. Addison wept softly and clung to me. The hallway felt like an immense dark cave, littered with a few ancient candy vending machines, and lined with once-regal carpets now stained and faded. My arms and back burned with the effort of pulling Addison onward, but the echoing screams and gunshots kept me from stopping. Before I could ask to rest, Addison saved me the trouble. She collapsed on the ground and began to sob loudly.

"Addison, get up." I tried half hard-heartedly to pull her upright. "Addison, we can't stay here." But she didn't listen to me. She didn't even look at me. Liam and I exchanged a look, the light of his headlamp blinding me for a moment.

"Should we carry her into a theater?" Liam's headlamp pointed and faded down the length of the long hallway, lined with double doors that led into movie theater rooms. We both looked back toward the echoing sounds of battle. Were we far enough away?

Tucked against the wall next to us was a refreshment counter, a board above listing the prices of popcorn, candy, and sodas. It was waist high, better to hide behind than nothing at all.

"Let's just get her behind there for now." I pointed at the refreshment stand. Liam tucked the gun back in his holster and groaned as he lifted Addison and we moved behind the counter. As soon as he sat her down, Addison curled into a ball and continued to weep. Behind us were cabinets that had once stocked popcorn and other treats. The door creaked open, revealing a space just big enough for a child to hide.

"Addison," I crouched beside her, trying to make my voice gentle. "I found a place for you to hide. As long as you stay there, and stay silent, nothing can hurt you." She froze, and then, to my surprise, she crawled inside, and curled into a ball. It reminded me of a wild kitten I had once caught in a trap. Once it realized it couldn't escape, it tried to hide from me by simply pressing its tiny wet nose and face into the corner and refusing to acknowledge me.

Liam slowly shut the door and I let out a small moan as I slid to the ground. Inside the cabinet, Addison was quiet. Liam slid to the ground beside me, his shoulder touching my own. He pulled off his headlamp, not clicking it off, but instead placing it on its head between us, so that the light lit the carpet a golden red and cast a soft halo of light around us. Neither of us spoke. In the distance, the sharp cracks of bullets tore the night.

"Not the greatest hiding spot, is it?" I said, too exhausted to move.

"Maybe the best hiding spots are in plain sight." He winked at me, and despite everything, I smiled. "Do you know how to use that?" he asked, nodding to the knife Gabriel had given me, still clenched in my left hand.

"Yes," I said with a touch of annoyance. "I can take care of myself."

He laughed, a deep chuckle. His shoulder was warm against mine. Though I'd learned to survive alone, I was glad he was here.

"Here," he reached into his back pocket, pulling free a flashlight no bigger than a pen. "It's my spare." I took it without speaking, clicking the light on once, then abruptly off.

"You okay, Ara?"

His sincerity made me uncomfortable. I didn't know how to answer the question. Men were out there dying for Addison . . . and for me. And they were led by a man I hated.

"I'm fine." I'd been saying that a lot. I wondered if I would ever mean it.

"It's going to be all right. I won't let anyone hurt you."

The way he smiled almost broke my heart. Because I knew his words were a lie, even if he didn't. No one could protect anyone in this world. Just like I couldn't protect Emma or Sam, like my father couldn't protect me.

Suddenly Liam tensed.

Voices, from the other end of the hallway. Terror settled in me. I looked at Liam, both of us coming to the same realization. This wasn't an attack; it was an ambush.

"They're going to surround the men," I whispered. Liam and I stared at each other in horror. They would take Gabriel's men by surprise, and this time there would be no recovery. Worse, what if they came for us after? They would find beautiful, timid, defenseless Addison. I could only imagine what they would do to her. I tightened my grip on the knife. I would die before they took me.

"One of us has to warn them." I glanced over the counter. "You have to go, Liam. Now."

He looked over the counter one more time. Then back down at me, hesitating, "Are you sure you'll be okay?"

I raised my brows again. "I told you—"

"—you can take care of yourself," he finished, the same sad smile on his face. He bent down next to me, and this time the hesitation on his face was different. "You're not even going to wish me good luck?"

It took me a moment to understand what he meant. I leaned forward and pressed my lips to his. Then I gave his chest a shove. "Now go!"

He pulled back, grinned, and was gone before I could catch my breath, his light disappearing into the darkness.

TWENTY-ONE—KADEN

The trees' limbs had frozen—they made a strange cracking noise below the building howl of the storm. The horde crept forward, and any hope that the clan would notice us seeped away like the warmth from my body. Snow swirled about us like a great cloak, masking our approach. With each step forward, Colborn's words grew louder in my head. *You're one of us.* He was wrong. I would never be one of them.

And yet, here I was, stalking through the dark, trying to decide if Gabriel deserved to die.

Through the falling snow, I could just make out the abandoned movie theater and the hazy figures on the other side of the glass. A fire burned in the back of the room, and several of the men held torches. The light blinded them from us. *Gabriel, you fool, where are the sentries?*

I switched off the safety on my gun and readied myself. One shot was the only warning I would give.

One of the side doors slammed open in the wind, and I froze.

A man stepped out. He was tall, with blond hair and wide shoulders, framed from behind by the light of the torches. I fought my instinct to move. He couldn't see us, not with the light inside. To move would be a mistake—

A crack rang through the night the same moment the man in the doorway shuddered and fell.

"No! Wait!" My words were lost in the roar as the men jumped up and charged the building, unloading their guns into its glass walls. They screamed and howled. The night came alive.

Then I ran with them toward the building, rushing toward men I'd once called brothers. Before us, the glass walls shattered and fell. The sound of gunshots, breaking glass, and screaming filled the night. I took advantage of the madness, pulled up my hood, and charged into the din.

Inside felt like a den of hell, all dancing shadows, madness, and screams. They'd brought the horses inside, and I used one of them for cover, running low and fast. Then I vaulted over a pool table turned on its side and took cover. The men behind it raised their guns.

"Don't shoot! It's Kaden!" I recognized Boden.

"Kaden, what are you—"

"There's no time—where's Gabriel?"

He pointed to the hallway behind us. Of course, he was back there, probably hiding like the coward he was.

Behind me the clan was organizing, firing back, and holding the horde at bay, at least for now. The door to the hallway burst open, more men rushing forward as I slipped by them.

And before me, at last, stood Gabriel. But for one sick moment, I didn't see him. I saw the high cheekbones, the light gray eyes, the dark hair of his brother. Everett. The man I had loved as my own brother. The man he had killed. The door shut slowly behind me, for a moment muffling the sounds of battle.

Gabriel hid his surprise well, taking me in and then dismissing me just as quickly. He continued with his orders, almost as if I weren't there. "Thomas, go in through the side, Brandon through the center. Stay low and keep them from advancing. We have the cover, so we hold and make them come to us."

The men left and now only Gabriel stood before me.

"Kaden, whatever you have to say—"

"Tell me the truth, Gabriel. Did you kill your own brother?" Surprise flickered in his eyes before a hardness descended.

"Kaden—"

"He named me his second, and then you went out together, and he never came back. Did you kill him?"

I didn't expect his answer, or the coldness of his delivery. "It doesn't matter how he died. Only that he did. And that you will never be clan leader."

I pulled out my pistol and aimed it at his head. My finger trembled. One small movement and I could end this. *You are one of us.*

Gabriel laughed softly. "This is why I am clan leader and you are nothing. You can't make the hard decisions."

And then he took a step forward, straight up to my gun, the metal only inches from his face. "You think you have what it takes to lead? Then pull the trigger."

Seconds passed. I stared at him, trembling. Before I could do anything, I heard the sound of running feet and Liam rushed around the corner. He froze for a moment when he saw the gun pointed at Gabriel, but he continued forward regardless.

"There're more men, coming from the back. It's an ambush, we need to hurry!"

Colborn was coming. I had only seconds to finish this. But Gabriel wasn't listening—his eyes were wide with shock, and his next words left me breathless.

"Ara's that way."

I felt as if a bucket of ice water had been dumped over me as I imagined Colborn and his men meeting Ara, alone and unprotected. And when I thought of her, of her laugh, her smile, the way she burned like a fire, I made my decision.

"I will never be like you, Gabriel."

Then I turned and ran, to save Ara and the last shred of humanity still within me. Because if I didn't find her, if I was too late and Ara was gone, I was afraid it would disappear forever.

TWENTY-TWO—ARA

Each heartbeat seemed like an eternity. Soon, voices filled the hallways, beams of light slicing through the darkness. Heavy footsteps and the sound of metal—weapons?—drifted down the hallway. It was impossible to know how many there were based on sound alone, but at least six beams of light sliced through the darkness, running over the ground and up the walls.

My body stiffened, one hand holding the flashlight, the other gripping the knife so tightly it hurt. I tried not to think of Liam, Addison, or Gabriel, but focused instead on the footsteps and hushed voices of the men as they came down the hallway. None of them spoke, but the closer they came, the larger their shadows grew on the wall, huge and unsubstantial, like demons. Even so, their voices were that of men. They would bleed the same as anyone.

I held my breath, not daring to move.

They came closer, until they were mere feet from me. If one leaned over the counter and looked down, they would see me.

But it turned out I didn't have to worry about choosing whether to stay or go, because at that exact moment Addison let out a low moan, and the shadows and voices all froze.

If I stayed, they would find us. I pushed off the ground, clicked on the flashlight, and ran like I had never run in my life. The beam of Liam's flashlight swung wildly before me, a giant, flashing sign, but I needed to draw them away from Addison and in the pressing darkness there was no alternative. My footsteps were swift, nearly silent, the voices confused, calling out behind me. I glanced back, watching as a single beam of light separated from the group of men, a massive form lit behind it.

Fear burned in my veins, and this time I didn't look back, running down the hallway. My heart screamed *run, run, run*, but the darkness around me pressed tight, offering protection that the storm outside wouldn't. *Hide, Ara, it's dark, he won't be able to find you.*

A door on my left loomed in the darkness, and without hesitating I threw myself through it. No lock. My flashlight lit a narrow stairway with an ugly maroon carpet that led up. Not what I'd been hoping for, but too late now. I took the steps two at a time. At the top of the narrow stairwell was a wooden door, its top portion glass, with a faint light leaking through the glass. *It must lead outside.* I threw myself inside and locked it, buying myself a few seconds as I spun around to look at the room—and realized my mistake.

The room led nowhere, dominated by several huge pieces of machinery covered in dust. A tiny, dirty window showed the theater below, where the side wall and roof had collapsed inward. A tree lay where moviegoers had once sat, the entire theater covered in snow that reflected what little light came from the open sky.

This was the room from which they'd once projected movies. And there was no way out but the way I had come.

A body slammed into the door and I screamed and spun. My flashlight lit on a mountain of a man, with a braided beard, long hair, and a coat of matted fur. His hair was wild around his face, and his mouth was an angry, gaping hole. The doorknob shuddered, refusing to turn, and the man smiled at me through the glass, so that I dropped the light of my flashlight to the floor, cold to my core. He took a step back, his dark eyes trained on me as he kicked the door. The impact shook the room. Once, twice, and then a third time he slammed into the door.

The door held.

There was a sudden breath of stillness, like the eye of a hurricane, as we each stared at the other.

Then suddenly, he turned and was gone.

I watched in disbelief. Seconds ticked by. My body thrummed with adrenaline. Had he really left? Maybe he'd gone back to rejoin the fight? My heartbeat filled the silence. I spun my flashlight back to the glass, but it revealed nothing. My legs trembled as I took a small step forward. Then another. Keeping a body length between me and the door, I peered through the glass.

The stairwell was empty.

My flashlight moved left and right, casting grotesque shadows, but still I hesitated, equal parts worried it was a trap, and that if I didn't move now, I would lose my only chance to escape. *There's no reason he would know you're a female . . . even if your hair is down, it's dark. Maybe he just figured it wasn't worth it and went back to his men.* My hands trembled as I stepped forward, legs weak, heart fluttering. If he had left, I needed to go before he brought reinforcements or something to break down the door.

The empty glass beckoned. I set the flashlight on the ground, knife still clenched in the other, as I lifted a shaking hand for the doorknob and—

The glass shattered. I screamed as it rained down on me. A monstrous hand reached through the broken pane, searching for the doorknob. It clutched the knob, moving to unlock the door—

And I buried my knife in his arm.

An inhuman howl filled the air. I pulled out the knife, ready to plunge it back in again, when the lock finally clicked and the door swung open, sending the flashlight spinning away, the room flashing bright then dark until the light hit the far wall and stopped.

He stood framed in the doorway. Blood flowed down his arm, but he didn't favor it or even move to stop the flow.

He focused solely on me.

I dragged myself back through the broken glass and stumbled to my feet. Blood dripped off the tip of the knife as I held it pointed at him. It suddenly seemed pitifully small. He towered over me. He stepped forward, glass crunching underfoot. I took a step back. His eyes slowly traveled over my body.

"I knew Gabriel was hiding something," he said, "but I had no idea it would be this good." The knife wavered, my hands refusing to hold it steady. He continued forward, and my back hit the wall, ending my retreat.

"You got me pretty good." He rolled his shoulder forward, and though blood seeped down his arm and dripped off his fingers, the way he said it made it seem as if it were only a scratch. "Don't be afraid of me," he said softly, the same way you might talk to a frightened animal. He took another step toward me, and though he smiled, his eyes remained cold.

"Come any closer and I'll kill you." My voice trembled. I held the knife in front of me.

"It doesn't have to be like this." He looked down at the blade in my hands. "You could come easily. I won't hurt you."

"Go to hell," I snarled and lunged forward.

He sidestepped the knife, much faster than I had expected for someone his size. He used my momentum against me, knocking the weapon from my hand and then slamming me into the wall. My head made a cracking sound and I saw black. He put his hand around my throat, crushing me, forcing me to raise up onto my tiptoes. I clawed uselessly at his fingers. I couldn't breathe. Black spots peppered my vision.

"Pretty little thing, aren't you?" His voice was in my ear, his full body pressed against mine. Tears ran down my face. I tore at his fingers.

Finally, his grip loosened and I sank back on my heels. I gasped in air, but now his hands traced all over my body. I felt sick. He cupped my chin and forced me to look at his face. His breath smelled like rancid meat and his beard scratched my skin. He was too close, but I couldn't pull back. He wiped away a tear that ran down my face.

"Shhh, don't fight, I don't want to hurt you." Then he gripped my shirt at the collar and ripped it down the front. The cold air hit my bare skin. I screamed and tried to drive my knee into his groin. He buried his fist in my stomach. The pain bent me in two, all air forced from my body. I wanted to curl into a ball and die, but he forced me flat against the wall. I thrashed, but weakly, still gasping. He dug into my hair, pulling back my head.

"We'll get you trained in no time." Then his mouth was on mine, hot and awful. I couldn't breathe again, couldn't feel anything but blind, terrible panic. His hands moved down, working at the zipper of my pants as I thrashed against him. I tried to scream, to breathe, to do anything, but he was everywhere.

And then, just as suddenly, he was gone.

His eyes rolled back in his head and he fell away from me. I looked down in shock at his body. For a moment, it seemed as if time stood still.

Finally, I looked up.

Another man stood before me. His chest heaved, a pipe clenched in both hands. Blood stained his clothes. His eyes were wild, a deep green I would have known in a different life.

"Kaden."

He caught me before I fell.

I heard his voice from a distance, but I couldn't understand it. Sounds and sensations warped and twisted, building inside me like a whirling storm trapped within a tiny chamber. Everything seemed to tilt and blur, and I collapsed to the floor.

"Ara! Ara, you need to look at me." His voice came from a great distance, like I was at the bottom of a well. It was painful to look up, to move or think. But something in his voice stirred me. I looked up into his eyes—I'd forgotten how green they were. It was like looking into a memory.

"Ara." His voice was soft and low. He crouched next to me. "Are you okay?"

It was Kaden, but at the same time not. His eyes were harder, older with a weariness in them I hadn't seen before. His jaw was rough with stubble and he was covered in dirt—and blood.

He reached out and I jerked backward. He stopped, slowly lowering his hand, his lips pressed tightly together. I realized that

I was wrapped in a tight ball, my fingers digging painfully into my legs as I held them clutched tightly to my chest.

"Ara, we aren't safe here." He said it clearly, patiently, but I could hear the fear underneath it. "We need to leave. Now." I nodded numbly but still didn't move.

He stood, and I watched him carefully. He took off his jacket. The side of his shirt was ripped, and I saw the mangled scar of a wound I didn't remember from before. This more than anything else made me come awake. I focused on unfolding my arms and legs one at a time, and then forced myself to stand.

I flinched as he moved to give me his jacket, but this time he didn't react, only stepped back slowly. His eyes traveled over me, over my ripped shirt and my bruised face. His shoulders and jaw stiffened, rage in his eyes. I was glad he didn't say anything. I wasn't sure I could answer. Instead of draping the jacket around me, he held it out to me in silence. Without looking at him, I took it, wrapped it around me, and zipped it up.

A tension hung there, thick and heavy, like a physical weight had been given to everything unspoken between us. I wanted to apologize, to beg his forgiveness, to tell him I should never have left him and Sam, but no words came out. It felt as if the world was closing in around me, and I would be engulfed if I tried to surface and face it all. I closed my eyes and focused on the scent of his jacket. It smelled . . . like home. Like fall mornings, dust on the road.

"Are you okay?"

I nodded, not able to manage more. He kept a careful distance between us, and I realized for the first time we had both changed. The easy feeling I had once felt around him was not exactly gone, but changed. He watched me as carefully as I watched him. He seemed to conclude that I was going to be all right, then he pulled a pistol from his belt and turned away.

"We need to go." He cocked the pistol, and I still didn't understand. He hesitated and glanced at me, looking uncomfortable but determined. "Turn around. You don't want to see this."

I suddenly understood. I looked at the other man on the ground, the man who would have raped me if not for Kaden, and the pistol in his hand.

"No, don't." The words surprised me. I pushed off the wall and placed my hand on Kaden's arm. Our eyes met, and below all the anger and hurt, I saw him. The Kaden that I missed. His arm was warm and solid, and I let it anchor me to reality. He lowered the gun slowly, giving the man on the ground such a look of hatred that I wondered if he knew him.

"Just—just leave him there, okay?"

Kaden slowly put the gun back in the holster. It was an odd moment, both of us surveying the other. In the past he would have smiled, or made a joke to lighten the silence, but he didn't now. He was more rugged than last I had seen him, his easy, graceful swagger gone.

I bent over and picked up the crowbar. There was blood on one end, but I forced myself to carry the weight.

"Did you know him?" I stared at the man, unable to look away.

"Yes. His name is Colborn. He's the leader of the horde." We both stared down at him, an unspoken question rising between us. If he wasn't dead, he deserved to be. But for some reason I couldn't let Kaden kill him. Not for Colborn's sake, but for Kaden's. I knew too well that some stains could never be washed away.

Kaden gently took my hand, pulling me away from the body. "We need to go."

I nodded numbly and followed him out. A shiver ran down my spine as I closed the door to the room. It felt like leaving a graveyard.

We walked down the stairs, and Kaden pulled out a flashlight I hadn't noticed before. I realized I'd left Liam's flashlight behind, but I didn't turn back. I never wanted to see that room again, and I wasn't going to ask Kaden to go back either. He carried himself differently now. His face was serious and focused. Had I not known him, I would have been afraid of him. He looked like a man who would walk through hell for what he wanted—or already had. He cracked open the door to the hallway, spun his flashlight each way, seemed to measure something in his head, then looked back at me and hesitated.

"What's wrong?"

He looked up at the ceiling, as if he considering not telling me, then he let it out.

"Trying to decide whether to do the safest thing and leave, or to do the more dangerous thing and screw them all over." He looked from the exit sign over to where Colborn's men had come from. I wasn't loyal to Gabriel's men, but the decision was easy. Ralph had always been kind to me. I would never have the chance to say a final good-bye to him, but maybe I could send him off with a final screw-you to his killers. He would have liked that.

I pushed past Kaden. "Let's get these bastards," I muttered. *For you, Ralph. Even though I know you would have preferred a song.*

We ran down the hallway. I fought to suppress a hysterical, rising panic that threatened to overwhelm me. It felt good to be running, to put physical distance between me and what had almost happened, but it also made me want to run faster, to give in to the panic. But I couldn't lose it, not now. Kaden ran beside me, and though he pretended not to, I felt him watching me, measuring me, as if to see if I would fall.

So I kept running.

"Brings me back," Kaden interrupted my thoughts, "to getting chased by those wolves." He laughed, and I tried to smile, though the memory was more chilling than fond. I could tell he'd set his pace to mine, and though it chafed my pride, my legs burned with enough pain to swallow what little remained.

I paused when we passed the hallway where I had left Addison. The cabinet was empty. Addison was gone.

"You coming?" Kaden called softly.

I pushed onward, sending up a silent prayer for Addison as I did. There was nothing more I could do for her now.

We reached the end of the hallway, and he stopped me, grabbing my shoulder.

"Wait." He zipped up the jacket he had given me to my chin, and pulled the hood over my face. He tucked a few strands of hair back into the hood, the brush of his fingers strokes of warmth.

"Do you trust me?"

"Mostly."

He smiled. "Hold your hands behind your back like your arms are tied, and keep your face down. Hide the crowbar."

I did as asked, tucking the crowbar up behind me. He pulled the gun from his holster, and then he shocked me, pushing me roughly forward and pointing the gun at my head. He kicked open the door in front of us.

Three scrawny men stood up. Behind them was a line of horses, all tied to old metal railings once used to lock up bikes. If not for the white clouds of breath that came from each, I would have thought the horses were statues, each dusted with a fine layer of snow. Kaden pushed, forcing my head lower.

"Colborn sent me back with a prisoner. He needs you all in there—NOW!"

Two of the men jumped up and scurried inside. The third stopped and peered closely at my face. I stared at the snowy ground.

"Colborn told me to stay and guard the horses and I ain't—"

I swung the crowbar as hard as I could. The shock of the blow came all the way up to my shoulders. The man crumpled.

Kaden looked at me in shock. "You've changed."

I couldn't tell if he thought that was a good or bad thing. He nudged the man lying facedown in the snow. He didn't move.

"We gonna do this or what?" I said with a bravado I didn't feel. Kaden only grinned and pulled a knife from his trousers. I raised my eyebrows in surprise.

"How many weapons do you have hidden on you?"

He grinned back. "Care to find out?"

I didn't have time to answer as he moved down the line and began untying the horses. Most of the ropes came off easily, but a few were frozen to the bar. These he sawed off. He worked quickly, completely at ease beside the enormous animals. I kept a careful distance. Each time he untied one, he slapped it on the rump and it took off into the night. Even if they didn't run far, it would have been impossible to track them in the growing storm.

I came up to the last horse, and he turned a quizzical eye to me. I smiled. Red. I'd never thought I would be so happy to see a horse. His thick red coat was dusted with snow. His brown eyes turned to me, and he bobbed his head up and down as I slowly approached. I didn't know much about horses, but I knew Red was beautiful.

"We don't have a saddle. Do you think you can ride without one?" Kaden asked as I approached the last horse.

"Well, someone gave me a lesson on riding bareback a couple months ago, but I wasn't really listening."

My voice felt flat, but Kaden still smiled. "Instructor too good-looking?"

"Something like that."

"Doesn't matter. I can; I just wanted to see if we should keep two horses. But Red can carry us both." He slapped a mean-looking black horse on the rear, which sprinted away and aimed a kick at me as he passed. Relief filled me. I really *had* listened to Kaden's lesson, but there was a big difference between riding a horse bareback in a corral in full daylight versus riding one bareback at night into a growing snowstorm.

Kaden walked over to me, and for a moment his hand rested on the small of my back. Red pawed the ground as Kaden approached.

"Hey, Red, 'bout time we left the horde, don't you think?" His voice was fond and deep, and he ran his hand over Red's long, graceful neck, then untied him. Red danced forward, his coat like a burst of flame in the storm.

Kaden threw the lead rope over Red's shoulder and, in one graceful motion, vaulted onto his back. Not only was there no saddle, but there was no bit in the horse's mouth, just a rope around his neck. That wasn't part of his bareback lesson. How did he plan to steer him?

He reached down and held out his hand. "Care for a ride, pretty lady?"

I wasn't ready to jump on the back of the enormous, powerful horse, even if he was beautiful. But then I met Kaden's eyes.

I gripped his arm just below the shoulder and jumped, letting him pull me up behind him. Red moved beneath us, eager to be off, and I wrapped my arms around Kaden. The ground looked much farther away, and Red's warm body beneath me felt unsafe. I scooted as close as I could to Kaden. He had no jacket now that I wore his, and I could feel his muscles as he shifted and moved. I looked at the building, silent as I thought about everything I had left behind.

"Thanks for coming back for me," I whispered.

He glanced back at me. "Sorry it took so long." Then Red leapt forward, and there was nothing but the cold wind, Kaden's warmth, and an exhilarating, terrifying fear, like flying, or falling, or both.

Though death lay behind us, and darkness before, I felt something I hadn't in a long time.

Hope.

TWENTY-THREE—ARA

The world had disappeared into a fury of white that left no room for anything but moving forward. My world began to contract as the cold clawed deeper and deeper inside. I was so tired of fighting. Part of me longed to close my eyes and disappear into the swirling world forever.

The city around us receded. Trees became dark monsters that loomed suddenly up out of the gale and then disappeared just as quickly. My world became only Red, his warmth seeping into my legs, and my hands clutched around Kaden.

Time passed, impossible to measure.

Red kept his head lowered against the driving force and trudged forward. Kaden had stopped directing him, but still he walked onward. At first Kaden trembled, but then he grew still. His eyelashes, coated with a dusting of snow, were tightly closed. I was wearing his coat—he had nothing to protect himself from the cold.

Warmth spread through my body. With it came numbness.

Not quite peace, but a lack of pain and feeling. Red continued to trudge forward, but more and more slowly. I felt myself nodding, resting on Kaden's back. Sleep beckoned like an old friend.

The numbness that had crept its way up from my fingertips now moved into my heart. Heaviness descended over me. I noticed dimly that Kaden's head now rested on his chest. Red had stopped moving. When had that happened?

The storm around us devoured space, color, time. I gazed out into the nothingness.

Then I saw her. Emma.

Beautiful Emma, running and laughing, dancing through the snow in an ivory dress. Her dark hair fanned out behind her, caught in the wind as she danced away from me.

"Emma, wait!" The howl of the storm overpowered me. But I couldn't let her go. Not this time. I fell off Red, crashing to the ground with a surprising amount of pain. My limbs didn't work like they should, but desperation forced me forward.

"No, wait, Emma, please . . ." Her mocking, singsong laughter tormented me, coming from everywhere at once as I stumbled after her. The storm was absolute, everywhere. I couldn't see Red or Kaden anymore. Hysteria rose in me, but I kept going. She was right in front of me, she was right—

I collided with a wall. Pain lanced through my fingers as I folded against the rough texture of the brick, letting myself feel and see something other than the blinding snow.

I had found our salvation. But it wasn't what I wanted. I wanted *her*.

It was too cold to cry or do anything but shuffle down the wall. Only a few steps over I stumbled on a raised porch. A faded red front door appeared through the swirling snow, and my stiff fingers fumbled with the doorknob. It was like my fingers no longer belonged to me, so stiff and bitingly cold. When finally the door opened, the storm forced its way into the house.

I turned back to the swirling darkness. "KADEN! RED!" My words were ripped away by the howling wind.

An idea began to form in my mind, dependent on one critical detail. I moved down the wall, eyes trained on the ground. My fingers tingled with a burning pain. Maybe this house didn't . . .

But then I saw it.

A green garden hose, tucked behind a bush, still attached to the house. I grabbed the end of it and walked back out into the storm. The storm was a billowing white mass all around, attacking and buffeting my face, howling and ripping at my clothes. But it didn't matter: the hose was my lifeline.

"KADEN! KADEN!" The storm ripped my words away from me. Then: a flash of dark hair. Emma. I surged after her.

The form grew, but it wasn't Emma. Instead the tall body of Red materialized, the snow coating his head and the lump on his back that was Kaden.

"Red, come." I pulled the rope connected to Red's halter. He raised his head, looking at me with sad, brown eyes, but didn't move. My body trembled, showing me how weak I was. If Kaden fell off him, or he refused to move, there would be nothing I could do. I cupped his beautiful head in my hands.

"Please, Red. Move." This time I turned and walked, pulling him after me. The rope didn't tighten. My throat tightened, tears blurring my vision as the hose led us back to the house. We reached the open door and Red's ears swiveled forward, sensing the shelter, and he stepped around me, moving inside. As he did, the top of the doorway caught Kaden and he tumbled from Red.

THE LAST SHE

My attempt to break his fall was pathetic and we both ended in a heap on the ground. I dragged him inside and then forced the door closed.

The house was frigid, even if we were out of the wind and snow. We needed a fire.

"Kaden, do you have a lighter? Kaden!" I shook him, partly out of panic, partly out of the need to not feel alone. His eyes stayed closed, lips blue and his face an ashen white. With no response, I searched his pants pockets, finding only his flashlight from earlier.

I ripped off the jacket he had given me earlier and wrapped it around him. His breath seemed to come too slowly. Red stood in the corner beside an empty coat hanger, his head down again. His coat was thick and coarse from winter, so I buried my fingers into the warmth. When they could bend again, I turned on Kaden's flashlight, and then grabbed Red's lead rope and pulled him after me.

I wasn't exploring this house alone.

The living room we stood in was mostly intact. There was an old fireplace and a couch with dark green flower print. Pictures still hung on the wall, but I was careful not to direct the light to them. I didn't want to know who lived here, what souls might still haunt this house. On the couch was an old throw, and I wrapped it around me, trying to keep in the heat.

The windows shuddered as the storm tried to batter its way inside, but Red's slow clopping filled the house with a comforting noise. His breath made clouds in the darkness, his earthy scent contrasting with the dusty, lifeless smell of the house.

The living room opened into a kitchen with a dining table lined with wooden chairs. I left Red in the center of the room

215

and began to open and close all the cabinets and drawers. Quiet desperation filled me.

Matches. Somewhere there had to be matches.

My trembling fingers made searching difficult, my body growing increasingly jerky and frantic as I pulled out drawer after drawer, my mind racing. Was it just me, or was the flashlight starting to fade? What happened if it died before I found matches? What if they didn't even have matches? The house was surprisingly organized, as if the inhabitants had intended to come back, but I ruined that now, ransacking every cabinet and drawer with no regard for the once owners.

Finally, I heard that familiar rattle of thin wood inside a cardboard box. My fingers searched and came up with a box, suddenly sure in their movements as I freed a single match and struck it to life.

The light flared—a tiny flame pushing away the darkness. My breath caught as I stared at it. There were so many times in the forest, with my father, that our fire had beaten away the cold and dark, the difference between life and death. As it burned, I felt like he was here, watching over me even if Emma wasn't. The flame burned down to my fingertips before a single breath killed it.

Then I made my way through the house, collecting books, wicker baskets, chairs; anything that might burn well. It took patience, and time, to coax the fire to life, but my father had taught me well. The flashlight faded further, and I turned it off to preserve what little battery it had left, the fire now casting enough light to see inside the dark house. When the flames roared, I dragged Kaden closer to the heat source. His clothes were damp, so after a moment's hesitation, I pulled them off. The girl I'd once been would have been uncomfortable undressing a man, but I felt only fear. If Kaden died, I would be truly alone.

"Don't you die on me too," I said to Red, but his ears only flicked forward briefly. He would probably outlive us both.

Kaden's shirt stuck to him, but I couldn't afford to be gentle. I pulled it up and off him. The light from the fire lit his full chest, revealing the twisted scar that hadn't been there before. His socks were wool, and mostly dry, so I left them, moving onto his sopping jeans. The material clung to him, and I had to hold my fingers up to the flame to heat them enough to manage to pull them off. He wore black boxers, and I struggled for a moment of indecision before I felt the bottom corner. They were wet as well. Finally, I covered him with the small blanket from the couch, and used his knife to cut both sides of his boxers and then pull them off. I'd never seen a man fully naked, and I didn't want this to be the first time.

I covered him with the jacket and small throw blanket, but it wasn't near enough. The room was warmer from the fire, but barely, and I would need dry clothing as well.

I took one of the last pieces of wood and held it for a moment in the flame. When it caught, I used it as a torch to move down the narrow corridors to the back of the house. They were too close for Red to come with me. In the darkness my thoughts ran wild. Had there been a red *X* on the door? I couldn't remember. What if someone had died in this house and the bodies were still there?

But Kaden needed me. So I pushed forward. The first room had soft pink flowery walls and a white crib. I shut the door quickly. But the second room was an adult bedroom. I stripped and gathered all the blankets into a pile, then added what clothes I could find to it. There was too much to hold with the makeshift torch, but it was already fading, so I went into the adjoining bathroom and tossed it into the empty bathtub. The last of it flicked and I forced myself to leave the light, pick up the pile of musty blankets, and make my way back to the living room. My feet stumbled once, but the flickering light of the fire guided me back.

When Kaden was covered with the blankets, I stripped out of my pants and shirt. There was nowhere to drape my clothes next to the flames, so I laid them and Kaden's jacket over the back of the couch. Then I pulled on the odd assemblage of clothes I'd managed to find in the room and crawled under the blankets, adding my heat to Kaden's. He was deathly cold and still, his fingers frozen, and I held them against my side, gasping at the sudden chill. I forced myself to leave them there for sixty seconds, and then rubbed them for another minute, trying to get the blood flow back. I did the same with his feet.

The fire cast shadows all around the room, and lit Kaden with a warm, flickering light. A blush heated my cheeks at the thought of what he was—or wasn't—wearing. His eyes were still clenched shut, but a redness had returned to his cheeks. I pushed a bit of hair out of his face, my fingers lingering.

The fire slowly warmed the room, pushing away the dark thoughts. With the fire roaring, and Kaden by my side, I fell into a deep, colorless sleep.

~

When I woke hours later, the room felt different, though I couldn't decide what had changed. The fire had died down to embers and the storm still raged outside. It seemed to be night. I got up and pulled on Kaden's jacket, the cold making me swift. A pile of books and other things to burn stood by the fireplace, and I hopped from one foot to the other as I fed the flames.

"Ara?" Kaden's voice startled me, and I whipped around. His cheeks were pink, a soft color having returned to them. He blinked, confusion written on his face.

"Kaden." His name came out as a rush of breath. He smiled in the semidarkness. Over in the corner, Red's head came up and his ears twitched. "I was afraid you . . ." I stopped, not sure how to continue. His eyes were closed, and a strange expression covered his face.

"Ara . . . am I naked?"

My cheeks burned, and I turned back to the fire, adding more wood. "Your clothes were soaked."

"And you undressed me?" His voice was full of mock indignation.

"Of course not. Red did, I told him not to get hooves-y, but you know Red."

Kaden's laugh broke the silence of the house. It was a full, booming noise, and Red jerked his head upright at it. I joined him, high on the fact that he was well.

Soon the fire roared again, fed by chairs and other belongings no longer needed. Kaden watched me throughout it all, and I felt a tiny bit of discomfort grow in me as I walked back to my side of the blankets. Now that the fire's glow lit the room I could see him watching me. Still, I wished I'd had the foresight to maybe put some blankets on the couch.

Kaden watched me and gave a half-wicked, half-understanding grin. "Just come sleep for now, Ara. We'll figure it all out in the morning." He smiled and moved over a bit. I scooted in next to him, careful to keep space between us.

"I like your new outfit—those socks are really great." I surveyed what I wore, realizing for the first time I was wearing men's slacks, a red and blue polo, and polka-dot socks.

"I liked your boxers." He only laughed at my rebuttal.

And just as easily the awkwardness was gone. The blankets were warm, and I let myself relax. A tension still lingered between us, but that was an entirely different matter, one I didn't think would go away anytime soon.

So we talked and joked and laughed, not speaking of those we had left behind, content to live in this small moment of happiness.

TWENTY-FOUR—ARA

Snow drifted down as I ran through the pine trees. Their scent was thick and sweet, their limbs heavy with winter. Through the branches I saw a flash of bare feet, the end of a dress, a limb but never her whole body. I didn't need to see her to know who it was.

Emma.

Her hair flew out behind her, a rippling cascade of black. No snow touched it. I could hear her laughter, though I couldn't see her face. No matter how fast I ran she stayed out of reach. My body moved too slow, straining to catch her, to call out to her, but she never turned.

Reality slowly bled into the dream, and with it came heartache.

My back ached, and the scent of rot and mildew lingered under the heat of the fire. Still the storm howled outside, battering the windows, making the house creak and sigh. My mouth felt sandy and dry, and my stomach was so empty it hurt.

I opened my eyes slowly, unwillingly. Weak sunlight filtered through the windows and a chill spread over the house. It was morning, but I didn't want it to be.

Emma was gone and I had failed her in every way imaginable.

I forced myself out from under the blankets. The cold sucked my breath from me, and I danced as it bit at my bare arms. My clothes had dried before the fire, stiff and uncomfortable on, but at least dry.

When the fire crackled and lit up the room again, it cast its glow on Kaden. He slept, his lips parted, his face free of expression.

Red lifted his head from the corner of the kitchen when I came in. The room reeked of piss.

"Nice, Red."

He shoved his warm, wet nose into my hand, and I gave him a small smile. It was hard to be mad at such a beautiful creature. I buried my face in his neck and wrapped my arms around him. No one was truly innocent in this world, but there was something peaceful about an animal with no hate in his heart.

Red followed me around as I searched the kitchen, sticking his head over my shoulder and in general being a nuisance. But I didn't make him leave. He was warm and solid, a comforting presence. The pantry still held an assortment of canned goods, mostly sweet corn. There was also a half-empty bottle of whiskey. I held it in my hands for several moments before uncorking it and taking a swig.

It burned my throat and I coughed, eyes full of tears. Red snorted and reached out with flapping lips. I pushed his head back.

"Not for you, Red. I'll get you some water."

Most of the supplies in the kitchen were useless to me, but I found a few big pots. Two I filled with snow and sat in front of the fire to melt for water. The cans I emptied into another pot—green beans, kidney beans, and chicken soup. Once the pot was filled, I placed it on the fireplace. The largest pile of cans was sweet corn, so I dumped eight of them into a large stir-fry pan, and set it in front of Red. He sniffed it for a few seconds and then began to eat. I laughed at the way his lips flapped and the food disappeared. It didn't take him long to eat it all.

"Kaden," I whispered at his still form. He turned over, blinking the sleep from his eyes, his hair a mess. A thrill ran through me that had nothing to do with the cold.

"You want some soup?"

"Mmmm," he grunted as he sat up. I turned, busying myself with stirring the soup and stoking the fire.

"Your clothes are dry, but you might want to grab some new boxers," I said without turning back to him.

"What happened to mine?"

"Red ate them."

"Damn it, Red! How many times do I have to tell you not to eat my boxers?"

I looked over my shoulder. Kaden had pulled on his jeans and was standing next to Red, stroking the horse as he rubbed his neck up against Kaden in a way that probably would have knocked me over. My stomach dropped as the fire lit the planes of a hard stomach. I guess he decided he didn't need underwear or a shirt. He turned and caught me watching, and without thinking I blurted out, "Your jacket and shirt are on the couch."

"Thanks."

"The soup will be ready soon," I said, keeping my eyes firmly on the fireplace and stirring the pot. When it was ready, we both sat cross-legged in front of the fire, bowls in hand—I'd broken all the kitchen chairs into kindling. The crackle of the flames was the only noise as we both ate. There were so many nights where I had sat alone, knowing nothing but the company of a fire, with only my father and our dog, Loki. And now I sat with someone else. Someone who—if I were being honest—I didn't want to lose again.

We'd been separated for most of the winter because I'd chosen to leave him. I wasn't sure how to apologize, or at least explain, what I'd done. But I also felt like I needed to say something; there was something heavier in Kaden's eyes that wasn't there before.

"What happened to your side?" I asked. "The scar is new."

"Princess, were you watching me as I got dressed? I'm scandalized."

"Seriously, what happened?"

This time he didn't joke. He stared into the fire, his eyes distant and cold when he finally answered, "I killed a man."

It was clear he didn't want to discuss it further, so I took out the whiskey bottle, drank deeply, and passed it to him. He stared at the amber liquid, then tilted his head back and drank as well.

"Kaden . . . I'm sorry," I whispered, unable to look at him. "For everything."

"Come here, princess."

I didn't move and he cocked an eyebrow at me, the devilish smile I knew now back in place. He pulled me into his arms, ignoring how I tensed at first, and cradled my head against his chest.

His voice was gentle when he spoke. "You were doing what you thought was best for your family. Like I was doing what was best for mine."

Tears filled my eyes and I let out a breath, and the truth with it. "I thought I saw her, in the snow yesterday."

"Who?"

"Emma. My little sister. I saw her in the storm. I ran after her, and then I found this house." Tears ran down my face, but I didn't try to stop them. Kaden stroked my hair. "I ran after her. And last night I dreamed of her. But I can't catch her, no matter what I do." My voice was a whisper now. "We left her, Kaden. My father and I, we left her. Everything I've done, coming back to this city, going to the medical center, trying to find our house—all of it was to fix what I did, but I'm not sure I can ever fix that."

I wept in his arms, and he rocked me gently, letting me mourn in a way I didn't realize I needed. When my tears slowed, I realized I had never been this close to him before. A small white scar hid in the cleft of his chin, another stretching down his neck and disappearing beneath his shirt. His eyelashes were long and dark, and laugh lines fanned out from the corners of his eyes—one of the only signs he was older than me. He smelled of pine and sweat and dirt and Red.

"Maybe there is nothing left for me here," I whispered.

He hugged me tighter. "That's not true. I'm here. And you shouldn't give up on Emma."

"But she wasn't real. The snow, the cold, that's all it was."

"She led you here, Ara. She saved us both. Why does it matter if she wasn't flesh and blood?"

I thought of Emma, of my father and my mother. I thought of my promise to myself and to them, and how lost I had become in all this. Then I pulled back and stared at him.

"Kaden, you need to go back to the clan. And find Sam. And I need to go back to my house. For Emma."

Pain marked his eyes and mouth, but I pushed past it. "Sam is in trouble. You need to go back, you need to protect him, Gabriel threatened—"

"Stop." I froze at the anger in his voice. "Just stop and think. Why do you do this? Why do you push everyone away? You just told me you were sorry for leaving me and Sam, and now you are going to leave me again? You said you're sorry for leaving Emma? Then don't do the same thing again!"

"I made a promise." Seeing her again, in the swirling snow, I had remembered my father's words. I needed to go back to the beginning.

"You don't have to do everything by yourself." He was angry, all fire and desperation. How could I make him understand?

"Kaden, I have to go back—"

"No. Just stop, Ara." He took my head in his hands and forced me to look at him. "When I found you there, with Colborn, I—" he stopped, voice low and strangled. "I've never wanted to kill someone like I did then. I don't know what I'm becoming. I'm losing myself. But I know this: If you go, I'm coming with you. There is no other way."

"Kaden, I can't let you, you need to go back for Sam, you need—"

But he wrapped his arms around me, and this time his mouth found mine. He might have intended it to be a chaste kiss, but the moment our lips met was like gasoline on a flame. His kiss swept through me, and I was surprised at the hunger that surged within as I kissed him back. He made a fist in my hair, pulling me closer, his lips crushed against mine until it was impossible to say where one of us ended and the other began. Everything slipped away but the feel of his arms, lips, his body pressed against mine. My breath came in gasps. I laced my fingers through his hair, electrified. It was like standing on the edge of a cliff, breathless and terrified and burning. Like nothing else existed.

Then he pulled back, his face inches from my own, both of us breathless and wild-eyed.

"I won't let you leave me again. We go together. Tomorrow, we go back to the clan and get Sam and Issac. Then we leave and go to your house." Even though he stated it, I saw the uncertainty, the question in his eyes.

I said nothing, drowning in green depths that refused to release me.

"Promise me, Ara," he said. "Promise me we do this together."

I thought of Emma, dancing away from me in a world of shadows. Of Sam, and how he looked at me with such hope. I stood at a crossroads, a boundary that, once crossed, would never allow for return.

"I promise."

TWENTY-FIVE—ARA

We left the house early the next morning, leading Red behind us, with what little supplies we'd managed to find. It was strange at first, walking so boldly—I was more accustomed to lurking. Even so, with Kaden walking beside me, I found myself smiling and laughing. Sometimes he would stop and pull me to him, and with his lips on mine, arms holding me close, I forgot about everything but him.

We spent the day talking about our lives before all this; school, jobs, parents, friends, flings. Red's footsteps made a steady rhythm as we walked, the only thing save the sun that measured the passing of time. Snow covered everything, melting away as the sun rose. A few trees held tiny green buds that hinted at spring.

Maybe it was my determination to enjoy every moment with Kaden that made the day pass so quickly. Before it seemed possible, the sun had sunk lower, painting a red-gold path to the clan. A bell inside the clan began to ring, a bold note reaching out across the city.

"One of the sentries must have seen us," Kaden said, his forehead creased in worry. He had hoped we could sneak in and out. But for once, the worry in me was gone. We had a plan. Get Sam and Issac, gather supplies and four horses, and then ride away at first light. With horses it wouldn't be hard to find my house. Maybe just a day or two. I would be home, and I would no longer be defenseless. *I'm coming, Father. I'm almost back to the beginning.*

Kaden interrupted my thoughts, swinging up on Red and holding out a hand to me. "Well, if they already know we're coming, we may as well hurry up and get there. I'm starved."

I grabbed his hand and swung up behind him. Kaden pushed Red into a gallop, and I clung to him as we ate up the ground. The gates were thrown open, armed guards on either side. My arms wound tighter around Kaden, uneasy at the number of men gathered there. It looked like the entire clan had come to witness our return. Every sound died but Red's hooves on the concrete.

"Kaden!" someone called out.

A flash of red hair moved through the crowd.

My heart leapt and I slid off the horse. "Sam!" I shouted, pushing through the crowd, wrapping my arms around him and planting a kiss on his forehead. I turned, expecting Kaden to be right behind me. To my surprise, he was still on Red's back, staring at the men around us. Sam and I stood side by side, looking up at him as the red sun lit him from behind. On the ground, I suddenly saw what the others had, and understood their silence. He looked like a conqueror of old.

He let the silence build, then grinned suddenly. "So, you lazy bastards think you can take a break just because I left? If you don't get back to work, I'm taking my woman and leaving for real."

The parking lot erupted with laughter. Red bobbed his head up and down. Kaden held him steady while shouting out directions. "Issac, gather men for a watch. Jack, go get the fires burning, I'm hungry as hell! Brandon and Thomas, meet me in the office in five. And the rest of you, get your lazy asses to work."

It was like a wave had swept over the men, and they jumped alive with purpose.

Then, finally, Kaden dismounted and pulled Sam to him, crushing him in a hug and whispering something in his ear. Sam pulled back, a determined look on his face. To my surprise he turned and took my hand. "Come with me."

Kaden gave me a wink as I followed Sam into the clan. It was a flurry of activity inside, messier than the last time I'd seen it, but with new purpose. Sam led me to a back room with a couple of cots and a single candle at the center.

Sam lit it and then turned to me. "Sleep, I'll go get some food."

I was asleep before he returned.

~

"Where's Ara?" Kaden's voice drifted over to me. I kept my eyes closed, wanting to drift back into oblivion. I wasn't sure how many hours had passed, but the room felt cold.

"On the cot," Sam whispered back.

The cot groaned as they both sat on it together. Then, silence. The warmth of the blankets threatened to pull me back under, but this time the silence was charged. Finally, Kaden spoke.

"Things are worse than I imagined." I was surprised at the heaviness in Kaden's voice. He had sounded so sure on the walk here, so ready to leave the clan. But here in the dark he was a different man than the one who had ridden in like a conqueror.

"Alex, Michael, Kevin, Parth, Loukas, and Frank are all dead," Sam said, voice full of sorrow. "Issac and I buried them outside the perimeter."

"Do you know who did it?"

"No . . . things were bad, Kaden. Gabriel hasn't been here for months. We tried to keep it together but without a leader, men were stealing things, fighting, deserting."

Kaden's reply was so low I almost didn't catch it. "Things are still bad, Sam."

"Not so bad we can't fix it. Those who want to leave have already left. We can build the clan we want this time—without Gabriel."

"And if I become the next Gabriel?" Kaden's normally teasing tone was off-key.

"You won't. You aren't like him." Sam was vehement, but Kaden gave no response. The silence made me uneasy. The men wanted Kaden to stay, and why shouldn't they? Kaden would make a great leader. I'd spent so long thinking of honoring my father's words I hadn't really considered what might come after. I wished I could sit up and read Kaden's face.

"What happened to Gabriel?" The question burst out of Sam, like he'd been holding it back for some time.

"I don't know. But if I had to guess, I'd say he's dead." Kaden's voice was hard and clipped, but like any younger brother, Sam wouldn't leave it be.

"What happened?"

"I led an attack against him." This time the silence was different. I opened my eyes a crack. The candle at the center of the room lit the faces of the two men. Kaden's was cast in darkness, his shoulders hunched over, fingers wound together, pressed against his forehead. In contrast, Sam stared at him, his eyes wide with disbelief.

"You led an attack against Gabriel . . . or the men of the clan?"

"Both."

"Why? Why would you attack your own men?"

Kaden sighed, his face buried in his hands. I wanted to spring up, to defend him, but my own shame stopped me. Kaden's next words cut like a knife.

"To save Ara. To save myself." This time Sam held the silence. Kaden's voice became pleading. "Sam, let me explain."

"Explain what, Kaden?" There was a bitterness in Sam's voice I had never heard before. "That you've forgotten where your home is? Or that you left your own brother?"

"I would do anything to protect you." Kaden's voice rose.

"But you didn't! You left me! *For months*. And now you've attacked your own family, and you don't even care!"

"This is not our family," Kaden said, low and urgent. "You are my family. Issac is my family. Ara is my family. The reason I came to the clan was to keep you safe. Now the clan can't keep anyone safe. I was trapped, I couldn't get back—but I did what I had to do, and now we have to do it again. We need to leave now, Sam, before it's too late. The clan is self-imploding, and we don't want to be here when it does."

"You're right, the clan did keep us safe, and now it needs us to help save it. You can't just pick and choose who you're going to protect and send everyone else to hell. These men will follow you, no one else. Even Ara looks to you now. You have a responsibility—"

Kaden jumped up and grabbed Sam's shoulders. For the first

time I saw them as brothers—by the anger in their eyes, the stubborn set of their jaws, the strength in their arms. But there was no forgiveness in Sam's eyes, only disappointment.

"Sam." Kaden took a deep breath. "The only duty I have is to protect *this* family. You. Me. Ara. Issac. No one else. I told you we would find a new home. Now let's go find it while we still can."

Tears filled Sam's eyes and he took a heavy step back. Kaden's hands fell away. For several moments, Sam simply stared at Kaden, and when he finally spoke his voice was dead.

"You're right. You aren't like Gabriel. You're a coward."

He turned and left.

Kaden stood frozen, staring at the door. Then he swore and followed after Sam, shutting the door behind him. The lock clicked in place and I was left with only the candle for company. The candle burned lower and lower, but neither of them returned, and finally the candle sputtered out. Alone in the darkness, I wondered if it was selfish of me to want Kaden to leave with me, to journey back to my home. Like me, he was now torn between his old family and his new one.

I didn't have to wonder long. An hour after dawn, the bells began to ring.

TWENTY-SIX—ARA

"How many?" Kaden asked. Issac, crouched before our small group on the roof, swept his binoculars across the hills surrounding the clan. Rain fell, washing away the last of the snow and casting the landscape of buildings in a gray haze. The sun hid behind the clouds, giving the day a feeling of perpetual dusk. I shivered as a cold trickle ran down my back.

"At least two hundred," Issac said. "Maybe three."

Kaden swore.

"What do you think they want?" Sam lay on his belly on the edge of the roof, looking down at the men patrolling the parking lot that surrounded the clan. The fenced-in area was closed and locked, the exact opposite of the building below, where men swarmed to arm themselves and build blockades at each of the entrances.

Kaden's eyes darted back and forth. Even Issac was unusually still. But Sam's eyes were bright with excitement.

"Why wait for dawn?" Kaden took the binoculars from Issac,

though I wasn't sure what he expected to see in the rain. "If they wanted to attack, why announce their arrival?"

As if to answer his question, there was movement on the road. Kaden forced me down. The four of us held our breath.

"Ara, go back inside. Now."

I made no move to leave.

A single man walked down the road that led to the parking lot, and as he crested the first hill, I realized he carried something thin and long across his shoulder. I sank lower, thinking it was a gun, but then I noticed something white on the end, flapping in the rain and wind.

A white flag. The sign of a truce. I met Issac's eyes.

"They want to talk. We need to go out there," Sam said eagerly.

"You can't be serious." I turned to Kaden, who stared straight ahead. "It's obviously a trap."

Kaden lifted the binoculars one final time before turning to Sam. "Sam, take Ara down to the gun room and lock yourself—"

"No. I'm coming with you!" Sam said, and all of us turned to Kaden. I could see what his decision was before he even opened his mouth.

"Well, at least you'll die together," I snapped, then regretted the words. "Kaden, please, think about this." I reached out to touch his arm. "We were going to leave." *We were going to go back to my home, remember?* "You don't have to do this. You don't have to lead the clan."

There was a moment of tense silence where no one moved. Then Issac stood up and adjusted the rifle slung across his back.

"I'll take her," he said. I bristled at his words; I didn't need an escort—they needed a lesson in stupidity. Then Kaden met Issac's eyes, and I saw something pass between them: fear.

"I'll go get some men together." Sam could barely contain the excitement in his voice. He ran across the roof and disappeared down the ladder. Kaden watched me, but I turned away, refusing to meet his eyes. I heard him leave the roof as well.

Then it was just Issac and me. The rain had slowed its incessant pounding.

"We should have left the clan while we still had the chance." I met Issac's eyes through the rain. "What if something happens to them?"

"Then we go on."

"I envy the peace you find in darkness." My words stung of bitterness, but Issac didn't move.

"Some find God in the light, I found Him in the darkness." Then he turned and left. His footsteps were muffled, and he made no sound as he disappeared down the ladder. He didn't demand I follow him as Kaden might have, and he didn't make me go first as Sam might have.

He left me in silence.

I would have preferred someone to argue with, something to distract me from the gnawing worry that reached deeper than the chill. The rain fell, unrelenting and unforgiving, as I shivered on the roof.

Then I climbed down the ladder into the chaos of men preparing for war.

~

Kaden strapped a gun across his shoulder, then another knife across his waist. He had gathered a small group of men in the weapons section of the clan, and I stood on the threshold,

watching with a mix of anger, fear, and disbelief. Kaden radiated energy. It was impossible not to see him the way they did.
Dangerous. Powerful. In that moment, he was an unstoppable
force; an avalanche plunging downhill.

A shock ran through me when his eyes suddenly met mine.
He pushed his way through the crowd until he stood before me. I
wanted to yell at him, to tell him this was stupid, to beg him not
to go. But instead I stared past his shoulder, as if I didn't care he
was there.

"I'll be back. I promise." He tucked a bit of hair behind my ear.
Still I stared away from him. Then, without warning, he pulled
me to him. His body smelled of rain and leather, and he was
warm and solid. He tilted my chin up and kissed me. Some of the
men whooped and catcalled but drawing back I saw only his eyes.

Then, just as quickly, he was no longer mine.

He turned, a devilish smile lighting up his face. "Let's go greet
the bastard at the gate!"

They cheered, and the crowd surged forward with the eager
strides of young men ready to rush into danger. Stranded alone,
behind them, reminded me of the moment Father and Loki
left me behind. The memory used to bring only sadness, now it
brought an anger that flushed heat through my entire body and
curled my hands into fists. He shouldn't have left me. Emma
wasn't the only daughter he abandoned.

Maybe that was what men did best. They left.

The men followed Kaden to the front door. A barricade made
of chairs, tables, shelves, and other odds and ends had grown
there in the past few hours. Now the men moved a small section
aside so Kaden and his group could pass through. The barricade
closed behind them, sealing us in. And them out.

TWENTY-SEVEN—KADEN

Twenty men followed Sam and me, each carrying a gun with a knife strapped to his waist. I'd instructed the men not to fire unless in self-defense, but as the rain leaked through my hood, violence felt as inevitable as the weather. This world was soaked in blood; why should this be any different?

The mud squelched beneath my boots, the rain washing the world in grays, but I saw only her accusing eyes, and heard Sam's angry words. We'd gotten back only last night, but already I wondered: Was I wrong to have stayed? It felt like no matter what I choose, there was no way to protect everyone I loved.

Beside me, Sam's eyes burned bright with excitement against the gray shadows of the day. His fingers reached up to touch his gun, then back down to his side as we walked.

The man waiting at the gate grew into a solid form through the shifting haze. The white flag leaned up against the fence, no other weapon as far as I could see. As we came closer, the dark angles of his face came into relief, and his lips drew back, a flash of white.

"Liam, what the hell are you doing here?" I laughed, calling out to him. The mood changed as quickly as the wind. Liam was one of us. Several of the men shouted greetings, laughing, and almost as one they relaxed, hands leaving weapons as we gathered by the fence to greet him.

"It's good to see you, Kaden."

"Missed us so much you decided to come back? We could use your help in the stables." I kept my voice light, posture relaxed, but my hand still draped over my gun. Something was off. Liam smiled, but not with his whole face. He hung back from the gate as if afraid of me.

Liam shifted on his feet and looked down. "I've heard some stories about you, Kaden. Unsettling things." The murmurs and laughter of my men grew still. I lifted my chin.

"They aren't true, none of them," Sam suddenly said, and I held up a hand. He fell silent, looking mutinous.

"You know me better than most men, Liam. Believe what you want, I'm not here to convince you otherwise."

He nodded slowly, all the while sizing me up, as if trying to decide if I were the man he knew or some demon who'd replaced him. *What had he heard?*

"I've come with a message, Kaden. I'm not sure you'll like it."

"I'm not one to kill the messenger." It came out colder than intended. His look felt like a betrayal. This man had been my friend. How many nights had we talked beneath the open sky?

Liam nodded. "Gabriel has come back for the clan. He wants peace, Kaden. Things can be the way they were. Give him back the clan, and he will pardon you and everyone else."

I froze.

No.

He couldn't be back.

Behind me, the men muttered and shifted, and I felt their eyes on me. Cold hatred pounded through my entire body, overcoming the reflex that wanted to insist he was wrong, that Gabriel was gone. I'd told myself that he was dead, that Colborn and his men had killed him.

But the cynical part of me understood. Why wouldn't he still be alive? I hadn't seen him die, and the bastard was half cockroach. Gabriel had returned for the clan.

The men shifted behind me, but I kept my voice lazy and cold. "Anything else?"

Liam swallowed. A look of sadness washed over him. Sadness and something worse. Regret. We no longer smiled at each other. We were on opposing sides of a divide that went deeper than blood.

"You have until dawn tomorrow." Then he turned and walked away, leaving behind a dirty white T-shirt made into a white flag.

The rain swallowed him whole.

~

The rain finally came to a stop as we walked back. It seemed almost a different group than the one that had walked out with me. Quiet, watching me, waiting for me to say something. Instead, Liam's words rang in my ears. Gabriel was alive—and back.

Back inside the building, the clan felt different. Men patrolled the sides and doors, but when we entered, they all paused and turned to me. For a moment I felt like the boy who'd killed his father and burned down his home.

"Liam met us at the gate." My voice betrayed nothing but confidence. "He told us Gabriel has returned for the clan."

The men shifted uneasily. Several glanced at dark corners, as if Gabriel might be hiding here already.

"He wants peace. At dawn tomorrow, I will go negotiate terms." I paused. "Any man who wants to leave before then is welcome. The rest of you . . . keep the watch."

Then I walked back to the room for Issac and Ara. I wanted to run but forced myself to walk confidently, as if everything were fine.

The men were watching.

Before I made it to the door, I turned. There, following me silent as a shadow, was Sam.

I pulled him close to me and dropped my voice. "Sam, I need you to do something for me." He nodded, eyes wide. "Go up to the roof and see how much of the clan is surrounded. Then go to the kitchens and get carrots, three torches, and a lighter. After that, come to the gun room."

He nodded again, but slowly this time, as if trying to decide whether I was playing a joke on him. "Go!" I said, and he took off running.

I took a deep breath and opened the door. The scent of wood lacquer and smoke hit me. Ara jumped up from the bed, but I held up a hand. "I need you both to listen to everything I have to say. Gabriel has come back for the clan. I'm guessing he already has us surrounded." Fear flashed in Ara's eyes. "I have a plan, but I need you both to trust me."

Issac stood up. "I am with you. Always."

Ara took a slow steady breath. "What do we do?"

We stood in a triangle, united, even as my legs felt weak . . . What if I was wrong? "We wait until dark."

The rain came and went for the rest of the day, and the men rotated between patrolling the fence and pretending to be busy inside. While we waited, I'd had Ara strap on a small dagger and hide her hair under a hat. Then I told her to leave her backpack of supplies and take only what was essential. In the end, she took out only a lighter and stuffed it in her pocket.

It took Sam a couple hours, but he returned before sunset with a black rubber bucket with carrots in one hand, and torches and a lighter in the other.

"I went up to the roof," he said, voice low. "We're surrounded, but Gabriel's men are stretched thin."

Ara's eyes met mine, and I nodded, throat too tight to speak. Together, the four of us made our way through the building. Most of the men were gathered around the large central fire, seeking a sense of community as darkness fell. I kept our group to the shadows, but none of the men looked up as we passed. The kitchen was deserted, the small back door opened to the scents of rain and wet earth. Clouds choked out the light of the moon, the night so dark that the fence was barely visible. In the distance, the torches of two patrolling guards floated away from away us, disembodied lights burning through the night.

We stepped out into the darkness, our breaths instantly turning to white clouds, and fear crept down my back, quick as the cold. I turned to Sam and Ara. "Ara, we need to get you out of here before Gabriel realizes you're with us. The two of you—" Sam's chest swelled "—wait till there's an opening in the patrol and then sneak through the trees. Issac will cause a distraction, and when the guards are occupied, climb the fence and run to the high pasture. Find Red. He always sleeps in the far corner, by the gate. He'll come if you have carrots. Get the painted mare, too, if you can, but if not, just take Red and run as fast as you can. Wait for me in the old cathedral."

I pulled Sam close and whispered in his ear: "If I'm not there by sundown, keep riding."

Then I turned to Ara. She regarded me at a distance. I stepped forward, ready to say my farewells, but she stopped me.

"No," she said. "No good-byes. I'll see you soon." She stepped forward, pressing her body against mine and wrapping her arms around me.

"I'll see you soon," I whispered. It felt like too much a good-bye despite what she'd just said. Then she pulled back and took off into the night. It made me smile, even with the chaos around us. Whatever happened when the sun rose tomorrow, Ara was strong. Ara would survive.

Sam went to follow, but before he could, he turned back. "The distraction, how will I know?"

"You'll know. Now go!" He gave me one last glance, as if waiting for me to call the whole thing off, then took off after her. They disappeared into the night.

A moment of silence passed. Issac came to stand beside me, his movements like the trees that rustled in the breeze. After the choking smoke and scents of the clan, the crisp, cool spring air felt like a salve to my worries: What if I had just sent Sam and Ara into more trouble? Issac's voice shocked me from my reverie.

"Are you going to tell me what this distraction is, or should I just go light a cow on fire?" Issac said dryly.

"While that does sound entertaining, what I need more than anything is time. As soon as Gabriel finds out Ara is here, he'll never let her go. Which is why I want you to tell him that she's here."

I continued. "We need time. And what will buy us the most is if Gabriel believes he has the upper hand and Ara is trapped here. He'll tighten his hold and look inward and give them time to escape. It's our best chance."

Issac nodded seriously. I lifted the torches out of the bucket and handed them to him. He took them as calmly as if he were going out for a Sunday walk, not about to speak with the enemy. If something happened to him, it would be my fault. But I'd gone too far to stop now.

"When you get to the fence, light the torches and draw out as many men as you can. Ara and Sam will have their chance. Then ask to be taken to Gabriel. When you meet him, tell him that we have Ara. Tell him—" I stopped. Gabriel needed to believe this. "Tell him you're doing this for peace. For me, Sam, Ara, and the men of the clan. So no one else gets hurt."

"What about you?"

His question surprised me. I had assumed he would be worried about his own safety, heading out to the enemy. But as always, Issac put others before himself.

"I've got a few tricks up my sleeves, but if everything goes well, I won't need them. I'm going to give Gabriel the clan, and hope that it's enough."

"Will it be?"

I met his eyes. I could lie to everyone else, but not Issac. I said nothing.

Issac nodded slowly and looked out into the night. There was an odd moment where I wondered what was going through his head. Was he afraid? Angry? Doubting?

"*Behold, I am sending you out as sheep in the midst of wolves…*" Issac said with a faint smile, as if the words were a joke only he understood. Then he stepped out into the night. A flash of panic went through me. What if this plan failed? What if they shot him on sight and this was the last time I ever saw my friend?

"Issac?"

He turned. My throat thickened. I wanted to thank him for being my friend, for being a better father than the man the world had given me. I wanted to say something deep, something true, something a hero would say at the end of the story.

But I was only a man.

"What will God think of you lying?"

A flash of white as he smiled. "Let's hope I don't have to ask Him."

Then he turned and was gone. A fear like death choked me, and I hoped Issac was right after all. That maybe God still cared, and maybe he heard the prayer I sent up now.

Protect him.

Protect us all.

~

"Whatever happens today, I want you all to know, it's been a privilege." Morning sunlight leaked down from the skylights, illuminating the remaining men of the Castellano clan: if we were even that anymore. Some had left in the dead of night to join Gabriel's horde, but the men I spoke to now were ones with which I'd worked side by side, men I would have trusted with my life. "I'm gonna miss your filthy smell, your ugly faces, and your complete lack of hygiene." They laughed, and my stomach twisted. Despite everything, I was going to miss this place. It was the only home I'd known since the world ended.

I hadn't been able to sleep after Ara, Sam, and Issac had left, so I'd sat around the fire. One by one the remaining men had joined me. We talked about old times, told stupid stories, mostly about girls we used to know, laughed at overused jokes, and passed the night together.

Now dawn had arrived and there was only one thing left to do. A lump formed in my throat as I looked at the men, trying to think how to say good-bye.

"Don't get all sappy on us now, Kaden," Jake called, and the others laughed.

My eyes went to the main doors at the front of the building, knowing who waited beyond them. Then I swallowed and gave the men a final smile. "Well, we're burning daylight." Together we filed out of the Cabela's.

The day had dawned clear and bright, the puddles and mud the only reminders of the rain. The sun offered my first full glimpse of what we were facing, and even I was shocked. Hundreds of men lined the perimeter. I'd thought Gabriel and Colborn would have destroyed each other, but somehow, they'd joined forces. Another day I might have found this inspiring. Now I just wondered how exactly we were going to escape this.

Gabriel stood at the gate, and standing beside him, a full head taller, loomed Colborn in his shaggy fur coat. *Should have killed him when I had the chance.*

We approached the gate.

"Kaden, so nice of you to join us," Colborn called out, his voice mocking.

"Wish I could say the same," I called back. "But last time we

246

met I didn't quite finish saying good-bye. Won't make that mistake again." His eyes glittered, and a cold smile snaked across his face. I dismissed him and turned to Gabriel, but not before scanning the men surrounding him. Worry filled me. Issac wasn't here. Where was he? Had he already escaped? Maybe he was far away, waiting for me with Sam and Ara at the cathedral.

"Gabriel." I nodded to him.

"Kaden." He wore a button-down shirt. A part of me wanted to mock him for dressing up.

"Glad to see you finally found that special someone, Gabriel. Mind if I ask how this happened?" Maybe I shouldn't have, but I had to know why.

But Colborn answered before Gabriel. "I woke up with a nice bump on my head, after I'd found my own special someone." My hands trembled as he smiled at me. *You'll never touch Ara again, you bastard.* "And I realized, I'm tired of raiding and killing . . . and leading, what did you call it? A horde? I decided it was time to settle down, make some friends. And who better to show me how to run a clan than Gabriel." His hand fell on Gabriel's shoulder, the smile he gave him one I recognized. Even if I was leaving this all behind, a sudden fear twisted in me for the forty odd men who'd chosen to remain with me, as well as the clan men who had sided with Gabriel. Colborn was going to kill Gabriel the first chance he got.

But it wasn't my problem. Not anymore. "It's all yours." I gestured behind me. Gabriel thought he was expanding, but really he'd signed his own death warrant teaming up with Colborn. The clan was dead, and the horde only grew.

"Where is Ara?" Gabriel said, finally getting to the words I knew he'd been dying to ask. Victory bloomed inside me, and it took all I had not to smile. If he had to ask, then she was gone. My plan had worked. Ara and Sam were free.

"Gone."

Gabriel stared at me, still, but Colborn's eyes flashed and he stepped forward. Rumbles rose from the other side of the fence. I didn't move, keeping my relaxed posture, though I longed to reach for a weapon, anything to not feel so defenseless. But I'd purposefully worn nothing. No reason to give them an excuse to shoot me.

"She's here, I know it. Issac told me the truth," Gabriel said, but his eyes darted to the clan and then back to his own men, seeming to finally realize that Issac was nowhere to be found.

"Then search the building, Gabriel. Search the men. Search the world over." *Because you'll never find her. Everyone I love is free now, you've got nothing on me.* Nothing but the men standing behind me, but even Gabriel wouldn't hold my mistakes against them.

Still Gabriel said nothing. Someone in the crowd coughed and the sun beat down on our small, ragtag group, small against the horde before us.

"Your men may leave in peace," Gabriel said. A wave of relief washed over me. "But you stay." It shouldn't have been a surprise, but the shock must have shown on my face.

"You're right," Gabriel said. "I could search the world. But I'm betting if I have you, I won't have to." Behind me, a soft click. One of my men removing the safety on his gun. Across the fence, I watched as hands shifted to guns, and men set their feet in a wider stance, Colborn smiling as he watched it all unfold.

"Easy," I shot a look behind me, and raised my hands. "Let my men go, they aren't part of this. And I'll come with you." I turned to Jake, nodding him forward. His eyes tightened, but he nodded back.

My feet felt heavy, my chest tight, as I walked the final feet to the gate and unlocked it. This wasn't how it was supposed to go, but Ara, Sam, and Issac were free; it seemed like too much to ask that we'd all make it. The men began to trickle out behind me as I made my way over to Gabriel and Colborn. Two brutes who stood beside Colborn instantly patted me down, checking for guns and knives, though I'd been careful to wear none. Jake gave me a final, sad smile as he passed. He had told me he was going north, looking for some fabled sanctuary, a city where the new tech still worked and women still lived. I hadn't the heart to tell him it was a pointless quest, not when he'd stood by me.

"Send units one and two inside, check the main building before we move in," Gabriel murmured, and men began to pour through the gate, but all I could think was: *Really, Gabriel, units?* Only Gabriel would see this whole thing as a chance to reorganize. Too bad he had no idea he'd partnered with the devil himself.

As men passed me by, most unable to look me in the eye, I felt a strange surge of loneliness. If I wasn't at the cathedral by sunset, would Sam take Ara and leave? Gabriel had always trusted Issac, and I had hoped Issac might help me now, but he wasn't here.

The only person who could help me was myself . . .

Two burly men stood on either side of me, but Colborn and Gabriel both stared at the main building, the Cabela's letters still clinging to the side, and spoke in low voices. A chill ran down my back at the sight of them working together. Their army surged through the gates. The woods were only a mad dash to my side—could I make it?

Before I could decide, a strange drumming came from behind me. Fast and hard.

The men on either side of me turned in confusion, but I understood what it was a moment before they did. I lunged sideways, bowling one over, then ran for the noise.

A red horse burst from the trees, sprinting straight at us. My heart dropped.

Sam.

He lay flat over Red, and though filled with fear I was also overwhelmed with pride. They surged forward, a force of nature, and with a sudden twist, I sprinted away from the men. One of them called out behind me, but I didn't turn to look. Adrenaline made everything sharp and clear: the earth flying up behind Red, the focused determination on Sam's face.

Red's legs devoured the earth. Just a few more strides. I pictured myself grabbing his neck, swinging onto his back, digging in with my heels, and bending low as we flew through the woods. Red would run with everything in his heart, and they would never catch us. I'd mapped out the fastest route back to the cathedral. I knew the trails of this city. We could disappear into the sunset and never come back.

But just as I'd almost reached them, Red reared up into the air before me, his legs striking out and flailing, as if he'd meant to hit me. I fell backward, as one of his hooves streaked past my face, disbelief filling me. Why had he tried to hurt me?

A gunshot broke the world in two.

Red screamed as the bullet took him full in the chest, where Sam had been just a moment before.

Red's chest exploded and a noise not of this world escaped him. His legs flailed in the air, trying to gain purchase, and then he fell backward, and I felt the impact on the earth.

Sam!

I lay stunned on the ground, just feet from Red. Behind me, shouts rose, and a gunshot cracked. *Sam. Protect Sam.* More gunshots. I flinched, but the shots continued, and when none ripped into my flesh, I glanced over my shoulder, cold horror creeping up my throat as I finally understood. The men who had surrendered with me now rushed back into the din. Jake led them, screaming, "FOR KADEN!" I'd been so careful not to wear any weapons . . . but I hadn't thought about theirs. Bullets ripped through the air, confusion as men yelled and shots rang out. Gabriel's voice rang out, and Colborn's laughter, but whether they were trying to stop or encourage the men, I couldn't decipher. All around me was madness, but only one thing mattered.

Sam.

I crawled around Red. My beautiful horse lay on his side, his eyes glazed. Blood seeped from his chest. He gave a soft nicker as he saw me. "Hey, boy," I whispered. A fresh dose of misery shot through me. He had deserved to live out his days in a pasture of green grass, not die on a useless battlefield. This wasn't even a war worth fighting. The world had ended, but still, all we could do was fight and kill each other. What were we even fighting for? I laid a hand on Red and crouched behind his body. Even in death he protected us. Behind him, Sam lay in a crumpled heap, his long, thin limbs spread out around him. He hadn't been crushed but flung off. As I crawled closer, I saw a rock jutting up from the ground just next to Sam's head, smeared with blood. Sam's eyes were closed. Blood pooled beneath his head.

"Sam, please, no . . ." I slowed in terror. He was still. I was frozen, unable to move, to reach out and check for a pulse.

My hesitation was a mistake. Hands seized me from behind. I screamed and thrashed, screaming "Sam! *Sam!*" Still, he didn't move.

All around me men died. My men. My family. I watched it all happen as I was forced to my knees. Right in front of me, one of my men held up his hands, trying to surrender, then jerked as bullets tore into him.

They had returned to protect me, but instead they died. I screamed and fought, trying to rip myself free, until something hard and heavy hit the back of my head.

~

The first sensation that returned to me was sharp, searing pain, followed by the desire to sink back into oblivion. Slowly, the pain concentrated to the back of my head and I tried to sit up, only to find my hands and legs bound. *Sam. Where is Sam?* And then the image came back to me, of Sam lying prone on the ground, blood gathering around his head.

"SAM!" Blood streamed down my face, hot and sticky in my eyes and mouth, but I didn't stop calling for him. Someone had to hear me, had to come eventually. I writhed on the floor, lower than the lowest of all creatures, until my voice gave out. Time passed, impossible to measure.

Finally, the door slid open. Blinding light. Was it possible the night had gone and the next day had come?

"Sam? Where is Sam? Is he okay? He hit his head—someone needs to help him." The two men acted as if they couldn't hear me, grabbing me and hauling me upright. Blood rushed in my ears, and I swayed and saw black. If not for their iron hold I would have fallen.

"Sam," I croaked as they dragged me forward into sudden blinding light. I blinked, bringing into focus the parking lot and the main building ahead of me. A sudden realization: they'd been holding me in one of the quarantine sheds behind the main building. But I couldn't think beyond that. The sun beat down on us, and a crowd was gathered in the empty parking lot space we used for soccer matches. There were more men than I'd ever seen before there, and for a moment I wondered if my ears weren't working from the heavy silence. But I could make out our steps on the cement, my breathing. Heavy silence hung in the air; not the empty silence of a deserted square but of hundreds of men.

The two men dragged me to the front of the crowd, the faces swimming in and out of focus. With no warning, they released me, and without their support I collapsed to my knees, a single cry of pain tearing from my throat. Before me the once-barricade had been transformed into a stage of sorts. But it was the men below the stage who drew my eye. Bloody, bound, and kneeling. I barely recognized my men. Jake met my eyes, the two of us staring at each other in mutual horror. A jagged cut ran down his face, and his eye was swollen shut. His shirt was stained with blood and a cut on his leg still leaked blood. He tried to smile at me, but it came out more as a grimace. These men were the last of those who'd fought for me. Seven. Seven men from forty. But one person wasn't with them.

Sam.

"This is what becomes of men who betray their leader." Gabriel's voice rang out from the top of the stage, clear and cold. Beside him, like a monstrous shadow, stood Colborn.

"He stands here accused—" Gabriel continued.

"Where is Sam?" My voice was gravel, but I stared him down, terrified at the pity in his eyes. Behind him, Colborn smiled.

"Your brother is dead, Kaden. Colborn saw to his burial. I'm sorry, but we all lost brothers today." My ears were ringing, my chest drowning in something thicker than air. I saw him again, his limp form, the blood a dark pool beneath his head. He had come back to save me. Sam was dead, and it was my fault.

The moment I'd lost my little sister Kia, I'd devoted my whole life to finding Sam, protecting Sam. All of this was for him. How could I still be breathing, my heart pumping, if he was gone? The world faded. I didn't even realize someone had approached until he slapped me, the stinging pain whipping my head sideways.

"Kaden!"

The words brought me back. I looked up into the clear, blue eyes of Liam, stunned. He swallowed, and then dropped to one knee and lowered his voice, so that he spoke only to me. "I know your grief, I lost my own brother three years ago. But there are seven men here who will die if you do nothing. Mourn the dead later. You have a chance to save the living now."

His words bounced around in my head, meaningless. He pulled a scrap of fabric from his jacket and wiped the blood and sweat from my face. When I could see again, he spoke low and steady, holding my eyes and forcing me to hear him.

"When you ran, Jake and your men returned, and in the battle six of Colborn's men died. Colborn wants to kill you and your remaining men for justice. Gabriel has offered a deal." Here he stopped, and I saw the regret spread across his face. "Colborn has agreed to let your men go, if you die in their place." He stood and stepped away, stranding me before hundreds of eyes. For the first time in hours, I thought of the one other reason I had for living. Of Ara.

But maybe it was better this way. She was free, and without Sam, my world was dark. I bowed my head.

"I agree."

TWENTY-EIGHT—KADEN

A sliver of light pierced a corner of the shed, lighting swirling motes of dust. Tiny specks danced into the light and then disappeared into darkness.

There was no way to get comfortable in a metal shed with both my arms and legs tied, so I had stopped trying. Dried blood caked my forehead and my shirt clung to me, soaked through with sweat. Yesterday Gabriel had told me Sam was dead, and I could die to save the last of my men.

So why didn't the bastard just kill me already?

Time warped, measurable only in the beads of sweat that rolled off my head. Hours might have passed, or only minutes.

Finally, footsteps approached, heavy and evenly paced. Someone big but not in a hurry. Chains rattled outside the door. How dangerous did they think I was?

The door creaked open. Light flooded the shed, the sudden glare blinding me.

Several men entered. The warmth of the sun touched the side

of my face, but I kept my eyes closed and turned away. Scraping noises and heavy thuds echoed in the small shed, the scents of grass and trees wafting inside, mixed with the aroma of some sort of food. It seemed impossible I could be hungry, but my stomach tightened at the smell. Still, I resisted the urge to look until the door had slammed shut again. Finally, I looked up.

Colborn.

He sat on a folding chair at a newly erected table. The new, savory aroma now made sense. Sitting on the table were roasted vegetables, fresh bread, and meat. My mouth watered. A pitcher of water stood next to the food, and I felt dizzy just looking at it. Colborn watched me through the darkness, leaning back on a folding chair, comically small beneath his enormous frame.

"Seems only right a man gets a good last meal," he said. Unlike Gabriel, he hadn't dressed up to take back the clan, still wearing the ugly matted fur coat. His beard was long and dirty, his eyes burning coals in the dim interior.

"For old time's sake, come eat," he said.

"Old time's sake?" I laughed. "Would that be the first time I met you and you forced me to kill a man, or when you forced me to lead an attack against Gabriel and the men of the clan?" He opened his mouth, but I cut him off. "Or maybe when your men slaughtered mine? Is that 'old time's sake'? Or the fact that you demanded I *die* to save the men who fought for me? Which of those old times are you talking about?"

Colborn grabbed the knife beside the plate and used it to pick his teeth, then licked the side of the blade.

"Sharp," he finally said, letting the knife catch the reflection of the light cutting through the doorway. Then, with the grace of a panther, he moved from his chair and crouched before me. I froze, catching the blade's glint. True, I'd stared death in the face many times, but it seemed a cowardly way to die, bound and helpless at the feet of another man. But Colborn ran the blade first through the bonds around my feet and then my hands. He was skillful and quick with the blade, though a single mistake could have taken off one of my fingers.

Then he stood, thrust the blade down into the wooden table, and sat again.

It took me several minutes to rub the feeling back into my hands and legs. Then, without any other real option, I joined him at the table.

"Eat." He gestured to the food. I needed no other invitation. Like a starved animal, I shoveled in food with my fingers and drowned it all down with the pitcher of water. Only halfway through the meal did I realize something tasted slightly off. My stomach clenched uneasily. Poison? Then I reached for the water. At least poison would be fast.

Besides, poison was too easy, and not at all Colborn's style. Still, the food didn't sit easy.

When the food was gone, I kept the knife in hand, staring down at the sharp end of the blade. Colborn caught my eye and grinned. I stared at him for a moment, gripping the end of the blade, before slowly setting it down between us. His eyes flashed with disappointment.

"Why do you always fight your nature?" Colborn leaned across the table. "Take the knife and bury it in my heart, I know you want to." His neck pulsed with blood, so easy to spill, but I did nothing. His smile dared me, exactly the reason I couldn't. I was done being manipulated. The weight of everything crushed me with a bone-deep weariness. Why fight? A world without Sam wasn't a world worth fighting for.

"You don't know me," I whispered.

"I knew you the first day I met you." The certainty in his voice was unnerving. He was baiting me, but I wouldn't let him win, not when he had taken everything else from me.

"You made me kill that man. I didn't want to."

"I didn't kill him, Kaden. You did."

My insides gave an uneasy twist. "What do you want, Colborn?" I asked, finally meeting his eyes.

"Justice."

I spread my hands wide. "You have it! Sam is dead, soon I will be too. The good men of the clan are dead, a bastard rules, and if I'm not mistaken, his second will kill him eventually." A cold, catlike smile crept over Colborn's face. "Make him suffer at least. That is the only justice this world knows."

He reached across the table and in one graceful motion reclaimed the knife.

"You're right." Colborn leaned back and put his hands behind his head, the picture of ease. "Justice is an ideal that the weak demand but only the strong can deliver. But you misjudge me. I've always respected you. I will give you justice. In one week, you will be executed, but not by a bullet or hanging. Those are the deaths of a coward. I will execute you myself."

Fire ran through my veins. I met his eyes and finally understood.

"Two men, two knives." Colborn leaned forward, and I saw excitement burning there. He dropped his voice to a whisper. "One of us walks away. One of us dies. Justice. Vengeance. Blood. Whatever you want to call it." A roaring river rushed past my ears, but I forced myself to focus on Colborn.

"And you came only to tell me this?" Something wasn't right. Something was missing. Colborn laughed, his features twisted and terrible.

"There's no deceiving you, Kaden. You're too much like me." He laughed again, and a terrible premonition grew within me. A deep instinct told me to run, but a dark curiosity kept me rooted in place. "You see, Kaden, I respect you. Like you, even. That's why I have to kill you. Now that bastard Gabriel, I can't wait to slit his throat. But you, it's going to be difficult. Maybe even impossible. Which is why I hope you'll forgive me for this."

He moved faster than a cobra strikes and buried the knife through my hand, pinning it to the table.

I didn't realize the screaming was mine until I clapped my other hand over my mouth.

A fat bubble of blood pushed up and around the knife before running down my fingers.

"I would say I won't let you suffer, but unlike Gabriel, I'm not a liar. You will suffer, Kaden. I will break you. And then you will die." He stood, and even the small movement as he brushed the table burned my hand like it had been thrust into a fire.

He opened the door and then looked back, silhouetted by the light outside. "You know, Kaden, it took me forever to butcher that damn horse. I'm glad you enjoyed it." He waited to see the confusion on my face. Then he slammed the door, thrusting me into darkness as his booming laughter receded.

TWENTY-NINE—ARA

I crouched in a grove of quaking aspen, shivering in the bitter cold. The birds were fully awake, mocking me even though the sun hadn't yet broken the horizon. As much as I wanted to bury my numb fingers in the warmth of my mare's coat, I stayed where I was. The clan gate lay in full view below. So far it had only been guards patrolling the perimeter. No sign of Kaden, Sam, or Issac.

As I'd drawn closer to the clan, it had grown harder to control my mare. In the end, I'd led her closer on foot, and then tied her head up to keep her from grazing the fresh green shoots pushing through the damp ground. When the sun had risen over the tree line, with no sign of them, I made my way back to my mare. Two days ago, Kaden's plan had worked, and Sam and I escaped to the old cathedral. But Kaden and Issac had never shown. Then, yesterday, I'd woken in the cathedral, alone, with a note tucked in my palm.

Ara,

I want you to be free to make your own decision. I'm going back to the clan for Kaden and Issac. If all goes well, we'll be here at sunset. If not, I send my love. I hope you find what you are looking for.

Sam

But they hadn't returned. And if they hadn't come for me, then I had to assume something had gone wrong, and they were being held as prisoners.

A cold wind wove through the trees, shaking the aspen leaves and tugging at my hair, the lone mark of red in the landscape blooming with spring. On the way here I'd passed wild onions, dandelions, chickweed, squirrels, rabbits; food enough to last the summer through. And I had a horse. I could leave right now and go home. Back to the beginning.

For the first time, I didn't want to.

Not if it meant abandoning Kaden, Sam, and Issac. I had regretted leaving my sister and losing my father for so long. The beginning my father had spoken of, whatever it was, would be there in a day or a year. Kaden, Sam, and Issac needed me now. I wouldn't let them become only memories and regrets when I had the power to stop it.

My mare nickered again, nodding her head up and down when I pushed through the trees and buried my fingers in her coat. When my fingers warmed, I tied a note around her neck. I'd ripped the paper from the back of a hymnal.

Gabriel,

Meet me at Phillipi Park at noon. Come alone.

—Ara

When it was secured, I slapped her on the rump, sending her running down the hill in the direction of the clan. She galloped for the fence, her tail streaming out behind her. I crouched low and watched as the guards took her inside before I melted back into the trees. They would find the note, and then bring it to Gabriel. There was no guarantee he would come alone, but being the sole person responsible for bringing me back to the clan seemed like something that would appeal to him.

With nothing else to do, I began the journey to the park. It wasn't far from the clan—we'd passed through it on the way here, and I'd seen the sign still standing, announcing its name. As I walked a pair of rabbits ran before me, and my hands twitched, aching for a weapon. I missed hunting; the singular devotion to a purpose, the simple pleasure of an honestly earned meal.

I reached the park well before noon, and ate some dandelion, the bitter leaves choking out my hunger a bit. Then I climbed one of the tallest trees in the park, perching there like a hawk as I looked out at the park around me. The playground was rusted now, but the swing set still stood, encased in ivy. Squirrels chased each other in dizzying circles below, and for once I didn't try to think of a way to kill them. *I wonder what you would think of this all, Father. Would you be proud I didn't desert my friends . . . or angry I put helping them before honoring your final instructions?*

From my vantage point, I saw Gabriel walk up the hill and

into the park well before he saw me. He was alone. Or at least appeared to be. When he was twenty feet away, I swung down, landing lightly on the ground.

"Ara," he said in that calm, measured voice. "I'm glad to see you well."

Can't say the same, Gabriel. His clothes were tidy, his hair long enough to cover the gaping hole where his ear should have been. And there was a gun strapped to his waist.

"We were worried about you," he said as he came closer. "You'll be happy to hear Addison is fine. Adjusting to life at the clan well. She misses you."

I didn't fall for the guilt trip. Instead, I took a step back, keeping space between us. "Are Sam, Issac, and Kaden all at the clan?"

"Why do you ask?"

"I'm here to negotiate for their release." I glanced to where the trees framed the edge of the park. I'd hoped the somewhat open layout would keep me safe, but now I wondered if it even mattered.

"What are you offering in this negotiation?"

"Me."

His eyes showed no emotion, just cold calculation. "What are your terms?"

"Issac, Sam, and Kaden all go free," I said without hesitation.

"I can't promise all of that."

"Why not?" Anger crept into my voice. I'd felt peaceful before, watching the squirrels play, but now I wondered if that time might have been better spent making a weapon.

"Issac is loyal to the clan. If he wishes to leave, then he is free to."

"And Kaden and Sam?"

He took a hesitant step forward, as if he wanted to comfort me, but I stepped back, holding on to the space between us. "What about Kaden and Sam?" I said again.

He sighed. "Kaden is fine. For now. He's being held."

"And Sam?"

This time he didn't try to reach out to comfort me. He just looked me in the eye, and said, steady and quiet, "Sam is dead. There's nothing I could have done, his horse threw him."

His words should have ripped through me like a bullet. Instead I felt blank, disbelieving. Sam couldn't be dead. I could still hear his voice. His note was still folded in my pocket. He was misinformed, or lying, because Sam couldn't just be gone.

"When will Kaden be released?" I said, refusing to accept Sam was dead.

"He won't, Ara. His men killed many of ours. Kaden is going to be executed."

I tried taking deep breaths, but my lungs felt suddenly shallow and tight. It was like the moment my father left, the moment I saw my sister's eyes weeping blood. *Too late.* I'd come back to save them, but they were already dead.

No. Kaden wasn't dead. Not yet. I took a deep, shuddering breath, pushing away everything but the fact I could save Kaden. "You can stop it."

"It's done, Ara."

"Let him go, let him live, and I'll be yours. In whatever way you want."

His eyes hid some emotion I couldn't decipher. My legs felt weak, heavy with despair at the thought of what would happen if he said no. I held my breath, finally exhaling when he said, "The men won't like it; you as a prisoner, after what happened with Sam and Kaden."

"Then make them believe I want to be there. Make everyone believe."

"How?"

"I'll marry you before the clan." I forced the words out. "A wedding that shows I choose to be with you. If you promise you'll let him go."

"He's already stood trial," he held up a hand, stopping me before I could interject, "but the execution isn't for another week. A wedding would cause a lot of attention. One of the guards might forget to lock the door to his cell. He could slip away in the festivities."

I felt numb, so much so that it felt like another person stepping forward, holding out her hand, and saying, in a steady but distant voice. "Then we have an agreement?"

He shook my hand. I barely felt it.

"We do."

THIRTY—KADEN

Days passed.

If I thought the cell was hell before, it was nothing compared to now. The heat suffocated me during the day, and the cold tormented me through the night. They'd added a bucket for waste, but besides that, the shed was bare. I'd used my shirt to bandage my hand as best I could and managed to at least stop the bleeding. Still, it ached with a dull, constant throb and was swollen and warm to the touch. I couldn't bend my fingers, much less grip a knife.

Worse than the pain was the silence. I found myself hoping Colborn would return, if only for company. I entertained dreams of moments long forgotten: Sam and I playing on a baseball diamond; Red and I galloping across green hills; Ara, smiling in my arms, laughing as I whispered in her ear.

Footsteps crunched on the gravel outside.

I opened my eyes, leaving behind a field of grass and Ara's smile. The doors opened, and I was blinded by the sudden influx of sunlight. A tall, lean man stood in front of me.

"Issac." My voice was a croak. "Took you long enough."

He stepped inside, bringing a cool breeze in behind him. The two guards left the door open and moved a short distance away. I couldn't find the strength to stand, but he folded himself onto the metal floor beside me.

"Here. Drink." He lifted a bottle of water from the bag he carried. Water ran down my chin as I guzzled the bottle, not even caring how weak I must look; my skin sallow, my hand wrapped in a bloody bandage of a shirt.

"Any food in that bag?" My voice was a croak. Instead of answering, he pulled out two more bottles of water and then a book. I recognized the leather cover and many leaf-thin pages, and tried not to grimace. A bible. *Not sure God can help me now, Issac.*

"They searched it before I came in. This was all they allowed." He dropped his voice a notch, "There're antibiotics in the water."

Tears pricked my eyes as the cool liquid slid down my throat. How could I ever have doubted Issac? It had taken him time to come, but it was all for a reason. He'd kept up the careful act of being on Gabriel's side. And now he'd found medicine I desperately needed.

More than that. He sat beside me now, even when it was far better for him not to be here.

"How you doin', Issac?" I said when the bottle was empty.

He looked sideways at me, a small smile on his face. "Better than you."

I laughed at his low, smooth voice. Never one for talk, our Issac. We sat in silence together.

"I went looking for Sam's body," he said suddenly, unexpectedly, and the pain hit me again, like a crushing blow.

"And?"

"The graves were unmarked. I'm sorry." I heard his unspoken words: *I'm sorry you didn't get to say good-bye. I'm sorry I wasn't there. I'm sorry he's gone.* He reached out to me and laid his hand on my shoulder. The touch was fatherly, and made me feel like a child, like I was reliving the moment I buried Kia. He stayed silent as I cried.

"There is no peace in this world," I said bitterly, still choking to find breath.

"There is only the peace we find," he said, slow and calm. He picked up the bible, holding it out to me, but I refused to take it.

"How can you still believe in God when He has taken everything from you? First your family, then Sam, soon me?" I didn't expect him to respond, and when he did his voice was calm and deep, like the ocean after a storm.

"Because He gave everything to me," he said simply.

"And so it's His to take back, just like that? Some cruel kid playing with us? I won't blindly follow a god like that." Issac didn't respond, and the anger in me grew. "You think He has given you these things? Well He has given me nothing, only what I have taken for myself, and He's taking even that."

Issac continued to look into the light. His hands were old and callused, and wrinkles lined his face. Still, it was impossible to think of him as an old man, just as it was hard to imagine a tree as old. He shrugged, as if to say, *I was never a man of many words.* Then he reached into his pocket and revealed an old leather wallet. He pulled out a tattered photograph and showed it to me. Issac sat beside a woman with bright eyes, and between them was a little girl throwing a white bow onto the ground.

"They're gone, Issac." The words were cruel, and I regretted them as soon as I said them, but I couldn't take them back.

"Only from this Earth. I will see them again."

"You really believe that?"

"Yes."

Despite our differences, I was glad Issac sat there with me, the silence and friendship of family between us.

"Time's up, let's go, Issac," one of the guards announced, looking back at us through the door as he stood and stretched. A sudden terror seized me.

"Issac, don't go." I couldn't face death bravely. Not alone.

Issac leaned over and placed his hands on both sides of my face. I stared up at him, looking into the face of the man I had grown to love. The first guard finished stretching and started to make his way over to us.

"I will see you again," he said. And for the first time in my life, Issac's words made me afraid. As the guards pulled him away, slamming the door and once more casting me into darkness, I wondered if Issac was saying his final good-bye. In the darkness, I held to the faith and strength in his eyes.

I had none of my own left.

THIRTY-ONE—ARA

"Who are the flowers from?" I pointed to the blush of color in the storage room that had been converted into a bedroom for me and Addison. The vase overflowed with blue, pink, and yellow flowers; a waste, really, to use plants for decoration and not food. But I suppose everything was blooming outside these walls, why not be wasteful? The scents of rain and earth taunted me on our daily walk outside. I should have been on my way home with Kaden; instead, my heart tightened every time we came back into the stench of unwashed bodies and lingering smoke of the clan.

"Addison . . . who are those from?" I repeated as I pulled my muddy shoes off.

"Find out for yourself." She danced away from me. For a moment I considered forgetting the entire thing. The only peace I'd had from her was when I'd first arrived and she'd given me the cold shoulder, angry at my abandonment. The silence hadn't lasted long. An hour in she burst into tears, wrapped me in a hug, and it was back to the unending dialogue. Then I thought of Issac—I'd been waiting for a message from him. So instead I made my way to the vase and pulled a slip of paper from beneath. It was written in elegant, bold cursive.

"The brightness of her cheek would shame those stars as daylight doth a lamp; her eyes in heaven would through the airy region stream so bright that birds would sing and think it were not night."

I stiffened when I read the signature. *Gabriel.*

Addison giggled and it took all my self-control not to tip the vase off the nightstand. What the hell did he think he was playing at? I'd agreed to a marriage—not love. And definitely not some twisted attempt at romance.

But then I saw it, written below Gabriel's note, two words written from a different hand.

Almost ready.

I forced myself not to react and laid down on the bed. There was only one man in the clan who could quote *Romeo and Juliet* from heart, and it wasn't Gabriel. It was a clever ruse for bringing me the note, and a reminder: we walked a dangerous path.

Outside the door, two armed guards stood. Everything we did at the clan was supervised by a team of men that rotated and didn't speak to us. I didn't even know their names. This separation didn't bother Addison, but it bothered me. I hadn't realized it before, but when I'd come to the clan at first, I'd helped the same as any other man. Now we contributed nothing, wasting manpower for guards and eating food we hadn't earned. The way the men watched us . . . it no longer felt friendly.

Maybe I was being paranoid, but keeping the two of us separate felt like a mistake. Kaden had thrown me into the fold, forced the men to see me as a person. Now those same men with whom I had laughed and joked either wouldn't look me in the eye, or watched

Addison and me with a sort of coldness that drove into my bones. In their mind, I had betrayed Kaden. I was going to marry Gabriel, while Kaden rotted in a cell. I would hate me too.

But maybe the biggest reason for the change was Colborn's presence at the clan. The moment I'd seen him, standing in the clan, it felt like my world had inverted. I'd made a deal with Gabriel to live here, but not to coexist with a maggot like Colborn. Every time I saw him from across the building, my skin crawled, both wanting to run away and to find a weapon and finish what Kaden had started. Whenever he saw me, he leered at me, talking about how strange it was that Gabriel had been hiding a female all along, and what else was he hiding? Gabriel had made a deal with the devil. But so had I.

"Maybe we could go outside again today," I said to Addison. I wanted to try talking the guards into letting us walk past the quarantine sheds in the back, where I'd overheard someone say Kaden was being kept. Yesterday, I'd asked to see Sam's grave and say good-bye. *Sam* . . . I pushed the thought—and sudden piercing pain—away. They'd said no, and maybe it was just as well. I couldn't think about Sam, or Kaden, or everything I'd given up. All I could do was hold on, pretend Gabriel didn't make me sick, and ignore the ball of ice that now lived inside me.

"I'll have to ask Gabriel," Addison said without looking at me. *Ask Gabriel, my ass.* He would say no for sure. "Besides, I already have a full day of activities planned for us."

I groaned and buried my head under a pillow. Life with Addison was like struggling through the mud and looking sideways only to realize the person next to you was playing in it.

"And it took the boys *all night* to get them here, so I expect you to be excited."

I flopped my arms a bit. Addison ripped off the pillow and hit me with it.

"All right, all right." I jumped up off the bed, holding my hands over my head to shield myself. "What is this activity?" I hoped it was something violent—archery, knife throwing, lighting stuff on fire . . .

Addison grinned at my sudden interest and backed up to the full closet where she kept her clothes. Mine were still in a backpack; I barely had anything, so I hadn't bothered unpacking.

She threw open the closet, and I froze.

Wedding dresses.

A closet full of terrifying white wedding dresses.

I couldn't have been more horrified if the closet had held corpses. She turned to rifle through them. I used the moment to compose myself.

"Addison, I don't think . . ." But she heard none of my protests. She dragged me closer to show me each one.

"Please don't say I have to wear one of these," I whispered. The closet looked like a fairy tale princess had thrown up over a winter wonderland. And not just that. I'd imagined myself someday wearing a beautiful dress and walking down the aisle, but toward a man I loved. Not a monster.

"They got every single dress left they could find!" She stomped her foot then started rifling through them again.

"Isn't there anything that isn't so—" absurd was the word I wanted "—white?"

"Most brides wear white," she said as if I were a child. I cringed at the word *bride*.

"How about this one?" I pulled out a green dress that had somehow slipped into the fold—bless the fashion ignorance of men. It was shorter, maybe for bridesmaids, and green like the forest. Or Kaden's eyes.

Addison raised her eyebrows. "It's *green.*"

"I like it," I said, favoring it all the more because she didn't. I held it up to my chest and twirled. Maybe if I was wearing this it wouldn't seem as real.

"Ara, you are impossible." But she hid a smile as she said it.

"Thank you."

"Fine, try it on and show me." She rifled through the dresses again as I put on the green dress. The space was easily the most decorated and livable room I'd seen for the last three years. They'd brought furniture, rugs, mirrors, clothes, and an actual mattress that we slept on together. I looked over at the lavender bedspread, a feeling of uneasiness sweeping through me.

Soon I would sleep in Gabriel's room. Soon I would be his wife, and he would take more than just my freedom.

I turned to the mirror. A young woman gazed back at me. Her hair was long and auburn, eyes wild and cheekbones sharp. She looked older than I remembered. Harder. The dress was beautiful. Just the color of Kaden's eyes. And suddenly I couldn't stand to wear it a moment longer. I tore it off, yanking as it caught in my hair and nearly shrieking when it took a clump of hair with it. I threw it on the ground and stood over it, my chest heaving, Addison watched me wide-eyed from the corner.

"You're right, Addison." I heard my voice from a distance. "Green is wrong. Give me a white one."

She pretended as if the moment hadn't happened and went on to dress me like a doll. I agreed with everything she said, nodding at all the right moments, holding onto a smile like a drowning man clutches a lifeline. She finally settled on a dress with an open back and delicate lace off the shoulders. As I wore it, I gave one last look at the green dress pooled on the ground. I pictured myself wearing it beneath a full sun, walking down an aisle through a field of wildflowers. My friends and family were watching me, but none of that mattered. All that mattered was that there, at the end of the aisle, sunlight highlighting his rakish grin, was Kaden. He waited for me, looking at me as if there was nothing in life he needed but me.

And I finally realized it.

I loved Kaden. I loved him with a pain that physically hurt.

And I could never have him.

THIRTY-TWO—KADEN

The door screeched open. I sat up, alarmed.

No. It wasn't time yet. I wouldn't face Colborn until tomorrow morning.

But right away I could tell something was off. Three men stood in the doorway. I backed up against the wall. My knees shook at the effort it took to stand.

The men said nothing, not looking me in the eyes as they seized me and dragged me forward. There was only a dull, blinding fear. Was this Gabriel's plan? A quiet execution? They dragged me out of the shed, and distantly, I thought I heard music, a guitar and singing, coming from the clan, but maybe I'd finally lost it. My feet stumbled, unsure, the sudden burst of colors and senses overwhelming. Open sky. Grass. A breeze.

I'm sorry, Sam. I'm sorry I wasn't the hero you thought I was. I'm sorry I failed you.

Then I realized: we were going the wrong way. The forest and the fence loomed before us. I looked back to see the walls of the clan at our backs. There was no one here. Wouldn't Gabriel and Colborn want to see me killed? They continued to drag me forward, saying nothing. When we reached the fence, they dropped my arms and I fell. One of the men, with a scraggly beard and beady eyes, pointed to the fence. I followed his finger. There was a small gap where it had been torn, and a hole dug out beneath it, big enough for a dog to slip under—or a person.

But I couldn't move. Was this all some sick joke? Then the bearded man shoved me, and suddenly my body reacted of its own accord, lunging forward and scrambling for the hole. I was like a rat. All I knew was I couldn't go back, I couldn't take another day in the steel box. I'd take whatever chance this was, and whether it led me to death or freedom, at least it led me somewhere.

The fence bit into my back, tearing through the thin fabric as I struggled to crawl through the hole. I scrambled and came up on the opposite side of the clan.

I was free . . . How was that possible?

A wisp of smoke came from inside the clan. Men patrolled the tops of the walls, but no one looked at me.

Could it really be so easy?

The cool shade of the forest beckoned, and despite everything I let myself believe it. I was free. Sam was gone, but Ara was out there somewhere. For the first time in forever, I let myself hope. I could find her. I knew where she would go: *back home*. I would spend every day of my life looking for her if need be. Hope filled me like a balloon expanding in my chest.

And then it burst.

Colborn stood in the shadow of the trees, leaning up against an oak, one leg cocked. A slow, viscous smile snaked over his features. He sauntered over to me.

I couldn't move.

"Gabriel's a cruel man, Kaden." He slung one arm over my shoulders, as if meeting an old friend, and forced me into a slow walk with him. His meaty arm dug into my bony shoulders, and I struggled to remain upright under the weight. A bird burst out of the undergrowth in front of us. Once I might have challenged him in strength, but now I was like a skeleton going up against a tiger. He dragged me alongside him.

"I would have just outright killed you, but that fiery redhead of yours got in the way."

No. He was lying. Ara wasn't here. She had escaped. The last time he'd seen her was in the movie theater when he tried—I couldn't think of it. I should have killed Colborn when I'd had the chance.

Colborn suddenly laughed. "Oh, come on, why can't things be like it was before? Your men killed some of mine, I killed some of yours, call it even." He shrugged. "You're like me. Not like that fool Gabriel. I would have killed him by now, but the man's got his uses. Working his fingers to the bone, stocking things up real nice for winter. Maybe I'll keep him around for a bit."

"Colborn, whatever you're going to do, just say it. Stop playing games."

He stopped and pulled his hand from my shoulder. I saw the eerie coldness in his eyes. He sighed. "Not as much fun as you used to be. No matter. I've got seven of my best men back at the clan right now. Saddled up on the best horses. We told Gabriel we're going out hunting. He didn't ask what."

He looked up at the sun, then started back to the clan, not even turning as he spoke. "I'd say you have a half-hour head start, Kaden."

I ran.

Not with the grace of a predator, or even the confidence of a hunter, but an injured deer before the wolf pack. I imagined Colborn behind me, throwing saddles across horses, dust rising as they snorted and pawed the ground. I'd caught, trained, and broken most of the horses in the stable; ironic now that they would be my undoing. But more frightening than the smile and dark eyes of Colborn was how weak I had become in my time as a prisoner.

My lungs seared, my feet were boulders, and each time I stumbled and plunged face-first into the ground it was harder to get back up. I wanted to crawl into a hole, close my eyes, and sleep forever. The shadows lengthened, the temperature dropped, and my pace went from a run, to a jog, and finally to a labored, painstaking walk. How much time had passed? How long until they came after me? I had no answers.

A howl ripped through the night. Then, rising with it, the baying of dogs.

THIRTY-THREE—ARA

Addison had brought in wildflowers and placed them in glass jars and old cans. It was beautiful, in a terrifying sort of way. The flowers contrasted oddly with the decor of antlers, stone, and logs that dominated the rest of the store. It felt like a hunting lodge taken over by a princess. She decorated the snarling wolves with garlands of wildflowers and lined the aisle with petals. Someone had found a guitar and they played it now, singing a sad love song that drifted up and out of the skylights.

"Would you prefer we had it outside?" Gabriel's voice came from behind me, and I tossed the note in my hand into the flames before I turned.

He wore a black tux, and it took me a moment to find my voice. "No. This is fine."

Across the store, I could feel Liam's eyes on me. Colborn had left a few minutes earlier, a group of his men following soon after. Outside, I could hear dogs braying and horses whinnying, like they were preparing for some sort of hunt. Of course, Colborn wouldn't want to be here for the wedding; he'd scoffed at it every chance he had.

"I'm ready," I said to Gabriel. His face lit up in a smile.

"Then I will tell the men." He turned to go, and I met Liam's eyes and nodded, before I followed Addison to the back of the store. She helped me into the wedding dress, and then we waited.

Gabriel had fulfilled his promise. Now I would fulfill mine.

~

It was the longest walk of my life, and yet the details seemed to blur together, as if I stood in the center of a waterfall and was watching everything happen from beneath the roar. Addison walked with me down an aisle lined with flowers. She held my hand and then handed me to Gabriel. Hundreds of men watched us. I looked into his gray eyes and felt absolutely nothing.

A man spoke before us, and I stood half listening as his words washed over me. I spoke when asked, repeated the necessary words, and pushed a small gold band over Gabriel's finger before accepting a twisted silver band inlaid with diamonds on my own.

But none of it really mattered. My mind was far away, in a field of wildflowers, in a green dress, looking past the swaying grass to the green-eyed man who waited for me.

"You may now kiss the bride."

I woke as if from a trance. We stood before the men of the clan, our hands joined yet a million miles apart. Gabriel turned to me, and I met his eyes. My husband. *You've done worse than this to survive. And you'll do worse to protect those you love.*

A silence fell over the clan. He stepped up to me and watched me carefully, as if I might break.

I leaned into him and brushed my lips against his. He froze, and then like a statue come to life he cupped the back of my neck with one hand and wrapped his other around my waist. His lips parted as he drew me to him.

The men around us roared, and he deepened the kiss. I let him. Then he pulled back, held out an arm. I placed mine on his as he led me back down the aisle. He smiled for the men of the clan, and I tried to see him the way they might. Handsome in his suit, his hair grown over the stump that remained of his ear. As we walked down the aisle, to the part of the clan Addison had prepared for the celebration, I caught a glimpse of myself in a mirror. The dress was stunning, all white lace and backless. My hair flowed down around my shoulders and over the bare skin of my back. Addison had braided in tiny white flowers. The bride in the mirror was beautiful, even if I didn't recognize her.

"Would you like to dance?" Gabriel held out a hand when we reached the section they'd cleared for a small dance floor. The smile I gave him Kaden would have known was fake, but I wondered if there wasn't also something posed in his own smile. He pulled me to him, one hand on the bare skin of my back as he led us in a slow dance. Someone played the guitar.

Addison had decorated the food tables with glass jars of wildflowers, and someone made something that resembled a cake topped with real flowers. The men gathered around the table, laughing and joking. Many shot me longing glances, as if remembering their sweethearts of old. We were at a dance, and yet there were no partners. I searched their faces, unable to meet Gabriel's. Issac and Liam's faces were missing.

I was married.

The full weight of it hit me suddenly. If not for Gabriel's arm around my waist I would have fallen. Was my dress always this tight? My breath came in short, tight gasps, suddenly unable to follow his lead. I wanted to be away from all the noise and people, but at the same time I was terrified to be alone with him.

I wasn't ready for this.

My face flushed and I felt dizzy, but I didn't let myself stop, or think about what was coming. Time slipped by faster and faster until he leaned over and whispered, "Do you want to leave?" I nodded, eyes on the ground as he took my hand in his own and led me away from the dance floor. Everyone stopped talking to watch us leave, a few catcalls following us. But he didn't lead me back to the small room in the gun room. He had converted one of Cabela's back storage rooms into a bedroom for us both. He nodded to the guards when we reached the room, telling them to take the night off. They leered at me, one giving Gabriel an exaggerated wink.

Then we were alone. He opened the door and I stepped over the threshold. There was a full bed with a white bedspread, and a wooden dresser with a vase of wildflowers on top. The door clicked, sealing us into a tomb of silence.

We stood staring at each other. The tension billowed like dark, heavy clouds, waiting for the first drop to fall.

"Could I have a moment?" My voice sounded faint, almost breathless.

"The bathroom is through that door."

I nodded and slipped into the bathroom. Then I put my hands on either side of the sink and tried to control my breathing. Addison had left a pink bag next to a potted plant, and a black silky robe next to it. I struggled out of the dress and then opened the bag. When I looked inside, I suddenly felt sick all over again. I took out what was inside, dressed, and then without looking in the mirror, pulled the black robe over me. *Breathe. Just breathe.* I forced myself to take three steadying breaths, then opened the door and stepped out.

Gabriel sat on the edge of the bed. He stood as I came out, his eyes traveling over my bare legs and black robe, which I held tightly closed. He was handsome—I couldn't deny that.

An eternity passed.

He stepped closer, bridging the small gap as I looked down at the ground, suddenly terrified. *Could I really do this?* I noticed a small pink stain in the beige carpet. He took my chin and gently tilted it upward. He waited to see if I would pull back, but when I didn't, his lips found mine, hot and hungry.

Then his hands were everywhere, digging into the black silk and my skin. I closed my eyes and leaned into him, lacing my hands around his neck. He held me flush against him as his mouth covered my neck. I trembled.

"I will make you happy," he said as he pulled back, my lips almost bruised. "I promise."

He kissed me again, deeply, his arms crushing me. He pulled back just enough to whisper into my ear: "I love you, Ara."

I buried the needle into his neck.

His surprise was worse than the look of betrayal. I forced the plunger of the needle down, enough tranquilizer to knock out a full-grown horse. Issac's note had said to only use half, but I wasn't taking any chances. His eyes widened and his body stiffened at the sudden pain, and I realized, in those few seconds, what he couldn't hide from me. He really thought I was his. He really thought I'd given up. Maybe he even thought he loved me, and that I would come to love him. He couldn't imagine any other reality.

I held him in a lover's embrace, our bodies pressed together, the needle buried inside him. Understanding dawned and he lunged for the door, but I was ready, locking my hands around his neck and tangling his legs. The needle flew across the room. We went down in a chaotic mess. Sharp pain lanced through my elbow as his full weight fell on me, but it only made me feel more alive. He fought against me, trying to tear me off him, but I thrashed and kicked and struggled.

He was stronger than me, but not for long.

He tore himself from me and, from his knees, began to yell, "Guards! Guar—" My foot smashed into his face, and he made an ugly, strangled noise as he went down. I fought like a cornered animal, lunging, kicking, biting—anything to keep him from the door. He shouted for help, and a sweet, viscous pleasure bloomed in me, understanding his mistake. The guards were gone for the night, the other men celebrating loudly. We were alone.

For the first time, I saw something carnal and ugly rise up in him as he fought me. He lost all his inhibitions, fighting with a brute strength that would have scared me if I didn't already see it fading. I matched his strength with a sort of fury I hadn't known existed within me. Each second he struggled less. His arms lost their power, his legs grew weak, until finally I pinned him to the floor beneath me. He stared up at me, a trickle of blood running down from his nose. His body went limp and I tensed, expecting a trick.

Instead he whispered, "Why? I thought . . ."

He was pitiful, eyes like a child, but I was far past pity or regret. I'd spent it all the day he'd told me Sam was dead, the day I'd left my sister.

Only rage remained.

"You thought I would just give up?" I spat at him. "It took Issac two days to find the sedatives, another three to put everything in place. But for all that time, it took me seconds to know I could never spend my life with you. You play with people, Gabriel. You think you own them. You think you're God. You are not." I shook him, but his eyes were already drifting out of focus. "I will make my own life," I whispered, adrenaline pounding through me. His eyes blinked closed and his head rolled back. I didn't know if he had heard me or understood. I didn't care.

He would know I had beaten him, and that was enough for me.

The floor creaked as I stood up, chest heaving, and took stock of the room. A chair was sprawled on the floor, but besides it and the small, empty needle, the rest of the room was untouched. The queen-sized bed was made, with large pillows and flowers strewn over the white covers. I pulled back the covers and proceeded to drag Gabriel up and into the bed, then tucked the covers around him.

A streak of blood ran across the floor, but there was nothing I could do about that.

Then I reached under the bed and pulled out a small back-pack. On top of it was a black T-shirt, dark jeans, and a baseball cap. Putting them on felt like reclaiming a piece of myself.

Then I sat on the bed and waited. The distant sounds of revelry rose and fell. My body pulsed with energy, like a bird fluttering madly inside a tiny cage. I wanted to open the door, to start down the hallway, but I knew I needed to wait till the men went to bed. Until then there was nothing I could do but pace the room.

Finally, I stood, unable to wait any longer next to Gabriel's still form. Every second I spent here was another precious second I could be putting space between me and the clan. I made my way to the door, then gave a final look at the room. Crushed flower petals lined the ground, and a dark streak of blood stained the carpet. Gabriel was an innocent lump on the bed.

I opened the door and stepped out into the hallway. The door clicked softly behind me, neat as a surgeon pulling a sheet over a body. The hallway ended, and the full room opened up before me. Fear rose in my throat like bile. The glass ceiling leaked moonlight on the high wooden arches, but below the tents and supplies were lumps and shadows in the darkness, only the farthest corner of the clan lit by a roaring fire.

The sounds of men celebrating rose around the fire, but the noise had changed. It was rowdier, and I heard a sudden crash followed by shouts and laughter. It sounded like they had found the alcohol—the same alcohol Issac had made sure would be included in the postwedding celebrations.

Each step forward was a torment. I didn't know if it was better to walk normally or slink through the shadows, so I simply walked quickly with my head down, heading for the kitchen.

The kitchen doors opened with a soft creak, revealing the long countertops and many abandoned stools. There was only one door besides the main entrance that led out of the clan, and both were always guarded. But there was no one here tonight. I breathed a sigh of relief, and crossed to the exit.

Outside, a moon lit the trees beyond the fence, and guards patrolled with torches and flashlights. But this time instead of heading for the fence I clung to the wall, moving through the shadows to a slight rise that took me to the stables.

A moment of regret hit me when I slipped inside and the scent of horse and hay washed over me. My eyes adjusted to the dim interior, bringing into focus the forms of horses, wooden beams, and a figure in the corner.

"Liam." I breathed a sigh of relief.

He wrapped me in a genuine hug—like cool water on a burn. "Everything's ready," he said. I nodded and looked around, even though I knew we had no time to spare.

"Thank you. For everything. You're sure you won't come with me?" The words seemed pathetically small.

"No, I can't." He didn't explain why. Really, we both knew. There was room for only one man in my life.

"Issac has the four horses just behind the western fence," Liam said. "There's a hole you can crawl under. When the barn goes up, the horses will go mad and run. All the stalls are open. That's when you should run."

I looked at the stalls, noticing several of the horses were missing and remembering the commotion from earlier, when Colborn and his men left. "Do you think Colborn knows something?"

Liam shook his head. "No. They said they were going for a hunt. Probably trying to make Gabriel mad by not showing up for the wedding. I figured it was better this way. Fewer people to notice you and Kaden are gone."

I nodded, looking down at my feet, angry with myself that I didn't know how to say good-bye to this man.

He laughed, then stepped forward and kissed my forehead.

"Good-bye, Ara. I will miss you." He ruffled my hair and walked out of the barn—and my life—forever. The scents of the horses rose warm and homey around me, and I sent them a silent apology for what I was about to do. Then I crouched down beside a pile of hay, and started the most dangerous fire of my life. When the flames licked high and hungry, and the horses had begun to whinny and shift with nervousness, I ran back into the night.

It took only a few minutes before the sounds of panicked horses rose through the night, and flames began to lick up the sides of the stables. Shouts came from the roof of the clan, as someone finally noticed the fire. *Too late.* Horses streamed out of the barn, galloping into the night, adding to the chaos as men shouted and ran. But no leader emerged among them.

The guards abandoned their fence patrols and took the opportunity to pace down the fence line. In the dark my hand made a soft *chink-chink-chink* noise as I searched for the red handkerchief his note said he would leave.

"Issac?" I called softly into the night. Something red showed at my feet, and I crouched down. A red handkerchief tied above a small gap between the fence and ground that I wouldn't have noticed myself. He should be here.

"Issac?" I couldn't call any louder for fear the men would hear me. Where was he? We needed the horses to put real distance between us and the clan.

The trees shifted softly in the night breeze, and the shouts and yells grew behind me. I didn't want to admit it, but I had to: I was alone. Some part of the plan had gone awry—Issac had done as much as he could, the rest I would need to do myself. The best thing to do was keep moving with the plan and hope to find him, and Kaden, later.

With raw fingers, I scraped out dirt, trying to make the hole below the fence deeper. Before I could check if it was deep enough, a soft voice cut through the night.

"I thought I'd find you here."

I spun, ready to fight, but the owner of the voice watched me with only sadness.

"Addison," I stood, slowly, suddenly terrified. All she had to do was call out, and the guards would be here in a second.

"I saw you sneaking out through the kitchen. Did you hurt my brother?" There were tears in her eyes, and I considered lying. Then I realized this might be the last time I ever spoke to her.

"Nothing permanent. Just a tranquilizer to put him to sleep."

She stared at me with those wide, uncomprehending eyes. "Why couldn't you have tried? He loves you."

He doesn't love me. He wants to own me. "I can't live my life in a cage. I won't. I'm sorry."

"It's because of the other man, isn't it? The one the others talked about. The handsome one who worked in the stables."

Every second I talked to her here was another moment I risked getting caught. Even so, I didn't want to leave things like this. "Yes, that's part of it." I reached out to her and took her hands in my own. "You don't have to live life in a cage either. You could come with me."

Before she could answer, a bell began to ring, the deep resonating booms like a death knell. Together we turned to look at the main building.

The barn blazed in the distance, but the fire had spread, yellow flames licking up the farthest wall of the main building. A few men tried to beat it out, but without water, I didn't see how they would.

"Addison," I whispered, fear growing to horror. "Gabriel's still inside."

She pulled her hands away from my own. In the growing light of the flames, I couldn't tell if her eyes bore regret, anger, or acceptance. "Good-bye, Ara."

"Good-bye, Addison." But she was already gone. It took only a few more moments to find the hole, smaller than I'd anticipated. I flattened myself to the ground and squeezed through, the chain-link raking sharp fingers across my back as I slithered out the other side.

I glanced back, worried someone might be following.

Instead, the night grew brighter, flames now reaching high across the entire building. Men streamed out, yelling, trying to organize a line of water buckets. Already I knew: it would be useless. The clan building would burn to the ground tonight, but I wouldn't be there to watch it. I'd wasted too much time here already, and my father's words beckoned me home.

I disappeared into the night.

THIRTY-FOUR—KADEN

I vaulted over the log and barely kept my footing. Behind me, the hounds howled, rising like a symphony of hell. They were closing in. My pants were soaked and muddied, my torso covered with angry red scratches where I'd stumbled through brambles. My breath tore through me, ragged and painful, and my side burned in pain. I'd waded through streams, thickets, and brambles, hoping to throw them off.

It wasn't enough.

I'd thought of climbing a tree and hiding there, but the thought of Colborn finding me cowering in a tree, laughing at me like I was a frightened animal, was repellant. So I stumbled toward a small clearing. I wasn't sure what I'd hoped to find there—a building, a weapon . . . salvation? But I moved forward regardless and crested the hill.

A beautiful meadow. Almost perfectly circular. Moonlight leaked through the clouds, touching a thin stream and long grass. Quaking aspen lined the perimeter—pale, thin ghosts with dark eyes.

The temperature dropped as I stumbled the last few steps down to the stream and collapsed on the bank. Sweat and blood greased my face so my vision blurred and I tasted rust, salt, and sweat. The soft gurgle of the stream contrasted with my ragged breath and the wild, frantic call of the hunt in the distance.

I was going to die.

My body had taken me as far as it could. But I wouldn't die being chased down and butchered like an animal.

The cold water stung as I scrubbed off the blood and sweat, washing away the animal and finding the man underneath. Then I paced down the bank until I found a thick branch, almost as if it had been left there for me. It was heavy but fit my hand well. *Remember, Sam, all those times we played ball in the park?* I tried to think only of him, of a boyhood where the biggest concern was hitting the next pitch or striking out.

The dogs came first. Sleek bodies streaking through bushes and around trees. The moonlight played a patchwork game, lighting up the hounds, then plunging them back into darkness. As they came closer, the white glint of sharp teeth showed, their fur matted and dark from where they'd waded through the streams to follow me. I'd spent my life working with horses and dogs, and had a higher opinion of them than many men. But there wasn't time for regret.

The first dog broke through the trees. He was small, his lithe body scarred. He snarled as he leapt at me, taking my slack stance as invitation. I swung the branch with the full force of my body and his neck snapped sideways with a sickening crunch. His yelp was high and cut short, and then the rest of the dogs surrounded me, barking and lunging.

My arms burned heavier with each swing. Twice the branch

connected, but I saw only writhing bodies and snarling fangs. One of the dogs managed to sink his teeth into my pants, almost pulling me down. I smashed his body with the branch, once, twice, and the fabric tore. He retreated with a piece of it in his mouth, but at least it wasn't flesh. The circle widened as the second dog went down, still barking but holding their distance. Their job had been only to find me, and now that they had, they waited for their masters to finish me. Or maybe they sensed already that I'd weakened.

A thunder of hooves rose from the forest, pinpricks of bobbing light moving through the darkness. Colborn's men. They gripped torches, though the light seemed only to distort reality instead of revealing it. They were demons in the night, shadows long and tortured, features malicious. I felt rather than saw his presence, and a strange sort of terror rose in me as Colborn appeared, riding the largest horse of the group, the light of his torch making him seem demonic.

I'd only looked away from the dogs a moment, when I felt a body hit me from behind. Adrenaline and instinct made me fight like a madman as the dogs contracted. I beat them back, but barely this time.

A shot ripped through the night.

The dogs whined, falling back from their attack, confused. I looked down. My chest heaved, torn with scratches and muddied, but still whole. And then, across the clearing, one of the men on horseback tipped sideways and fell off his horse. He didn't get back up.

The thump echoed through the darkness. And with it, the winds shifted. Another two cracks broke the night. The dogs whined, the circle around me growing wider as two more men dropped from their horses. One horse bolted into the night while the others high stepped and tossed their heads. The men were merely dark lumps trampled in confusion.

"Where is he?" Colborn's voice rose above the madness, and I wasn't sure if he meant me or the shooter. The remaining men fired into the forest, shots wild as the horses began to panic. Colborn fired again and again, as if every shadow were an enemy, but none of them seemed to realize the torches they held made them perfect targets.

The dogs still surrounded me, confused, ears down and tails tucked between their legs. I roared and swung viciously with my branch. They scattered before me and I ran.

The shots continued into the night, the confusion giving me cover. Behind me, Colborn kicked his horse forward, leaving the group behind as he charged after me.

Another two shots ripped through the night, but the pounding hoofbeats only grew. Still, I pushed myself faster. If only I could reach the trees, they would protect me.

A bullet ripped through the night and the dirt exploded to my left. I veered sideways, about to vault over the stream, when several things happened at once.

The bank collapsed. The opposite side of the embankment rose up before I could raise my hands. Sharp pain cracked through my head, blinding white for a moment, and in the next a blurry, tilting distortion. My heart pounded, *run, run, run*, but my body could no longer obey. The whole world became a mess of water and sky and earth as I twisted and saw a tilting version of Colborn reining in his horse and raising his gun.

The shot rang out.

But it wasn't his.

Blood and gore exploded from Colborn's throat. He choked, unable to breathe or stop the flow or do anything, the same way I could do nothing but watch. Finally, he fell from his horse.

Icy, cold water lapped at my chest, forcing me up and out of the water and onto the bank. Colborn's horse, a massive roan, had fallen with him, but now it stood, and ran back into the darkness where the other men and horses had disappeared.

It seemed a long time before the ground stopped moving beneath me.

Movement across the meadow. A man separated himself from the darkness. He took two slow, deliberate steps forward, then leaned on his rifle, as casually as if he had been out for a walk.

"Thought maybe you and God had given up on me," I called out as I limped toward him.

"Didn't you read the book I gave you? He always shows up in the end." Issac's voice was deep and husky, like the Earth itself had spoken. I hugged him. And for a moment, everything in the world was right.

Then the heavy scent of blood made me pull back. Something warm and sticky covered my hands, lit red by the moonlight.

"Issac?"

He tilted forward. I moved to catch him, but he was tall and broad shouldered, and I could only ease his way to the ground. He groaned as he lay down. If not for the growing stain across his stomach, he looked like a man stretched out to admire the stars.

"I need to bandage the wound. I'm going to see how bad—"

"Leave it," he whispered, but I looked anyway, only to wish I hadn't.

"You're going to be fine. We've come all this way . . ." Angry, disbelieving tears pricked my eyes. His hand covered mine.

"There is no peace in this world," I said bitterly when finally I found the words.

"There is only the peace we find." So simple. So like Issac.

"You really believe that? You really believe you can find peace somewhere?" I didn't want him to. As selfish and terrible as it was, I wanted him to stay. I wanted him to fight. I wanted him beside me to face a world that seemed so dark and terrible.

He lifted a hand. "Get the saddlebag from my horse. By the trees. Hurry." I looked out at the towering trees and was terrified to leave him. What if he wasn't there when I came back? But he stared me down, expectant, so I ran for the trees and ripped the bags from his horse. Back at his side, I knelt beside him and set the bag gently on the crushed grass.

"Open it." His voice was hoarse.

Clothing lined the top of the bag, but a small book fell free from the fold. A ghost of a smile came across his face.

"My bible. Don't use it for kindling." I laughed and set it to the side. I would protect it to the end of my days.

Next was a wallet, his initials engraved on it and a picture of his family inside. Tucked next to the picture was a scrap of folded yellow paper. He turned slightly, a spasm wracking his body.

"The yellow paper, you'll know . . . what to do." I nodded, even though I didn't understand, and set the wallet aside. The last item was a wooden box that fit in my palm. Inside was a delicate silver ring. A green stone glittered on top.

"Give it . . ." He stopped, and coughed, struggling to speak now. "Give it to Ara someday."

My heart pumped cement, my soul heavy. "Anything else, old man?" For a moment he almost laughed, and we were as we had always been—two men against the world. He smiled as he looked up at the stars, their brightness reflected, even as his own grew dim.

"Leave me here. Under the stars. Go find her." He closed his eyes, and this time his voice seemed removed from reality. "Find peace, Kaden." A smile hid in the corners of his mouth. He was teasing me, even at the end. Despite everything, he was still my Issac, steady and sure. Unfailing in death as in life.

"There is no peace in this world," I whispered back. But this time the words held no bitterness. Issac gazed at the stars, to the God he trusted more than I could understand, and breathed his last.

"There is only the peace we find."

THIRTY-FIVE—ARA

The midnight blue sky cracked in the morning fog, the sun almost here. I leaned over the fire pit and fumbled with a match. My fingers were stiff and clumsy, but with a quick scratch the match burst into flame. It died in my haste. I slid open the matchbox, and then paused. There, nestled between the red-tipped wooden soldiers, was a single, downy feather. Father was always hiding them; tucked beneath my pillow, stuck into my canteen, standing proud at the top of the trailhead. It had become a sort of inside joke between us; a small mark we could leave on a world that demanded we be invisible.

A crack came from the end of camp. Someone was coming. I tucked the feather back into the box.

Loki bounded out of the trees, the mountain slope rising behind him. Already I could tell that he'd plunged into the alpine lake below our campsite. His tail flung arches of water in each direction.

"Hey, boy," I roughed up his head as he barreled into me. He bounded back down the trail, to where my father had gone for

water. Soon he, too, emerged from the thick trees. He moved slowly, leaning to one side as he carried the water bucket in the other.

"No fire yet?" he called.

"If Loki wasn't soaking wet and spraying water everywhere it'd be a bit easier." As if to agree, Loki suddenly stopped running and shook his entire body. Water went everywhere, spraying the carefully arranged pile of twigs. Father laughed at the annoyed look on my face.

A flock of geese suddenly flew over us, their honks breaking the morning calm. Loki titled his head back to survey their V formation. His ears strained forward and he let out a high whine.

"How do they know where they are going?" I wondered aloud. I expected a joke, or even a funny story from my father. Instead he was quiet. His face was wrinkled leather as he squinted into the dawn. When he finally responded his voice was soft, the same tone he used when he talked about the whitewashed house he grew up in that had since burned to the ground.

"I guess there's something in all of us that leads us home."

~

The gravel crunched on the small dirt road as I bent over, hands on my knees. My breath came in ragged gasps, my knees trembled, and a sheen of sweat covered me even through the cool night. Still, I smiled.

I did it, Father. I'm coming home.

A breeze ran with me, lifting my hair, cooling the sweat on my forehead. Each step forward made me feel stronger, more alive.

After an hour, the dirt road became gravel, and my footsteps went from dull thuds to a steady *crunch-crunch-crunch*. Another two hours and the path joined a paved road. My steady jog ate up the miles one by one. My track coaches would have been proud.

The sky lightened in the east when I passed an old park I remembered, where a herd of deer watched me with wide, brown eyes. My legs burned and blisters rubbed against my heels, but I didn't stop.

If they caught me, it wouldn't be because of any weakness on my part.

The day melted by. I got lost several times—everything looked so much different than I remembered. Buildings had collapsed, roads were overgrown. Whole sections had burned down. But the closer I got to home, the more I remembered. No infected animals or other men crossed my path, a stroke of luck that felt personal, as if the city remembered me too.

There was the old theater Emma and I had snuck into. The diner we ate at on Sundays, its roof now collapsed in. My old high school. Something low and deep built within me as my feet brought me closer and closer. Even all these years later, my heart ached. *Home.*

I was finally going home.

And then I turned down the street where I'd grown up. Adrenaline pulsed through me, like I'd reached the end of a race and the finish line loomed up ahead of me. There was the tree under which we'd waited for the bus. There was Tommy's house. There was the mailbox my sister had once biked straight into. There was the blackberry bush we ate from in the summer.

There was home.

After everything I'd been through, it seemed to rise before me too quickly. The paint peeled and the hollyhocks wilted in front. An ugly red *X* stained the front door, faded from when I'd seen it last.

Now it was covered with a swirling black spiral, a mark I had never seen before. One of the windows was broken in. The grass was brown and dead.

But none of that mattered. None of that changed the swelling and bursting feeling inside of me. *I did it, Father. I made it back to the beginning.*

I stood on the front lawn and stared at my house. Kaden should be here with me. And Sam. And Issac. And my father. But I couldn't have made it here without them, so all I could do now was carry their memory inside me.

It seemed as if another woman paced across the brown grass. She was older, harder. She had loved and lost. There was blood on her hands. But as she stepped up onto the porch and stood before the maroon door, none of that mattered. Because this was the one door in my life that had always been open to me and would always welcome me back.

The door handle turned in my shaking fingers as the door creaked open and I stepped inside.

~

The sun cut beams of light through the dust so thick it seemed almost physical. There was a soft thud as the door closed behind me, sealing me into a tomb-like silence. I was home, but this was not the home I remembered. Dust and cobwebs clung to the ceilings and the light that filtered through the windows hit spirals of dust.

Go back to the beginning.

My father's voice echoed in my head. I stood in the middle of the living room, lost.

Go back to the beginning.

The silence mocked me. I wanted to scream, *I'm here! Father, I'm here! I made it! Help me!*

But the house was silent.

The floorboards groaned under my weight as I walked deeper into the house. The couches were ghostly lumps, and in the corner the lamp had tilted over, its bulb shattered. The curtains had faded, stained by the sun.

My eyes went to the pictures on the walls. Most of them still hung straight, courtesy of my mother, but a few were crooked, the way my father liked to place them. They were portals to a different world. There was an embarrassing picture of me in braces, hugging a tiny Emma in a pink tutu. Over the fireplace was a picture of my father and me in the backyard. I was soaking wet and grinning, my chin up, standing before a fully blooming apple tree. It was my third-grade birthday party, and we'd just had a water balloon fight and treasure hunt.

Next was a picture of Emma with her hair long, straight, dark, so different than mine. No one ever picked us out as sisters. Even now, she looked different than how I remembered her. Was it because I could only picture her with white, bleeding eyes? Or worse, because I'd forgotten her?

A creak from upstairs. Every cell in my body vibrated.

Someone was in the house.

It was difficult to breathe, to think. The mark on the door. I'd dismissed it, but what if it meant something? What if it meant someone lived here? What if it meant someone was waiting for me?

Anger burned away the pain. This was my house—I wasn't leaving. I'd lost too much to give up now.

My footsteps made soft creaks as I ghosted into the kitchen. Unlike the living room, the kitchen looked like a battleground. The island had fallen over, and the window that once looked out over the garden was now a gaping hole. Leaves and dirt had blown inside, and the tiny elephant figurines my mother had collected lay buried in the dirt. But the second drawer next to the dishwasher slid free with no complaint. Mother's knives gleamed—Father had always kept them sharp. I picked two, tucking the smaller into my belt and holding the other out in front of me.

The first turn was terrifying, blind to the narrow hallway that led to the staircase. My parents' bedroom was behind the first set of closed doors, but I didn't open it. The sound had come from upstairs. I eased my way up, wincing as the steps creaked beneath me.

The upstairs was darker than downstairs, even though it was daylight outside. The curtains over the windows were drawn, muffling the light. No obvious signs of life.

What had I really expected to find here? A clue? A map? *Bodies?*

I stepped onto the green carpet at the top of the stairs and looked around the room in which I'd spent much of my childhood. The TV stood in the corner, a black reflective eye watching me. Emma and I used to have sleepovers on the carpet. One of the shelves had fallen off the wall, and broken picture frames littered the ground. My bedroom was off to the left, the door closed, but ahead of me Emma's bedroom door was open a crack. Sunlight leaked through.

A shadow moved within.

My fingers were sweaty around the knife. I wiped them on my pants and paced forward. This was my home. Whoever was here was an unwelcome intruder.

I kicked open the door to Emma's room, brandishing the knife as a pungent smell assaulted me. My heart pounded, every part of me ready to attack.

There was no one there.

A small movement caught my eye and I jumped, swiping the knife through the air at . . . an orange cat.

He tilted his head at me, confused. Then his ears perked up, and he sauntered over to me, as unconcerned about the knife as I felt foolish holding it. His coat was glossy and striped, his tail bushy and held aloft like an exclamation point. Though he wasn't fat, he looked better fed and rested than me. He pushed up against me, twining himself around my legs and purring.

I stood for a moment looking down at him, trying to rein in my heartbeat. Then I laughed. He stopped meowing and gave me an affronted look. I tucked the knife back into my belt and leaned over and scratched his ears. He rose up on his back legs, pushing his wet nose against my fingers.

Emma's room seemed smaller than I remembered it. The bed was stripped bare and covered in tufts of orange cat fur. The ground was littered with skeletons of small mammals and, unlike the rest of the house, smelled of cat piss and rot.

"Be grateful I'm not hungry for cat," I said to him, but gave him another pet anyway.

Everything was knocked off the dressers and shelves, but I wasn't entirely sure I could blame this on my feline friend, as one of the windows had been smashed in. Leaves and dirt littered the carpet that had once been a cream color. Most of the wall hangings had fallen off as well. Only one of her drawings was still pinned to the wall, a horse running through the woods. I poked around a bit more, pulling a spare blanket out of the closet and wrapping it around me, but in the end, I set my two knives on the dresser and sat on the bed.

How was it I had finally found what I was looking for and yet felt more lost than ever?

The hopelessness of it all crashed over me. What had I really expected to find here?

This was no longer home. All that remained were ghosts.

I curled up on the bed, trying to come to terms with the awful, terrible knowledge that no one was listening. No one would hear and no one would come to comfort me.

Then something wet and cold touched my arm. Wide, golden eyes stared up into mine. The cat jumped into the circle I'd made with my body, turned a few times, then settled into the curve of my body like I had made it especially for him. He yawned, revealing a mouth of sharp white teeth and a sandpaper tongue. And then he went to sleep. I stared at him, shocked that this creature trusted me enough to crawl into my arms and fall asleep. How had he survived in this world?

But as stupid as he might be, he was also soft and warm. The gentle sound of purring soothed me. I lowered my head, careful not to disturb him yet grateful for his trust and company. I'd always been more of a dog person, but next to his small pink nose, I promised myself that I would never eat a cat, no matter how hungry I was. With sunlight pouring in, and the blanket wrapped tight around us, we both passed into oblivion.

~

I woke hours later, cold even with the blanket.

It was evening; I'd slept too long. The orange cat was gone.

More pressing than his absence was my painfully empty stomach and pounding head.

My legs screamed at me, cramping and seizing up. I forced myself to stretch and keep moving, then made my way downstairs. The inside of both my room and my parents' room revealed only dusty furniture and relics of the past. No bodies. No messages.

The kitchen was another puzzle. The cabinets and pantry were systematically cleaned out. I forced myself to think. Where would Mom and Emma have hidden food? Where would I? Where would Father?

The answer came to me with a smile. The pantry was stuffed full of cooking supplies—old pans, trays, and frosting decorations my mom had used on fancy cakes she'd once helped design for weddings. I moved all of this out, then felt for the hatch inlaid in the floor. It led to the small crawl space under the house. Father had taken me down here once, where I'd been delighted to find an entire mouse skeleton. The hatch heaved upward, the scent of stale, cool earth washing over. A few feet below, stacked on the crawl space floor, lay a pile of canned goods. My breath quickened even as my mind reeled.

What had happened here? Though I didn't want to face the ugly truth, it felt like a slap. There was still food here. And no bodies. So . . . what had happened to Emma? The question and stillness taunted me, until I suddenly couldn't take the house anymore. I slid the back glass door open and stepped outside.

Outside, beneath the tree, our tire swing was still there. The weeds were overgrown but my mother's garden still bloomed. Beneath the sky, in the fresh air, it was easier to remember the way things had once been. Father loved to make fires out here, so I decided to make one myself. Maybe it would help me remember what I was missing.

The day faded, and the flames grew higher, feeding my anger. I was being stupid lighting a fire, but I couldn't bring myself to care. The backyard spread out around me, lit in fiery shades—a hooded figure leaned up against the fence.

I fumbled to pull out one of the knives from my belt. "Who's there? What do you want?" My voice was high-pitched and hoarse.

The figure stood up straight. They were tall, bigger than me, and now fear worked its way into my body. I cursed myself for thinking a knife was enough of a weapon. For building a fire at all. But the hooded figure came forward slowly, confidently, not as an enemy would.

He stepped into the light.

All fear and hopelessness fell away when he smiled at me.

"I'd rather you kissed me, but I guess stabbing would be more your style, princess."

The knife hit the dirt, forgotten as we both moved at the same time. He crushed me into his chest, and for a moment nothing existed but me and Kaden.

I'd forgotten his smell: dust, sweat, and horse. We clung to each other. He cradled the back of my head, and I pulled back from his chest to stare at him. The fire danced across his face. There was a wildness to it; beneath his eyes were deep bruise-like shadows. But even if his face was lean, his jaw was still strong, his mouth teasingly arrogant.

"I missed you, princess." There was a weariness in his voice I hadn't expected.

"I missed you too." *Nothing felt right here without you.* "How did you find me?" I didn't want to let go, but he pulled a slip of yellow paper from his pocket and unfolded it, revealing a long line of numbers, dots, and names. In the firelight it took me a moment to realize it had been torn from a phonebook.

"Charles and Maria Edana, 3924 Blackhawk Ave." I stared at the names of my parents. So neat in cold, black ink. "We're the only Edana in the phonebook. I'd forgotten . . . Clever." Strange, to live in a world where last names no longer mattered. It felt like a betrayal to my family somehow, as if I had forgotten a small part of myself, and therefore them.

"It wasn't me," Kaden whispered. "It was Issac." He drew a shaking breath.

"Where is he? What happened?"

"He's dead."

Numbness covered me, a slow, deep ache. This time our embrace was different. Like if either of us let go, we would drown.

It didn't seem real. How could Issac be gone? I half expected him to walk through the darkness, to smile and tell me this was all a misunderstanding.

Later we sat before the fire, staring into the embers while holding a silent vigil. Kaden wrapped a blanket around us both and I leaned against his shoulder. Occasionally I got up to stir the pot I'd filled with canned food, now simmering over the coals. We didn't speak. At some point, when the tears came, Kaden pulled me to his chest. He held me as I sobbed, stroking my hair.

Neither of us said anything, which somehow felt right. Issac hadn't been a man of many words. In the darkness, I could almost imagine that nothing in the world had changed. My sister would come outside to annoy me soon, or my father would come outside on some pretense to make sure "that boy" wasn't making a move. Issac would emerge and sit with us.

"He died to save me," Kaden whispered. He folded in on himself, his knees clutched to his chest.

"He loved you. He's with his family now."

Kaden stared into the flames. "Do you really believe that?"

His words caught me off guard. His eyes were hard, challenging me. I felt his anger, so I paused before I answered, thinking of the answer I wished someone would have given me.

"Yes. I guess no one can really know. Still . . ." The slow, entrancing flickering of the embers reminded me somehow of Issac. "There's something beautiful in believing without really knowing. Issac would have called it faith." But I realized as I said it that I wasn't sure exactly where my faith had led me. To an empty house full of secrets? Or to a man I loved and a new beginning?

"He didn't deserve to die." Kaden thrust a stick in the fire, and the sparks jumped up, a sudden flare. "He had a plan. Four horses, all with saddles and bridles. Food. Equipment. Weapons. Medicine. A map of the country. All those times he disappeared, I thought he just liked being alone. But he was planning a life for us. We could have gone wherever we wanted." He paused and glanced at me, as if suddenly considering something he hadn't before. "He even thought of how I could find you, if we were separated."

Shame burned a hole in my chest. I hadn't considered what might have happened to Issac when he hadn't made it to the fence. I'd thought only of myself. But Issac had thought of Kaden and me before himself, and paid the ultimate price for it.

Kaden must have realized my own train of thought. "I didn't mean it like that. It's not your fault, Ara." But his voice was miserable, and I heard the blame he didn't put on me placed on himself. That, too, I understood. How often had I blamed myself for my father's death?

"So how did you get here? Issac never told me the plan," he said.

I heard the pain in his voice as he said Issac's name, but also the invitation to move the conversation somewhere less painful.

"We couldn't talk directly, so we passed notes back and forth to figure out the plan. And then, I sort of . . . tricked Gabriel."

"Tricked him how?" A smile hid in the corner of his mouth, and as much as I wanted to make him laugh, I also walked a thin line. There was no way I was telling Kaden I had fake-married Gabriel.

"I got him alone, without guards."

His eyebrows rose. I pushed on, knowing he'd like the next part. "And then . . . I stabbed him." My left hand slashed through the air.

Kaden laughed, then when I didn't correct him said, "Wait, are you serious?"

"With a needle. Issac had tranquilizers, we used them." Even now, there was no regret in my voice, only a vicious sort of triumph. The only pain came from realizing how much Issac had helped me. And how I would never have the chance to thank him.

A wind brushed through the trees, stirring leaves and tossing sparks from the fire. Goosebumps raised on my arms as I thought of Gabriel. It took me a moment to realize why. Kaden had found me . . . but I'd also told my last name to someone else: Gabriel. On my very first day at the clan, I'd signed my full name on his list of members.

I'd forgotten who I was. But that didn't mean Gabriel had.

"So, then what'd you do?" Kaden interrupted my thoughts, his teasing eyes and smile made me swallow my fear, at least for now. Maybe I worried over nothing.

"I burned the clan to the ground."

"You're lying!" But he threw his head back and laughed as he said it, his whole body shaking.

"I'm not."

He kept laughing, and I tried to keep the smugness at bay by adding, "But I only really meant to burn down the stables." And now I was laughing too. It bubbled and overflowed, a carefree, devilish feeling. I'd forgotten what it felt like to be around Kaden: wild, unburdened, like an eagle diving off a cliff for no other reason than it could.

"I'm picturing you bursting out of the stables on a giant black stallion"—he could barely talk he was laughing so hard—"one hand holding an American flag, the other a pistol, and the other flipping off Gabriel as you ride off into the night."

"How many hands do I have in this? Seven?"

"At least. You're also brandishing a sword, wearing a coonskin cap, and carve a giant *A* into the wall before you go." When he laughed, he looked so much younger and happier. I wanted him to stay that way. "You amaze me, Ara." There was a heat in his eyes that made me flush. I picked up the stick he had used earlier and used it to push a few logs into place. Then his voice changed to a longing whisper. "I saw a herd of horses on the way here."

"Really?" When I turned back, he sat much closer than before, our legs and sides touching, his eyes inches from mine.

"A beautiful, roan stallion leading them too. Almost as big as Red." His smile was sad. "Maybe I'll catch one for us." He cleared his throat, looking away. "So . . . is there a bed in there?"

"Several. I spent the day curled up on one with a cat, actually."

He leaned back in mock outrage. "Oh, I see how it is. First chance you get and you shack up with someone else." He pulled me up and draped the blanket around me. But he didn't move toward it.

"Did you find anything?" he nodded toward the house.

"Nothing." Bitter disappointment filled my voice.

"Maybe tomorrow we can look together."

I shrugged. The truth was, there was only one thing I wanted to do tomorrow. But I didn't want to think about that now. Kaden was here, and safe. That was enough of a victory for today. We walked a shadowy tour of the house.

"My parents' room." I gestured inside to the relatively simple room. The bed was made, the covers tucked in, as if waiting for someone to return. "It's the biggest bed in the house. But . . ."

Kaden pulled the door closed. "But that would be superweird."

I laughed, trying to be as smooth as he was, secretly unsure. Where was he going to sleep? Where was I going to sleep? I'd slept beside him before, but this felt different. Self-consciousness filled me when I opened the door to my room. The space captured an image of a strange girl, one who seemed so removed from the person I was now.

The walls were tacked haphazardly with posters of athletes of all shapes and sizes. My mom had a fit when she first saw it, but finally let them stay, pursing her lips every time she entered. I'd painted the room a dark blue, which I'd insisted would look like the sky just after sunset. It didn't. It was ugly. But I'd kept it because I'd done it, and I refused to admit I was wrong. The bed was still made, a black duvet bursting with spiraling galaxies.

When I was younger, I loved astronomy. I'd wanted to study the stars. I then spent the last three years sleeping beneath them in the high mountains, where they were a thousand times more vibrant. *Be careful what you wish for.*

Kaden trailed inside behind me. He held his hands clasped behind his back as he leaned forward to look at one of the athletes on the wall.

"I knew you ran track but didn't know you were so *into* athletics."

"My coaches thought I could go to college on a track scholarship. I had the fastest 200-meter time in my school as a freshman."

His gaze trailed down to my legs. "Makes sense."

My closet still held most of my clothes, and it was a bizarre experience to dig through the bright colors and flimsy fabrics, snapshots of a world that no longer existed. A long sleeve black shirt still fit, but I must have grown taller, as the pants were at least an inch too short. Kaden stretched out on the bed, burying his face in one of the pillows as I changed. He seemed too tall and masculine for a bed that had belonged to an angsty teenager.

"Okay, I'm good." My hair was wild, and likely smelled of smoke and cat, but there was nothing I could do to fix that now. Kaden turned over but didn't get up, sprawling with his hands behind his head and gazing up at the ceiling. I followed his gaze, up to the glow-in-the-dark stars stuck to the ceiling. I'd forgotten I'd stuck them to my ceiling years ago.

Our eyes met and I looked away first.

He stood up slowly. "Do you want me to sleep in the TV room on the couch, or can I bring the cushions in here?"

His words surprised me. "Why don't you just sleep on the bed with me? There's room."

"No, I'll sleep on the floor." His words stung.

"We've slept together before." I couldn't quite hide the hurt in my voice, and when he touched my elbow I pulled away. "It's okay if you don't want to." My words were ice, but not enough to cover for my lie.

Kaden caught my chin in his hands and forced me to look up

at him. "I want to, Ara. But if I sleep next to you, I will want to do more than just sleep."

Oh. I had no response. The truth was, I'd been trying to survive for so long I hadn't really thought about what life with Kaden would look like.

"So, you don't want . . ."

He laughed at this, but when he saw the hurt on my face, he immediately stepped forward and circled my waist with his hands.

"Ara, of course I want to." His voice was low and warm. "You are beautiful, and I am only a man." He hesitated, and I might have teased him, if not for the fact I saw how carefully he chose his next words. "I'm just saying that we have time. I know you've been through more than most people have in their entire lives, but you are young . . . we have time, Ara."

"And if we don't have time?"

He stopped and tucked a strand of hair behind my ear. "We do. And I don't care if you are the last woman left on the Earth. It's still your choice, and no one else's."

You are my choice, I wanted to say, but he raised my chin and kissed me, soft and sweet. "Someday, when you are ready," he said.

Then, without waiting for an answer, Kaden swept his arms under my legs, knocking me off my feet and into his arms. I shrieked and grabbed his neck as he playfully carried me to the bed. The awkward moment passed, and he was playful and teasing once again. Kaden tucked me into the bed and pulled the covers up around me.

"Sleep, Ara. There's plenty of time to fight me tomorrow, and the day after that . . . however long you'll have me."

"I'll always want to fight with you, Kaden."

He laughed at my devilish smile. Then his face became serious.

He brushed his thumb against my lip, and suddenly I was burning. He leaned over and kissed me. It was like fire. He pulled back too soon, something in his eyes held carefully in check.

He made a bed of couch cushions on the floor next to me and we talked about what our lives would have been like had there been no plague. How we might have met. What jobs we might have got. Where we would have gone to college. Despite the darkness that surrounded us, it felt like, for just a moment, we made our own light that burned bright as a star.

THIRTY-SIX—ARA

I woke to the smell of a campfire and the sense that something wasn't right.

The scent was familiar; Father and I woke for three years to a banked fire in need of reviving, dew streaming on the tent, birds calling, and the forest coming alive. All those memories haunted me now. This house didn't hold secrets, only memories. I wasn't the daughter, or the sister, I thought I was. Whatever the beginning was, whatever he meant, I wasn't sure I would ever find it.

The feeling of wrongness persisted. I opened my eyes and raised my body just enough to look down at Kaden. He'd slept without a shirt, and even though he'd lost weight, his shoulders were still broad and strong, his stomach toned. He could easily have been one of the athletes taped to my walls. He held his right hand tucked gingerly against his chest, marked by a deep wound still inflamed on the edges. What had happened? Part of me wanted to roll over and go back asleep, but even with Kaden beside me, the wrong feeling persisted. Dawn leaked in through the windows and the scent of the fire—

Fire.

Terror overturned sense as I jumped up and flung open the door.

No.

A cloud of growing smoke reached up the stairs. "Kaden!"

Kaden jerked upright, voice slurring, "Was wrong?"

"Fire! Get up!"

I left him there and plunged downstairs into thick smoke. Instantly it became harder to breathe. A thousand thoughts tumbled through my head. *Had Gabriel found us? Why would he set a fire? Where was the fire extinguisher?* I turned the corner.

The kitchen blazed, flames reaching up the kitchen cabinets to the ceiling. Through the broken kitchen window, a breeze swept inside, fanning the flames higher.

The gaping windows. The fire I'd lit in the backyard last night and had failed to extinguish. The dried layer of leaves on the kitchen floor. All the pieces slammed together to form a single, horrifying conclusion. *My fault.*

A sudden crack and a burst of heat forced me to retreat. I ducked back around the corner and smashed into Kaden. He'd had the foresight to grab his jacket and held it over his mouth to breathe.

"It's too late!" he yelled. "Grab what you can! I'll throw what's upstairs out the window."

His words jolted me into action. We had minutes, maybe less. There wasn't time for regret. I hadn't had time to search the house fully, and if my father had left anything, now it was burning. Thick smoke clouded my senses. What should I take? All that was left here were memories.

The heat forced me away from the kitchen, ducking low beneath the smoke to move into the living room. Noise came from upstairs, hopefully Kaden tossing our things out the window. The fire hadn't reached the living room, but the smoke was thick enough that I had to bend nearly in two and feel my way to the pictures on the mantle. I reached for the one in the back, the last family picture of us all. As I lifted it, something fell away from it, drifting away through the smoke and landing on my foot.

Something light, long and thin, with alternate dark and white marking: an Osprey feather.

Memories surged back, not from this house, but of my father, and our life in the mountains. All the times he had hidden feathers for me to find. An inside joke. But also, a symbol to mark the way. A symbol only I would have understood.

There wasn't time for another thought; a sudden burst of light and a roar threw me backward. Pain lanced through my head and side. *The whole world's burning, Father, but at least I've got you.* The thought tumbled away from me, dizzy and disoriented.

Somehow, I'd managed to keep the frame clutched to my chest, the only thing recognizable in a world of fire and smoke. Black spots clouded my vision. My legs weren't working, like they'd somehow been disconnected from my body. It was so hot. So hard to breathe, to think. So hard to do anything.

The flames grew. My body curled around the picture as thick smoke became my whole world.

Then a hand grabbed me. I was hauled upright roughly. The hands forced me through the clouds of smoke and unending heat.

Just when I thought it would never end, we fell through the front door into a burst of fresh air.

My body hacked and coughed, trying at once to expel the

smoke and inhale, but my savior didn't let me stop, pulling me away from the heat that burst out of the windows.

Beside me, I finally brought Kaden into focus, his eyes wild, his face red and blotchy. Brief disappointment rose in me—for one wild moment, I'd thought he was my father, come to save me again.

As soon as he caught his breath, Kaden hauled me up from the ground and dragged me across the street, swearing all the way. I clutched the picture frame to my chest. I'd almost just killed us both . . . but I couldn't think past the picture pressed against my chest.

We collapsed on the neighbor's yard across from my house.

I thought he would yell at me, but instead he silently clutched me tightly against him, stroking my hair and rocking back and forth. Burns covered my legs and hands, and my ears rang.

None of that mattered. All that mattered was the picture frame clutched in my hands.

"Princess, you will be the death of me," he whispered. I barely heard him.

I placed the picture on its face, and with trembling fingers undid the sides and opened it. Words abandoned me.

"What is it?" Kaden asked.

I tilted the picture frame so that Kaden could see what I did, the same moment a sobbing laugh burst out of me.

Taped to the back of the picture was a yellowing envelope. *TO ARA* was written in my father's long, sloppy hand. But even that seemed inconsequential compared to the date written just below. It was a month after I'd last seen my father, when he'd disappeared in the woods.

He was alive. He'd left this for me and marked it with a feather. He'd come back to the beginning. Just as he promised he would.

I was too consumed to speak, or even cry, the envelope clutched to my chest.

My father was still alive.

The knowledge was sweeter than a drug. It was like a dam had burst within me, water sweeping over a desert I hadn't known had existed within. He was alive.

And finally, everything was worth it. All the pain, the loneliness, the betrayal, the doubt. Everything I'd gone through was worth it.

I tilted my head back and wept, only one thought keeping me from being swept away into the indigo sky.

I did it, Father. I made it back to the beginning.

I made it home.

THIRTY-SEVEN—ARA

With a deep, steadying breath, I ripped open the envelope. For something so small, it felt like I held the universe in my hands. Inside was a thick, laminated page folded many times. A map. Tucked against this was the faded stationary marked with my father's hand. I set the map aside and unfolded the paper carefully. I cleared my throat and read.

My dearest Arabella,

I'm not sure if this note is written out of desperation or hope, but something inside me tells me you are still alive. I barely survived the river. I knew they were following me and I had to run. By the time I managed to throw them off and made it back, you were gone. Those bastards killed Loki . . . Best dog I ever had, and he died to save me without a second thought. Why is it dogs are so much better than men?

*I planned to come home and wait here for you, but
Emma wasn't here. There was only some damn cat. I
thought of shooting him, but she always wanted a cat,
so I left him there. There was so much I should have
told you, so many things I need to explain to you in
person, but instead, I will leave you with the one secret
I thought to tell you a thousand times but never could.
In the far north, there is a city of survivors. While the
rest of the world faded away, this city has progressed.
The wealthiest from all over the world gathered here.
Its mark is the black spiral, the same that marks our
door.
They collect women and bring them there.
No. Not collect. They hunt women, and they are sold as
the world's most precious commodities.
It's there that I go to look for your sister.
But Ara, I warn you now. As dangerous as the journey
will be, the city itself is a thousand times more dangerous. Our world has moved backward, while this
one has moved forward. It will be a world the likes of
which we have never imagined. Women will be beyond
precious. It would be impossibly dangerous for you to
follow me there, to help me find your sister.
And yet, I hope you do follow me. Again, I leave you
with an impossible choice. Enclosed is a map that leads
north, to the city I speak of. Guard it closely.
I miss you. I'm sorry. Without you, Emma, and your
mother, the days are endless. Perhaps my punishment is
to spend the rest of my life alone. Perhaps you are gone.
But I can't believe that. You were always the strong one,*

Ara. Something inside me, either faith or stubbornness,
tells me that I will see you again.
Come find me. Come find Emma and we can be a
family again.

All my love,
Your Father

The fire burned hot and bright, its noise a distant buzzing. A robin flitted through the sky. It seemed impossible that life could move forward in this moment.

"Are you okay?" Kaden finally asked. He stood a careful distance away, as if waiting for me to implode. With a sudden roar, the roof of my house crashed in before us, sending sparks flying into the air.

"I . . ." I stared at him. Not like I had before, when I saw him as a man that stood between me and my goal, or even as I had later, as a man who might help me get to where I needed. Instead, I looked at him as the person I wanted beside me wherever my path led me next. It was like seeing in color after a lifetime of black and white. "I love you."

Kaden froze, surprise reflected on his face. But then a slow smile melted through. It wasn't his usual teasing smile. It was different, like the sun breaking through clouds.

"I love you too, princess. Every crazy inch." He grinned at me. "How are you feeling?"

I knew he meant the burns on my arms, but I only smiled and shook my head. It seemed impossible to put it into words. "I feel like I could jump off a cliff and fly."

Kaden laughed. "Please don't."

"It feels like I'm alive again. Emma and my father are alive." I already knew what I would do. It wasn't even a decision; it was fate. "They are alive and I'm going to find them."

He nodded at this, and I realized with a surge of panic that I was assuming Kaden would follow me on this ridiculous quest.

"It will be dangerous, Kaden. Impossible even. I'm probably stupid to even try. You . . . you don't have to—"

He cut me off. "Just try to stop me." My heart leapt. "And of course there will be trouble. You attract it like no one I've ever seen." He saw the tears in my eyes and stopped, his voice suddenly deep and serious. "I'm with you, Ara. Always." He pulled me to him, and I was lost in the warmth of his lips and the strength of his hands. We would need to leave soon. To watch for danger and betrayal and selfishness and everything else that defined humanity. But in Kaden's arms, I remembered what else remained.

We turned to watch the black trail of smoke drift up into the clear blue sky. Far in the distance, the snowcapped mountains stood as silent sentinels to the world of men.

"Where to, princess?"

I spread the map out on the grass, tracing the lines. The way my father had taught me.

"North. We go north."

EPILOGUE

The world was fuzzy on the edges. It felt like someone had smashed a brick against my head. Repeatedly.

My body moved slow as a lame horse. The air was musty and cold, tinged with the scents of metal and earth. Slivers of light leaked in from the ceiling.

Underground.

I was underground . . . Why the heck was I underground?

The world spun as I pushed up, and my bed, a small metal cot, squeaked beneath me. The walls were made of metal. Underground, but not a cave. The room was small and rectangular, almost the size of a large RV. Shelves filled with pots, lanterns, canned food, and strange, rusted metal objects lined the farthest wall. Opposite me was another cot. It was empty except for a small pillow and a red sleeping bag.

Where was I?

I searched my memory but found nothing. It felt like opening a refrigerator, expecting a feast, and finding dust. Which was when I realized I was starving.

A sudden pain lanced the back of my head when I tried to stand. Black dots appeared in my vision. My knees buckled and I crumpled back to the bed. When the pain faded to a dull throb, I reached up and touched the back of my head. The sudden flare of pain kept me from probing further, but the touch told me my hair had been shaved off and the back of my head bandaged.

A blinding white circle suddenly appeared in the ceiling. Sunlight glared down at me. I shielded my eyes, barely making out the form of a body that descended a ladder into the room. The door stayed open above him, like a burning light that led to heaven.

He jumped the final few feet, landing with a thud, and turned to face me. Climbing down he'd seemed huge, but standing before me he was short, with a bulbous nose and deep frown. Like a grumpy gnome.

"You're awake. It's about time. Can't believe how much work it's been feeding two people." His voice was cool. Not unkind, more logical. Like a doctor assessing his subject. Distantly I remembered a hand feeding me.

"Where am I?" My own voice surprised me, deep and scratchy.

He unslung a canvas bag from his shoulders and began unloading odd pieces of metal onto the shelf.

"You know, sometimes the question itself is more important than the answer." He flipped over a small metal box.

"What do you mean?"

"I mean, wouldn't the better question be, who am I?" He placed the metal box back into the backpack.

There was silence as I tried to figure out what he meant. It just made my head throb more. "Who are you?"

He shook his head, voice low and angry. "No, boy, who are *you*?"

He returned to sorting through his backpack, but this time I didn't watch. Instead I let the question play on loop. Who was I? Why couldn't I answer that question? I raked my brain, searched every dusty corner. Nothing.

"I'm . . . I don't know . . . Why don't I know? What happened to me?"

He shook his head again. "What happened to the world? What happened to the bird after it left the nest? What happens to water when it leaves the sky?"

"I don't understand."

"Because you're asking the wrong questions."

Why couldn't he just answer my question? I spoke slow and clear, enunciating each syllable, "Why am I here?"

He sighed. The silence stretched out, so long I thought he wouldn't answer. But finally—

"I found you in a field with a group of bodies. All of them dead, but not you. Should have left you there, but you looked so much like my boy . . ." He trailed off, his eyes far away, his fingers tinkering with another small bundle of wire in his hands. He seemed to have forgotten me. When he looked at me again, a decision had been reached.

"But you're better now. I can't afford to feed you anymore. It's time you're off. On your way."

He turned as he said it, and I saw for some reason that he was ashamed. I didn't want him to be. Something told me I would be dead if not for him. I pushed myself up and swayed for a moment, saw black, and then found my balance.

"How do I get out?"

He pointed at the ladder, and I buried the sudden desire to ask more questions. It was difficult to ask the right questions when you didn't know who you were.

Even though my head pounded, my arms were strong, moving me up rung by rung toward the circle of bright light, until I climbed free. Clear, cool air washed over me, heavy with scents of grass, wildflowers, and running water. Thick grass spread out around me and high above the sun burned bright. The word tasted strange. I rolled it around in my mouth: ". . . Sun . . . sun . . ."

Sam.

"Sam!" I shouted. The man, whose head poked out of the hole like a groundhog, gave me an affronted look. "Sam!" I grinned at him. "My name is Sam."

He blinked twice and gave a small smile. "Maybe you are starting to ask the right questions. Good luck, boy . . . Sam."

And with nothing more he reached to close the hatch. Fear made my knees weak as I realized the second that hatch closed, I would be alone. Left with nothing but a name.

"Wait! What should I do? Where should I go?"

He laughed in my face. "What shouldn't you do? Where shouldn't you go?" The metal hatch slammed in my face, revealing a careful cover of greenery—if I hadn't just seen the door close, I would never have known it was there. Stunned, I stared at the spot where he'd disappeared and then smiled. Maybe I should have seen that coming.

I rotated in a circle. Jagged mountains rose behind me, capped with snow even in the summer. The sun hung above the horizon, lighting a vast stretch of forest like a golden ocean. In a few hours it would disappear for the night. I was alone, and knew nothing of who I was, or where I came from. Yet something about the forest called to me, as if it knew I belonged here, even if I couldn't remember.

I began to walk west, toward the sun, my heart rising and racing with the birds around me. The day was glorious, the sun bright, and I had found my name.

Who knew what else I might find?

ACKNOWLEDGMENTS

My first thank-you goes to the love of my life, Travis. Of every story I've read or written, ours is my favorite. Your first impression of me was a tall teenager wearing a homemade *Twilight* shirt in biology class: I always knew that shirt would bring about great things. You are selfless, kind, supportive, and the best husband, father, and friend a person could ask for. The night you said, "You could call it *The Last She*," I bet you had no idea it would end up here.

To Ella, thanks for always saying, "You can do it, Mommy!" You're usually trying to get another cookie, but I still appreciate the sentiment. To Kinsley, who just started walking, your smile and giggles make the world brighter. I love you both.

To Dad, thank you for giving me a love of the mountains, God, and adventure. I started writing this book at the loneliest time in my life, and I don't think it's a coincidence that the main character was a girl who had only the skills her father had taught her. Thank you for never hesitating to tell yet another bedtime story.

Which brings me to my next thank-you: Mom, thanks for putting up with Dad's endless bedtime stories! Mom, you are a strong, independent country girl from Kansas who gave me a love of reading and taught me the value of hard work and perseverance. You have both been so generous with your time in watching my tiny monsters—I mean kids—so I could write, and I'm forever grateful.

To Sadie, thanks for all those years spent playing horses, instead of dolls, and for being the best sister. To Luke, thanks for being such a cool brother that you didn't mind me dating (and marrying) your best friend. Also, thanks for always hogging the computer and television growing up. You gave me no choice but to become a voracious reader. Thank you to my wonderful mother-in-law, Diana, for reading so many early drafts and watching the kids so I could write.

A giant, worldwide thank-you to my Wattpad readers and friends. I always knew I wanted to be a writer, but you were the ones who made me feel like it could be more than just a dream. You believed in this story first, you made this happen, and I am grateful for every one of you.

To the Wattpad team, especially Deanna and I-Yana, thank you for believing in this story and pushing it to be everything it could be.

To Natalia: we met in fourth grade, where we decided we would be the same height forever. I am now six feet tall, and you're five foot two, but that hasn't changed our friendship. You were the first person I told I wanted to be a writer. In response, you gave me a green journal and told me to fill it with stories. I did, and I still have it, as a reminder that the dreams we have as children can come true. Thank you for being a lifelong friend.

To my friend and talented writer, Alex Constantino, thank you for endless encouragement, and many in-depth sci-fi discussions. Many thanks to The Idaho Wordsmiths, and especially to my fellow Idahoan authors, Brooke Urbaniak and Conda Douglas.

To my professors at the University of Wisconsin, Ron Kuka and Judith Claire Mitchell, thank you for helping me grow as a writer. Also, to that one guy in class who called my story "dope," thanks, man.

To my cat, Oliver: I've worked in a zoo, a large cat rescue facility, and majored in wildlife biology, but you are still pound for pound the most devious creature I've ever met. Thanks for being a great writing buddy and for ridding me of many breakable possessions.

And finally, my gratitude goes to you, dear reader. Thank you for being a part of this adventure. Until our next one.

ABOUT THE AUTHOR

H.J. Nelson is an Idaho native who graduated from University of Wisconsin with degrees in creative writing and wildlife biology. She began writing on Wattpad in 2015, where her story *The Last She* was one of the most read science fiction stories in 2016 and 2017. Since then her works have been optioned for television by Sony and garnered over twelve million reads. She has also written for brands like General Electric, Writer's Digest, and National Geographic. When not writing, Nelson has lived on a boat in the British Virgin Isles, worked in two zoos, and ridden an elephant through the jungles of Laos—though she considers raising two daughters her most dangerous adventure yet. You can sign up for her newsletter at hjnelsonauthor.com, or find her on Instagram at @h.j.nelson.

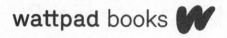

 premium

Supercharge your Wattpad experience.

Go Premium and get more from the platform you already love. Enjoy uninterrupted ad-free reading, access to bonus Coins, and exclusive, customizable colors to personalize Wattpad your way.

Try Premium **free** today.